THE GETAWAY

RONA HALSALL

B
Boldwood

First published in Great Britain in 2025 by Boldwood Books Ltd.

Copyright © Rona Halsall, 2025

Cover Design by Head Design Ltd

Cover Images: Shutterstock

The moral right of Rona Halsall to be identified as the author of this work has been asserted in accordance with the Copyright, Designs and Patents Act 1988.

All rights reserved. No part of this book may be reproduced in any form or by any electronic or mechanical means, including information storage and retrieval systems, without written permission from the author, except for the use of brief quotations in a book review. This book is a work of fiction and, except in the case of historical fact, any resemblance to actual persons, living or dead, is purely coincidental.

Every effort has been made to obtain the necessary permissions with reference to copyright material, both illustrative and quoted. We apologise for any omissions in this respect and will be pleased to make the appropriate acknowledgements in any future edition.

A CIP catalogue record for this book is available from the British Library.

Paperback ISBN 978-1-83603-128-4

Large Print ISBN 978-1-83603-127-7

Hardback ISBN 978-1-83603-126-0

Ebook ISBN 978-1-83603-129-1

Kindle ISBN 978-1-83603-130-7

Audio CD ISBN 978-1-83603-121-5

MP3 CD ISBN 978-1-83603-122-2

Digital audio download ISBN 978-1-83603-125-3

This book is printed on certified sustainable paper. Boldwood Books is dedicated to putting sustainability at the heart of our business. For more information please visit https://www.boldwoodbooks.com/about-us/sustainability/

Boldwood Books Ltd, 23 Bowerdean Street, London, SW6 3TN

www.boldwoodbooks.com

*For my readers – thank you from the bottom of my heart for all your fabulous support.
I hope you're reading this on a sunny getaway somewhere...*

PROLOGUE

Are we really going to do this? Nerves twisted in Maddie's gut as she held Tom's hand, their fingers clasped tightly together under the table. They were sitting in her favourite restaurant, on the next to last day of their two-week holiday in Split, Croatia, waiting for her new friends to arrive. Now the time had come to go through with the swap, it was hard to believe it was actually happening. Even a week ago, such a move hadn't been on her radar and here they were, about to do something adventurous for once. Something she hoped would reset their relationship after the bitter disappointments of recent months.

Everything had been going wrong. First was the news that a natural pregnancy was not going to be possible. Then the loss of the biggest client at the design agency where she worked, putting her job at risk. The final blow had been the sale of her flat falling through, meaning they couldn't continue with the purchase of their first house together. And on top of all that there was the worry about her dad's health after his recent heart attack and her mum having to give up work to look after him for a little while. The whole family had been going through the wringer and it would be wonderful to have a bit of time out, away from the stresses and strains.

This opportunity felt like it could be a new beginning, a turn in a new direction. She hardly dared to hope, but she had to, didn't she? Had to hope that she could re-shape her dreams and aspirations. Had to have faith that life had more to offer than the original fantasy of a suburban home and two kids, now that possibility had gone.

Her eyes strayed towards the door again, a fizz of excitement shooting through her body as she imagined a different future. Better, she hoped, because it wasn't just the last few weeks that had been bad, the last couple of years had been tough, with both of them facing knockbacks individually as well as their troubles as a couple. In some ways, it was amazing they were still together. Other couples would have been broken, but they were clinging on, still striving to build a future they both wanted, even if it wasn't what they'd originally planned.

They were sitting by a window, and she studied their reflections in the glass. Tom, stocky and compact, was perched on his chair, not quite relaxed. His square face was tanned after their holiday, his dark blond hair short at the sides and longer on top. A sensible haircut, rather than stylish. But that was Tom all over. What you saw was what you got and he had no time for fashion or frivolity. She liked that about him, after dating more stylish guys in the past, who spent their time checking how they looked and taking selfies. Tom was quiet and deep and wouldn't talk for the sake of it. That was another thing she liked about him. He was calm to be around, thoughtful and understanding. Given how measured and sensible he was, she hadn't been sure he'd go for this suggestion of hers. This unbelievable opportunity that had appeared out of left field, but had grabbed her so hard she was determined not to let it go. She needed it. *They* needed it.

Her face looked a bit thin these days, she thought, gazing at her reflection. And her long brown hair was in need of a cut, the ends split and frizzy, but she'd given up caring for a while. At least she'd managed to slap a bit of make-up on tonight and had made an effort.

What if they bail on us? Her stomach clenched. *What if it all falls through like everything else?*

She squeezed Tom's hand to get his attention. He was off in his own little world as usual, his eyes drifting round the crowded restaurant. He gave her a fleeting smile. 'What time did you say they were coming?' She could tell he was nervous too.

'I suggested we meet at seven.' She glanced at the oversized clock on the wall by the door. It was half past seven now. Maybe they'd agreed on eight? She frowned but shook the doubts away. No, it had definitely been seven. She gave an uneasy laugh. 'Alex seems pretty variable when it comes to meeting times. The other day, when you had that Zoom meeting, she was almost an hour late. She reckons it's because time doesn't have the same meaning living out here and being a digital nomad.'

'I thought you said she worked, though? Financial advisor or something.'

'That's right. She works through this portal, where they send her leads and she gets a commission. She showed it to me but I can't remember the name now.' She flapped a hand. 'You know me, I'm just not interested in that stuff.'

He grunted. 'I don't care what your work is, even as a digital nomad, you'd still have to be on time for online meetings with clients.' He sounded frustrated and Maddie knew how he disliked people keeping him waiting.

The muscles in her shoulders tightened another notch. She couldn't have him getting cold feet. Not at this stage. 'Maybe there's a problem and they've been held up.'

At that very moment, Maddie's phone pinged with a message. She pulled it out of her pocket and smiled with relief. 'It's Alex.' Her eyes scanned the text.

> I'm really sorry, but I can't make it tonight. I've come down with a tummy bug, or eaten something bad. Ed's just gone out to get some meds for me, but then he'll be with you. I'm so sad I won't be able to say goodbye in person, but I'll see you in a couple of weeks when you get back. A x

She turned her screen so Tom could read the message. 'There, I knew there must be something wrong.' She heaved a sigh of relief, before realising Alex's absence might put a stop to their plans. Her hand tightened around his. 'It's a shame you won't get to meet her, but if you hadn't been so wrapped up in your work project all week, you could have met her before now. Like I've told you many a time, they're a lovely couple. At least you'll get to say hello to Ed again.'

Tom's Adam's apple bobbed up and down and he shifted in his seat but didn't reply.

'You're still okay with the swap, aren't you?' Just asking the question made her queasy in case he said no. 'I mean, I don't want us to do it if you're not 100 per cent on board.'

He hesitated before he replied. 'If I'm honest, I'm sort of wavering. I know we've talked about this for hours, and you're keen on the idea, but... I'd feel more comfortable if I'd met both of them. It's not too late to back out.' He caught her eye and a weight landed in the pit of her stomach. *Does he want to back out?* A flash of panic seared through her body at the thought.

Her jaw tightened. *I'm not going to let this go. For once I'm going to think about me.* A steely resolve hardened her voice. 'I don't want to back out, Tom. I really don't. It's only for two weeks, you know. It's not a big deal really. And we get some extra time in this gorgeous city. I mean, how many other chances are we going to get to trial being digital nomads, at no cost to us at all?'

He nodded, his eyes sliding away from hers to his empty wine glass. 'I know. And I want you to be happy.' He heaved a sigh, sounding more downbeat than she would have hoped. It was obvious that he wanted to say no, but also didn't want to be the one to change their plans.

'Ah, come on now, don't play that game, putting the decision all on me.' Her finger tapped the table, like an angry woodpecker. 'You know this is something you've wanted to try for years, so don't start denying it now.' She dredged up some patience from somewhere and softened her tone, aware she was getting shrill. 'This is the perfect opportunity to give it a trial run. You know it is.'

She pulled her hand from his, her arms hugging her chest, annoyed at the way he was framing things. Backtracking. Well, she wasn't going to let him. This was just him getting cold feet, she was sure of it. He'd been a different man these last few days of the holiday, now he'd had time to properly relax, and it was this version of Tom she wanted to be with, not the wound up, closed off person he'd become.

When he stayed silent, she relented and took his hand again, their fingers linking together. 'Look, this is our chance to give the European life a try without fully committing ourselves.' She smiled at him, glad that he was properly listening. 'And if we like it, we are at a perfect crossroads in our lives to rethink our plans, aren't we?'

He nodded again, but still didn't reply.

'Two extra weeks, Tom. That's all.' She couldn't hide the note of frustration in her voice. 'I can't see that it's much of a risk.'

He fiddled with his glass, picking it up and draining the final drops of wine before putting it back on the table. Finally, he spoke. 'I'm not worried about us being here, seeing if we can work and travel. That bit I'm excited about. What worries me is them being in our apartment.' He started to adjust the cutlery, straightening his knife and fork, making sure the end of each handle was lined up with the edge of the table. 'You know what I'm like about my stuff. Everything in its place.'

Maddie clenched her teeth and gave a silent scream. They'd been through this so many times she couldn't believe she was having to say it all again. But she knew there was no point getting cross; the best thing was to stay calm and just repeat herself, however frustrating it may feel.

'Oh, Tom, they know about that, I've explained it to them. Honestly, I'm confident they'll be totally respectful. I've spent quite a bit of time with Alex while you've been messing with that project of yours. I mean, I've had to find my own entertainment most of this holiday, haven't I? And you're going to have to trust my judgement. As soon as I met Alex in that café and we started chatting, it was like I'd known her all my life.' She paused, wondering what else she needed to say to convince Tom. 'They're a good, solid professional couple.' She was running out of arguments, but found one last salvo to hopefully secure the deal. 'I know you've only met Ed once, but you two hit it off, with him being a fellow gamer and everything.'

Tom's mouth twisted from side to side as he thought. 'Yeah, he seems like a sound guy,' he said eventually. 'And you're right, I liked him.'

'When you think about it, this whole idea of the swap, the timing couldn't be better. Most of our stuff isn't even in the apartment, is it? It's in storage, packed up ready for the house move that should have happened and didn't. It feels like fate.'

She squeezed his hand, hoping she'd done enough to persuade him. 'We couldn't have planned it better if we'd tried.'

She smiled at him and ran her fingers down his cheek, wanting to wipe away the worry in his eyes. 'Like you said the other day, we just need to think of it as an Airbnb type deal.'

'Yeah, I know.' He sighed, his fingers rubbing his chin. 'I'm just worried about my computer.'

Maddie laughed. Tom and his bloody computer; it was like an extension of himself. 'It's locked in the spare room, and we won't be giving Alex and Ed that key, will we? Which they're fine with, so you don't have to worry. And I've told the estate agent we're staying out here a couple of weeks longer so they won't organise any viewings until we're back.' She sensed her powers of persuasion might not be working and pushed a little harder. 'Besides, Alex and Ed said they'd hardly be there anyway. It's just somewhere for them to crash in the evenings until they can find a permanent base.'

She caught a movement in her peripheral vision and felt her body sag with relief when she saw the gangly figure of Ed weaving his way through the tables. His long, dark hair was combed back from his face, hanging to his shoulders and in his loose-fitting clothes, he looked quite exotic. Definitely someone you might tag with the label 'traveller'. *Thank God.* She had a feeling if he'd been any longer, Tom might have talked himself out of the whole deal.

Poor Ed wasn't looking his usual cheerful self though, a frown wrinkling his forehead. She'd spent a fair bit of time with him and Alex over the period of their holiday, while Tom was busy, and he was normally a very personable, chatty guy. She'd never seen him without a smile on his face, but now he looked worried.

'Hi, guys,' he said, pulling out a chair on the opposite side of the table and flopping into it. 'I'm so sorry we've had to bail. I was looking forward to a night out but poor Al's in a bit of a state and I'm just hoping she's okay for the flight back tomorrow.' His fingers rasped over the stubble on his cheek. 'I don't know if it's something she's eaten or if it's the stress of the news about her mum. Hopefully it'll settle down once she's had this medicine I've picked up from the pharmacy.'

Maddie leant across the table and gave his arm a sympathetic rub. 'It's a shame she's poorly. Do you think you need to stay a few days longer to let her recover?' Her mind was already scrambling, wondering if they could extend their stay at the hotel.

Oh God, what if they don't have room? We'd have to go home. Now she'd set her heart on staying, the thought was unbearable.

Ed gave a shrug. 'I did suggest that but she's desperate to get back to her mum, especially with her starting chemo. I mean, that's why we've had to change plans in the first place. And being able to stay at your place has been a lifesaver. Honestly, we can't thank you enough.'

He delved into a pocket and pulled out a set of keys. 'Here you go. These are for the apartment. There's another set which we'll need to lock the front door when we go, so I'll post those through the letter box.'

He dropped the keys into Maddie's outstretched hand. Tom pulled the spare set of keys to their apartment from his pocket, hesitating, just for a second, before he held them out to Ed.

Maddie's heart did a backflip, delighted that Tom had acquiesced. Ed curled his fingers around the keys before stuffing them in his pocket. 'Don't you worry, now. We'll look after the place as if it's our own and keep it nice and clean, ready for when you come home. Like I said, I don't think we'll be there much anyway.' He stood, pushing his chair back against the table.

'I'll... um, I'd better get back. I'm so sorry to dash off, but we'll hook up in a couple of weeks, yeah? If you let me know your flight times, I can even come and get you from the airport if you like?'

Maddie smiled. Ed was such a thoughtful guy. Nothing was ever too much trouble and she knew he meant every word. She could imagine them staying friends and liked the thought of new people to hang out with. Alex and Ed were interesting company, easy to be around and were so loved up it had made her a bit jealous at times. They appeared to have the life she wanted, but now it was hers to try.

They said their goodbyes and Ed walked away.

It's low risk, she told herself, putting the keys in her bag.

What could possibly go wrong?

PART I
MADDIE AND TOM: CROATIA

1

MADDIE

Ten days ago

Maddie sat at the pavement table, in front of the café, enjoying the early morning sun on her face. She was indulging in a spot of people watching, while thinking about her partner and waiting for her breakfast to arrive. She sighed, wishing she could be sharing the experience with Tom, surrounded by the amazing architecture of the ancient city centre. But that would only be possible if they actually operated in the same time zone.

She was a morning person and he was a night owl and since they'd arrived on holiday, he hadn't climbed out of bed until lunchtime. It was more than a little frustrating, but she just got up anyway, unable to lie there for any length of time once she was awake. She'd used the time to do a bit of exploring on her own, not wanting to waste a minute of her holiday in this fabulous city.

Given the option, Tom would live the life of a hermit, preferring to chat online with his gaming friends rather than venturing out to meet with real people. But Maddie loved striking up conversations with strangers and visiting new places. Everyone had different experiences and a unique perspective on life and she always learnt new things when she chatted with random people. That's what she enjoyed about travelling.

A good conversation energised her, filling her with new ideas. In fact, she would say talking to people was her life fuel, the source of inspiration for the adverts she designed and, in a way, every conversation, all the time spent people watching, it was all research. Finding out what mattered to real people who might be customers for the products her clients were wanting to sell. What images attracted them? What would encourage them to buy? Those questions were never far from her mind and she was like an observant magpie, taking in the details of what people were wearing and how they were behaving, filing it all away for future reference.

In a lot of ways, she and Tom were like chalk and cheese, but still, somehow, their relationship worked. Probably because they gave each other enough space to be themselves, she thought, as she took another sip of her coffee. And they shared a love of strategy games, which they enjoyed playing as a team, but also against each other.

They were on a two-week holiday in Split, a stunning coastal city in Croatia with a history stretching back over two thousand years to Roman times. She'd been longing to come for ages, ever since her work mate had been the previous summer, and shown her pictures of the stunning scenery, raving about the amazing time she'd had. Ever since, Maddie had been drooling over the online pictures of the Dalmatian coast, with its turquoise seas and the myriad islands dotting the horizon.

Split was a busy port and already she'd enjoyed hours strolling along the promenade, watching the cruise liners come and go. Seeing all the little boats heading off into the bay. And she was just at the start of the holiday; there was so much more to look forward to, especially if they hired a car and headed up along the coast road. The scenery was spectacular, with the road bordered by the sea on one side and a long ridge of rocky mountains on the other. And then there was the city to explore with its museums and galleries and eateries. She gave a happy sigh, spoilt for choice as to what she wanted to do first. Thank God she'd insisted that they come.

It had taken months of wheedling to persuade Tom that he needed a break from his computer screen and the animated heroes and villains that he created for video games. The problem was, he got lost in his work, obsessed with his creations and there were times when she felt quite lonely. Thankfully, he'd just finished a project and had to wait for the next one to be signed off before he could begin, so it was the ideal opportunity for a proper break.

Maddie was a graphic designer, and understood the creative process, but her work was sociable, designing adverts for consumer goods, which meant she needed to understand the social trends and what was currently influencing buying patterns. Working out what images and colours would resonate. She loved her job, she really did, and she especially loved finding out what made people tick. Tom, however, increasingly lived outside of reality in his made-up worlds. The distance between them was starting to worry her, especially after the emotional turmoil of the recent setbacks, which had caused him to shrink away from her. She knew he was as disappointed as she was that a family was not on the cards for them, but she couldn't get him to talk about it.

She hoped a holiday would help to mend the fractures that had been appearing in their relationship. Lots of little niggles that made them snip and snap at each other in a way that was becoming a habit. But then, being squashed together in her small apartment hadn't helped. It had been fine working from home when it had been just her, but Tom had moved in once his flat had sold, while they were waiting for the purchase of their new property to go through. Their first real home together. When that didn't happen, they were stuck.

She'd had to go back to working in the office in the last couple of weeks because the lack of space was getting on her nerves. It was impossible to concentrate with Tom popping in and out of the living room where she was trying to work, en route to the kitchen for drinks and snacks. But the office environment didn't really work for her either as there were too many distractions and she found herself getting pulled into other people's projects rather than concentrating on her own. Her stress levels had increased to a point where she felt on the edge of exploding and she'd become tetchy with Tom, picking at him about little things that didn't really matter.

When she'd been rewarded with an unexpected bonus from work, she'd immediately decided to spend it on a holiday. They hadn't been away together for a couple of years and were well overdue for a break. Croatia was the sort of destination where flights were relatively cheap and she'd found a last-minute booking going for a song.

She was smiling to herself, picking up the crumbs of her breakfast croissant with a finger, when a voice interrupted her thoughts.

'Excuse me, I wonder... would you mind if I joined you?'

She looked up into the face of a very attractive young woman, with glossy black hair and caramel skin, eyes hidden behind an oversized pair of sunglasses.

A quick scan of the tables told Maddie there were no empty

seats and she decided it might be fun to have a companion while she drank her second coffee of the morning.

'Be my guest.' She smiled as the woman sat down. 'I'm Maddie by the way.'

'Alex,' the woman said, putting her bag on the floor. 'I'm sorry to butt in, but I told my partner I'd meet him here and the place is heaving. I can't find another empty seat.'

'No worries.' She held up her coffee and took a sip. 'I'll be finished soon.'

Alex pushed her sunglasses on to the top of her head, not needing them in the shade of the canopy. 'Oh, don't let me chase you away. He'll be a while yet, I would imagine, but I couldn't stay in bed a minute longer.' She rolled her eyes and combed her fingers through her hair, pulling it over one shoulder. 'Honestly, we operate in different time zones.'

Maddie laughed, drawn to this woman who seemed to have the same problem as her. 'Tell me about it. Mine's the same.'

They fell into easy conversation, commiserating with each other about video gamers as partners.

'How long are you here for?' Alex asked when there was a lull in their chatter and they were both sipping fresh coffees.

'Two weeks. This is day three, so I'm hoping Tom is just tired and he'll catch up at some point then we can make the most of the days.' She sighed. 'It seems to be flying by so fast.' She leant towards her new friend. 'I keep seeing these people working in cafés and I would love to be able to do that. You know, the whole working while you travel thing. Then I wouldn't have to think about going home at all.'

'Oh God, yeah.' Alex rummaged in her bag and glanced at her phone before putting it away again. She smiled at Maddie. 'We've been here three months and it only feels like days. I don't know where the time's gone.'

'Three months? So, you're living here?' The thought of living in such a beautiful place was like a dream to Maddie.

'We're part of the digital nomad crew.' Alex laughed, popping the last of her croissant into her mouth. 'There's quite a community. It's a great name for people who travel and can still work as long as there's an internet connection, isn't it?' She picked up her napkin and dabbed crumbs from her lips.

Maddie's ears pricked up. She and Tom had been discussing this very thing only last night when she'd seen a Facebook post, which had led her to an article and then an hour of online research. She'd first heard the term a little while ago but had never taken much notice because it hadn't been possible before lockdown. Now her employer had introduced flexible working, and she realised this was an opportunity she wanted to explore. Tom had been surprisingly receptive when she'd floated the idea, revealing he'd had plans to travel when he was younger, before life got in the way. The more they talked about it, the more it seemed like a great way to kickstart the next phase of their life together. If they weren't having a family, they were free to go anywhere and do anything.

It was weird how she hadn't thought about it in this way before, but she'd been locked into a pattern of thinking. And this was exactly why she loved talking to strangers. It occurred to her, if she could work from home, she could work from a hotel, or anywhere for that matter. As could Tom. In fact, he'd been spending a lot of time getting his ideas together for his next project while they'd been on holiday.

She beamed at Alex, wanting to know more. 'It does have a nice ring to it, but I hadn't realised how many people lived that lifestyle.'

'There are *loads* of people doing it. And there are so many apartments available for short-term lets. We're renting one now and it's way cheaper than living in the UK, just with rental costs alone. Yet we're earning UK pay. Financially it makes so much sense.' She finished her coffee. 'We're actually thinking about extending our stay a bit longer.'

Maddie was properly intrigued now, a bud of an idea blossoming in her brain. 'That sounds like a great way to build up some cash.' She leant towards her new friend. 'Tell me more.'

'It's brilliant, there's fast Wi-Fi everywhere in Croatia. I mean, as a country they've really invested in their digital infrastructure to attract travellers. And the locals are so welcoming, you soon feel part of the community. The truth is, this country runs on tourism, so it's like this symbiotic relationship.' She shrugged and smiled. 'It seems to work well.'

'That sounds idyllic.' Maddie's eyes scanned the café and sure enough she could see a handful of people with laptops on their tables. There was a background buzz of chatter and laughter. 'I do love it here. It's such a great vibe.' Maddie dabbed at the last of the crumbs on her plate, her mind absorbing everything Alex had said. A picture of a new life was forming, one built on adventure.

'I know and wow, the scenery. Honestly, get out on the buses and have a look, it's stunning. Or get a boat trip to some of the islands.'

Maddie pulled her tourist map out of her bag, inspired now to organise some trips out, whether Tom wanted to accompany her or not. She spread it out on the table. 'Come on then. Show me the best places.'

They chatted for over an hour, by which time, Maddie had a list of things to see and do, as well as some useful links about working in Croatia. They only parted when Alex's partner, Ed, appeared, all tousle-haired and bleary eyed. After brief introductions, Maddie stood to give him her seat, keen to get back to Tom and share her new idea. Excitement bubbled inside her and for the first time in many months, she felt optimistic. Life had plenty to offer if she took off her blinkers.

If Alex and Ed could enjoy this lifestyle, why couldn't she and Tom?

2

Maddie decided she needed to slow herself down, and took a meandering route back to the hotel to give herself time to think before mentioning anything to Tom. There was no point setting a hare running if it wasn't one she genuinely wanted to chase. But by the time she got back to their room, she'd done some mental arithmetic and was absolutely certain trying life abroad was an option they should consider.

Tom was in the shower, singing tunelessly when she entered the room and she waited for him to emerge before sidling up to him and giving him a lingering kiss.

He looked surprised, then grinned and pulled her to him. 'More of that, please,' he murmured, dropping gentle kisses on the base of her neck. She laughed and pushed him away. 'Maybe later, but I've had an idea and I really need to talk about it before I self-combust.'

He grimaced. 'Oh God, should I be worried?'

She gave him a playful punch on the shoulder. 'No, not worried. Excited, I hope.' She smacked his towel-covered bottom. 'Come on, get dressed then we can go to that café on the prom for lunch and I'll tell you all about it.'

It was a glorious day, a gentle sea breeze keeping the temperature at a nice level, the sun sparkling on the sea like a thousand starbursts. *Imagine if I could see that every day.* A thrill of excitement made her heart race, her lips curling into a smile.

At the café, Tom sat beside her, his hand draped round her shoulders as they took in the view. He seemed relaxed, not talkative, but lost in his thoughts, which wasn't unusual. She didn't mind the quiet. It wasn't one of those awkward ones where tension buzzed in the air; this was peaceful. Companionable. And how they used to be before all the stress of trying to move house and conceive a baby.

This was exactly what she'd wanted from the holiday: to reconnect with her partner.

'I love you, Maddie,' Tom said, out of nowhere. 'And I'm sorry if I've been a bit... distant.' He pulled her closer, fingers brushing her skin. 'I just let things get on top of me, but I feel better now that project's finished. At least we'll have a chunk of money coming in.'

That was the problem with Tom's work. He was self-employed and jobs arrived in project form, payments following the completion of set milestones. But the timing wasn't predictable because specifications and deadlines changed and Tom wasn't great at the admin side of things. Like many creatives, he'd found himself running his own business when he despised paperwork with a vengeance. Maddie had offered support, but he could get quite prickly and defensive if she suggested she could help with his invoices or filling in forms or organising his filing system. So, she'd learnt to leave him to it unless he specifically asked.

She was lucky that she was actually employed by the advertising agency she worked for, rather than being a freelancer, and although they'd moved to a more sub-contract model in recent years, she'd been with them for almost a decade and was part of the core team. She was grateful for her monthly salary, which gave them regular cash flow. There'd been talk though, of letting staff go after the loss of a major client and that worry sat as a permanent guest at the back of her mind.

If they decided to travel, they could live cheaply. And if they put a hold on buying a house together, they could rent her place out and have an income from that. Even if she had to go part-time, they'd manage. The more she thought about it, the better the idea sounded.

'I get so stressed about money,' he continued, his fingers pressing into her shoulder for a moment, the thought of it making him tense. 'I know I get tetchy. And I know I haven't been easy to live with, but sometimes I get pretty down. I want to be able to look after you, or at least be an equal partner in terms of bringing in money, but I always fall short.'

She could hear the heaviness in his voice, and it pulled at her heartstrings. She'd guessed he was feeling like this, but he'd never opened up about it before, going silent rather than talking it through.

'I can't see an end to it. Constant pressure just to get by.' He caught her eye. 'Everything's getting more expensive and I've been worrying about taking on a bigger mortgage for a new house. Then there's the energy bills.' He puffed out his cheeks. 'It's exhausting, isn't it?'

'Oh, Tom.' She leant her head on his shoulder, her arm round his waist. 'I love you too, sweetheart. And you're right, things have been a struggle recently, but I hadn't realised how much it was getting to you.'

'I've been racking my brains, thinking how we can change

things, but I keep coming up with a blank. And that's getting me down as well. I don't want to just work. I want us to be able to take time out, come on holidays like this.' He sighed again, like he had the weight of the world on his shoulders. 'I don't know what to do. It's like we don't even have time to live, do we?'

Tom's words brought a lump to her throat. He sounded so defeated and yet he loved his work. She knew he did, could visualise the excitement in his eyes every time a new project was approved. It was balancing the finances that was the issue. If they could get that right, she knew they'd be fine because their love for each other was strong. It was something she'd never questioned. They were made to be together, two halves of a whole. It wasn't their relationship that was the problem. It was how they'd chosen to live their lives.

She sat up straight. 'It's weird you bringing this up because that is literally what I wanted to talk to you about. And you know what? I might have a solution.'

His eyes widened. 'You do?'

She laughed, excited to tell him. 'I told you I had an idea, didn't I? You know we were talking about digital nomads yesterday?'

He nodded. 'Yeah, but I've never actually met anyone doing it.'

'Well... I just did. A couple called Alex and Ed, and I got chatting to them at the place I went to for breakfast. They've been here three months and couldn't say enough good things about it.' Her smile widened, hope blossoming in her heart. 'Why don't we give it a go? Apparently, Croatia is a great place for it. They have all the infrastructure we'd need. We could get an apartment over here and it would be so much cheaper than living in London. So, if we rented out my apartment instead of trying to sell it, we could even save some money. Or just not work so hard. Take our feet off the pedal for a bit.'

He gazed at her for a long moment and she could tell he was really thinking about it. 'What? You really think that could work?' He sounded dubious, but not like it was a lost cause at this point, which was encouraging.

'Alex reckons they save loads of money and they're thinking of staying longer. She told me you can get a special visa so you can stay here for a year.'

His arm dropped from her shoulder, his hand rubbing at the back of his neck, a sure sign he was feeling uncomfortable. 'A couple you just met told you this?' Maddie nodded. 'And you believe them?'

She was a bit taken aback. It seemed a strange question and she had an inkling she was losing her ground. 'Why wouldn't I? They have no reason to lie to me.'

'Yeah, well you don't really know them. And you do tend to believe everything people say.' He sighed. 'You just can't trust people these days. And everyone wants to make out they're living the dream even if they're really having a shit time. Social media has made everything a mirage.'

Her fingers drummed on the table, and she slapped one hand over the other to stop herself. She was riled by Tom's dismissiveness towards her new friends but she'd been snared by the idea of a different lifestyle and she wasn't going to let it go easily.

She loosened her jaw, told herself to calm down. Getting cross with Tom didn't work. He shut down at the first sign of conflict and either changed the subject or walked away. To have a proper discussion with him, on any sort of contentious issue, she had to make sure there wasn't too much emotion involved. If he felt challenged in any way, or believed he had caused upset, he ceased to function.

Obviously, this aspect of his character wasn't ideal, but nobody was perfect and she was still working out how to get round this particular obstacle so they could talk through their differences. She knew he was worth it though, because the good times with Tom filled her heart with joy and if she could navigate the rocky times, she knew their relationship could only get stronger. She loved him like she'd never loved any other man and although being with him could be frustrating, the challenges had made her think about her own behaviour and how she communicated. In the end, she thought it had made her a better person.

After taking a few moments to calm down, she took a deep breath and gave him her pitch. 'We're free to work anywhere we choose, right? So this could be perfect for us. You've got to admit it sounds like a win-win, doesn't it? I've had a bit more of a look online and it really does seem to be a thing at the moment. Especially among people at our stage of life. Getting to travel while they earn, before they decide to settle down.'

She pulled out her phone and found her internet history, showing him an article Alex had pointed her towards.

His mouth worked from side to side as he read, before he handed back her phone. 'Honestly... if it could work, that would be great.' Her heart leapt and she crossed her fingers under the table. 'Today, for the first time, I think I'm starting to relax. You know, it's good to have a bit of distance from... everything, not just work. It helps.'

She knew that the everything he referred to was not just their money worries or the day-to-day grind. Up until a couple of weeks ago, she'd been obsessed with starting a family and it had been an intense and emotional time when their hopes had been dashed.

They were still digesting the implications and it had been hard on him, seeing her so down about it, and believing that he might be to blame for her sadness. Turned out it was *her* body that didn't want to play ball and now she was trying to accept the situation. At this point, they had options. There was the IVF route and there was always adoption, but for the time being, they had agreed they needed a break, to really consider how they wanted their future to unfold. Now she could see that a bit of travel and living abroad might help to open their eyes to new opportunities.

She squeezed his hand, pressing her point home. 'Both our jobs are home-based, so I don't see what difference it would make if our home was over here for a while, do you?' The idea of it created a buzz of excitement that she didn't want to let go. A jump off the hamster wheel of their lives and something new to look forward to, now children were unlikely to be in the mix. The timing could not have been more perfect with the house sale falling through and she felt, in her heart, that this was meant to be. A pointer as to what life could be like for them if they could open themselves up to new ideas.

Tom chewed at a fingernail, his brow furrowed, lost in thought and she let him have space to think, not daring to speak in case she pushed him the wrong way.

'Yeah, but what if we rent out the apartment, and then we decide we don't like it over here? We wouldn't be able to go back, would we? We'd have to wait for months, which is a long time being miserable.'

Maddie shrugged. 'We could always do short leases. Or even Airbnb.'

It hadn't crossed Maddie's mind that coming here to work might be so disastrous she'd want to go home. As soon as she decided to do something, she fully committed to it, despite any setbacks along the way. Giving up was not part of her DNA and she wasn't going to give up on this idea either. She wanted it, she needed it and, in her heart, she felt Tom did too. Despite him being a bit of a hermit, he enjoyed being in new places. Even if it was a tussle getting him there. Money had been a stumbling block in the past but now she'd come up with a solution, Tom didn't seem to know what to do with it.

'Let's start properly looking into it, shall we?' Their eyes met and she gave Tom a hopeful smile. 'We'll do our research and come back to it in a couple of days, how about that?'

They had ten days of their holiday left, so she was hoping they could come to a decision before then. Maybe they'd come up with a way of not having to leave at all. She started to wonder if there was anything they had to get back for and realised there was nothing stopping them from extending their stay. Was it possible they could do this? Now the idea had hatched in her mind, she was determined to nurture it into existence. And if there was a way, she was going to find it.

Tom's face cracked into a grin. 'Yeah, let's do that. When I was younger, the idea of getting away and travelling was always on my mind.' He laughed. 'I didn't have anyone to travel with then, and I wasn't confident enough to do it on my own, but if you're up for it, I'm in.'

'We don't have to stop at Croatia. Alex and Ed said they've been to Thailand and Bali.' She gave a happy sigh. 'Can you imagine?'

She leant in to give him a kiss. This idea could be the making of them. *Or the breaking*, said the voice of doubt in her head, the one that saw the risks she often refused to see when she had an end goal in her sights.

3

ONE DAY AGO

The holiday sped past, Maddie and Tom ticking off lots of sightseeing trips from the list she'd put together. She'd settled into a routine of meeting up with Alex for breakfast, while their respective partners had a lie in, and they'd become firm friends. Sometimes Ed would join them, making them laugh with his observations and anecdotes. Once, she and Tom had bumped into Ed on the promenade, the men bonding over a chat about gaming, but they'd never managed to meet up as a foursome. Tom had always found an excuse. He had to work on developing his next project, or he had a chat organised with a friend he collaborated with from time to time. Or he'd organised a game night with his mates online. Maddie just went ahead and met up with her new friends on her own, determined to enjoy her holiday to the max and not let Tom's agenda stifle her.

Alex was bubbly and fun and made Maddie laugh. She was easy company and had helped Maddie to progress her ideas about renting in Split, giving her contact numbers and suggestions for everything they'd need to get themselves sorted. She was a walking encyclopaedia on the digital nomad life and the more they talked about it, the more possible the plan appeared. Even Tom seemed to be getting excited about it.

By the end of the holiday, they'd done a fair amount of research and things were looking more positive than Maddie could have hoped. They knew they could stay in Croatia for 180 days – six months – on a tourist visa, so there would be nothing to do on that score immediately. They'd looked for apartments and found a few in Split that would do. A bit smaller than they'd like, but they'd be okay in the short term and they could rent on a monthly basis, so they didn't have to commit to a longer let, like they would in England.

To make it possible, though, they'd need to let their apartment in London and how they should do that was the current sticking point. Tom was worried it was too risky and it was this problem that was running through her mind when she met up with Alex for breakfast.

As soon as Alex sat opposite Maddie, it was obvious something was wrong. Her eyes looked bloodshot and red-rimmed, her face puffy and tear stained.

'Hey, are you okay?' Maddie reached across the table and put a hand on her arm, giving it a gentle rub. Alex had a tissue scrunched in her hand and blew her nose. 'Oh... I'm fine, ignore me. Just had a bit of bad news, that's all.'

The waitress appeared and took their order and Maddie waited for her to leave before she continued their conversation. 'I'm so sorry to hear that. Is there anything I can do?'

Alex shook her head, gave a tight smile. 'It's just... life, I suppose. It's never straightforward, is it?'

'You can say that again.' She gave her friend's arm a squeeze, her voice gentle. 'I'm happy to listen if you need to talk. A problem shared is a problem halved, as the saying goes.'

Alex blew her nose again and stuffed the tissue back in her bag. 'It's my mum. She's just been diagnosed with breast cancer.'

'Oh my God, no wonder you're upset.'

'It's such a shock. You sort of think your parents are indestructible, don't you? She looks after herself, you know, she does yoga, has a healthy diet, runs half marathons. And she's only fifty-four.'

Maddie was stuck for a reply, because it seemed very unfair. But nothing about life was fair, was it? As she knew only too well from her dad's recent health issues. The thing was to look for the positives, that's what her friend needed.

'But that means the prognosis must be good? I know treatment has come on a long way in recent years.'

Alex's chin puckered and it looked like she was going to burst into tears, her voice wavering. 'I don't know. She just told me she had cancer and then she started crying, so I couldn't ask her any more. I mean I've loads of questions but Mum is one of those people who has blind faith in the medical profession. She'll just go along with whatever they say and won't ask about anything.' A tear rolled down her cheek. 'I'm so worried about her.'

Maddie moved her chair closer and put a comforting arm round Alex's shoulders. 'What about your dad?'

Silence for a moment.

'He died last year. It was a hit and run and me and Mum were just getting our heads round that and all the debts he left behind. She had to downsize and completely re-organise her life, you know, it's been a lot.' She paused. 'It's just me and Mum now.'

'Have you got other family members who might be able to support her? Siblings? Aunties or uncles. Grandparents?'

'Not really. Mum was estranged from her family when she

got pregnant with me. Some sort of scandal, but she won't ever talk about it and I decided a long time ago it was probably better not to know. And my sister moved to Dubai.'

Maddie's heart went out to her friend. 'Oh, that's hard, isn't it?'

The waitress came back with their coffees and a couple of pastries, putting them on the table before leaving them to continue their conversation.

Maddie could feel Alex's body shaking, like she was trying desperately hard not to give in to her emotions and she rubbed her shoulder again, feeling quite helpless. 'What are you going to do?'

Alex sniffed and pulled another tissue from her bag, dabbing at her eyes. 'I'm going to have to go home. Mum has nobody to help her and she's starting chemo any day now, she said. I need to be there for her. It's not fair to leave her to go through this alone. I can tell she's terrified.' She blew her nose. 'I'm terrified too. But I think it'll be easier to deal with mentally if I'm there and I can see for myself what's happening.'

'Yes, I'm sure that's the right thing to do, but I'll miss you. What about Ed? Is he staying or will he go back with you?'

Alex shook her head. 'I don't know. I haven't told him yet. I literally got the news while I was walking to meet you.' She tucked her hair behind her ears and seemed to give herself a mental shake, picking up her coffee and taking a sip. 'I have a feeling he'll be glad to go back though.' She sighed. 'We've been travelling for a while now and he's a big family guy. There are loads of brothers and sisters and cousins.' She flapped a hand, sounding thoroughly disheartened. 'Honestly, I've lost track. But he was planning on going back to visit anyway.'

Maddie was struggling to know what to say. 'Well, at least you'll be together. Because you'll need support too.'

Alex took another sip of her coffee and gazed over Maddie's shoulder, lost in her thoughts for a few moments. 'I can't even think straight. It's been such a shock. And we've paid for the apartment here, so we're going to lose that money.'

Maddie picked up her own coffee, glad of the warmth of it in her hands. 'Nightmare,' she murmured, reminded how life could spin in a moment, when you were least expecting it.

'Tell me about it. And when we get back, we need to find ourselves somewhere to rent. I can't stay with Mum because she's only got a bedsit. She moved down to work in London after Dad died, because she had to sell the house to pay off his debts and she wanted to be close to me. It's all she could afford and honestly, it's tiny. I mean, I love her to bits, but we couldn't go back to living together. That would be a recipe for conflict, especially if she's feeling poorly with the chemo. Mum is a big personality and needs her own space, if you know what I mean.'

Maddie took a bite of her pastry, Alex's news dragging her own mood down. 'I'm so sorry this is happening to you. And there I was envying you your lifestyle. In fact, Tom and I have been looking into following in your footsteps. You and Ed have been such an inspiration to me, the way you live your lives and the freedom you have. I think it's kicked me out of the rut I've been stuck in. So, thank you for that and... I've really enjoyed your company.' She reached over and squeezed her friend's hand. 'Is there anything I can do? Because I feel like I owe you a favour.'

Alex put her other hand over Maddie's. 'Thanks for the offer. That's so sweet of you.' She was silent for a few moments. 'Although... no... but maybe... OK... totally wildcard idea...' She sat up straight. 'I don't suppose you fancy doing a swap, do you? Would you maybe consider letting us stay in your apartment for a couple of weeks, while we get something more permanent sorted? And you can stay in our apartment here? It would literally be the most amazing help, because right now we have nowhere to go and everything costs so much in London.'

Maddie stared at her while her brain ran round in circles.

'Please,' Alex said, her eyes fixed on Maddie. 'We'll be the perfect house guests, I promise. In fact, you can come back with me now and have a look at our apartment before you make your decision, but you'll see it's pretty bloody amazing. We were so lucky getting it and it's way better than a hotel room. It's got a beautiful private patio at the back that gets the sun for most of the day. We have a swimming pool. And it's central for the cafés and the beach. You can even see the sea out the back.'

Maddie hesitated, unable to fathom how this opportunity had just landed in her lap. And Tom had agreed it was something they wanted to do. She didn't need his approval to make this decision, did she?

'Yes,' she said, before the sensible voice in her head told her she should be saying no.

4

Tom was busy tapping away on his laptop when Maddie arrived back at their hotel room an hour later, a definite spring in her step. She was bursting to share the plan with him, but also knew she had to get her approach right. He didn't like surprises and if she rushed things, his answer would be a straight up no. Then there'd be no budging him.

'I've got news,' she announced, hanging her bag on a hook by the door.

He looked up from where he was sitting on the bed and shifted his laptop off his knee, patting the mattress next to him. 'Come on then. Is it news I'll like, or something I'll be scared of?' He laughed. 'It's always one or the other with you, isn't it? No in between.'

She liked that he was teasing her. It was something he hadn't done in a while and it was another sign that his low mood had lifted. He'd definitely relaxed over the course of the holiday, and it reinforced her determination to follow her living abroad idea. Now that she had a way to make it happen, it was hard to stop herself from letting her excitement burst out.

She plopped down next to him on the bed, leaning in for a kiss before snuggling up, her head on his chest.

'I've got news too,' he said, a note of excitement in his voice. 'But you first.'

She adjusted her position so she could look at him and gauge his mood. Optimistic, she thought. More positive than she'd seen him in a while. She sat up and crossed her legs so she could face him, taking his hands in hers. 'Okay, so I've just met up with Alex and she's had some really bad news. Her mum's not well. It's the worst thing, a cancer diagnosis, and she's about to start chemo. Anyway, it means Alex and Ed have got to go back to the UK. Like straight away. In fact, I think she said they're trying to get a flight tomorrow.'

Tom's eyes widened. 'Oh no, that's terrible.'

'Yeah, really bad. But... and here's where it could be great for us because' – she paused, wanting her punchline to have maximum impact – 'their apartment here in Split is now available for two weeks.'

Silence. His face was suddenly blank and she wondered if he hadn't understood the implications. What it might mean for the two of them. Was his mind busy computing behind that vacant façade? She ploughed on.

'So... this is the really good news... Alex has said we're welcome to use their apartment for free, because it's all paid for and they can't get a refund. And she took me to see it.' Maddie still couldn't believe their luck and was having to stop herself from bouncing up and down on the bed with excitement. 'Honestly, it's gorgeous. Way better than those pokey places we've been looking at. And it's really central.' She pulled out her phone and found her photo album. 'Look, I've got pictures.' She held it up for him to see while she scrolled through, encouraged by his murmurs of approval. 'Good, isn't it?'

'Looks fantastic. But can we afford it?'

'You're not listening.' She laughed. 'That's the best bit. We don't have to pay anything.'

'What?' His startled expression suggested that he didn't believe her. 'Why not? How?' He rubbed a hand over his hair, looking completely flummoxed. 'I'm sorry, I'm probably being really thick here, but I'm not sure I understand.'

'We're going to do a swap.'

He blinked.

'As long as you're okay with it, of course. But it would really help Alex and Ed out because they're stuck for somewhere to stay in London at short notice.' Tom's expression changed from disbelief to concern. He stared at her.

'Don't you see what this means? We could try out living here at no extra cost to us and no risk either. In fact, we'll probably *save* money. It'll only be two weeks. So, we don't have to do anything official like sublet to them. It'll be like they're our guests in London and we'll be their guests here.' She grinned. 'Keeping it simple. Like an Airbnb swap.'

His dubious expression couldn't keep the delight from her voice or the smile from her face. This was a genius plan.

'It'll be a try-before-you-buy type of thing. Then we're not committed to being here, but we can test out the lifestyle. And we still have our apartment to go back to when the time is up. Even if we decide we don't like it and it's not going to work for us, we can manage two weeks, can't we?'

To her, it was too good an opportunity to miss. And if this trial worked, they could go home confident and motivated and find a longer-term solution, before setting out as digital nomads for real.

'Wow.' Tom's forehead crumpled into a frown, his mouth moving like he was trying to shape some words but was struggling to find the right ones. She gazed at him, waiting for him to say something else but after a couple of minutes of silence, she couldn't resist pushing her argument a little more.

'I know it's a lot to take in, but I just think it's fate and we can't ignore it.' Her enthusiasm was making her gabble, the excitement hurrying the words out of her mouth. 'You know… we've been handed this great chance to spend an extra two weeks here trialling a new lifestyle.' She kissed his cheek. 'And the timing is perfect, given all the bad luck we've had recently. Plus, it makes sense financially.'

She could hear the desperation in her voice and decided she was pushing too hard now. It would be better to back off at this point and let the poor guy process things.

So, she did and the room fell silent, Tom's hands fidgeting with hers, his eyes gazing over her shoulder at the blank TV screen on the wall. She cleared her throat and changed tack. 'You said you had news too?'

He seemed to come out of his trance then and gave her the briefest flash of a smile. 'Yes, yes, I do. I've got the go-ahead for my next project, and it's a quick turnaround, which is going to be a squeeze, but it means the money will come in quickly too.'

She gave him a delighted hug and another kiss. 'That's brilliant news. A bit of a relief really, because there wasn't anything else on the horizon, was there?'

'No, it's gone a bit quiet on the work front. But that's the way it is, when you're self-employed. Feast or famine.' He laughed, his mind on his work now. 'I'll probably get more enquiries once I'm busy.'

She gave him another hug, wondering if this was their turning point. After everything going wrong, maybe now they were going to hit a lucky streak. 'I'm really pleased, Tom. I know this is a project you've set your heart on.'

'It is. Because it's a new client for me and they're the market leaders with loads of best-selling titles, so if they're happy with this project, they've said there will be more.' He grinned at her, delight sparkling in his eyes. 'I've just got to prove I can do a good job in the time they've given me.'

'I'm so proud of you. I don't know how you come up with all these ideas.'

He laughed. 'No, well neither do I. It's my weird brain I suppose.'

'I love your brain.'

'And I love you, Maddie.' He was suddenly serious. 'Being with you is all I've ever wanted. And... and I've been meaning to say this for a while... you're more than enough for me.'

She swallowed, deciphering the hidden meaning in his words, which brought a lump to her throat. If they decided against IVF or adopting, options which they'd left on the table while they gave themselves time to think things through, there would only ever be the two of them. But that prospect was exciting now she'd realised they could roam the world if they wanted. Way more exciting than spending their days in London.

A slow smile spread across his face. 'I think your idea of staying here for another couple of weeks might be just what I need to get this project started. I'm so full of ideas and I don't want to jinx it by changing anything. I'm at the storyboard stage at the moment, working out the concepts and the characters, so it's doable on my laptop. A change of surroundings, being somewhere new, seems to have freed up my mind for some reason.' His hand squeezed hers. 'Perhaps you're right and it *is* meant to be.'

He pulled his laptop onto his knee. 'Let me show you this character I started working on while you were out. He's going to be the bad guy in the new game. Honestly, he is *so* cool.' He tapped a few keys and a giant of a man wreathed in what looked like seaweed appeared. He had crab claws for hands and his face was almost shark-like, with huge eyes and rows of pointed teeth. 'I'm going for islands and under the sea for my game worlds and, you know, I wouldn't have thought of that if I hadn't been here. Seeing all the lovely islands round the coast.' He laughed. 'It's right what they say about travel broadening your mind.'

Maddie smiled to herself, liking that Tom was a big kid at heart. Why on earth would she need children when she had him? 'He's amazing. The players are going to love him.'

Tom frowned. 'The bad news is I'm going to have to work for the rest of today because I've got to get some of these ideas firmed up before they vanish. And I've got a team meeting booked later with the rest of the people I'll be working with.'

She let go of his hands and climbed off the bed. 'That's fine. I've got my next work project to think about too. And I'll have to check with my boss to make sure they're okay about me being here for a bit longer, but I honestly can't see what difference it'll make.'

She could tell Tom wasn't listening, his mind already back on his project. But she needed confirmation that they were really going to do this. She was so excited she felt a bit sick, her stomach swirling. This would be the most adventurous thing she'd ever done in her life. The most impulsive thing she'd ever done, too, and although a part of her brain was asking her if she was mad, the other part was already celebrating.

'So... can I confirm with Alex that we'll do the swap and take on their apartment? She's leaving tomorrow so we have to make a decision today. I thought we could meet them for a last meal tonight, then at least you get a better idea who we're loaning our apartment to before we exchange keys.'

Tom was already distracted, tapping away on his laptop while he replied. 'Okay. Let's do it. As you say, it's a low-risk way of giving this digital nomad thing a go. And if we're ever going to do it, the best time is now, before we have any... family commitments.'

Oh God, there it is. She'd more or less decided she didn't want to subject herself to invasive fertility treatments and all the disappointments she anticipated. Nobody seemed to have a straightforward story to tell on that score. But he didn't know that and he was also thinking about adoption as another way forward. It wasn't a route she wanted to go down just yet. She didn't want strangers poking about in her life, judging her, deciding if she was fit to be a parent. She just hadn't confided that to Tom. But all that could wait – why spoil the moment?

'I've told Alex and Ed the spare room is out of bounds because it's your office. But we always lock that anyway because of the insurance on your computers, and all our personal paperwork is in the desk in there, so it's perfectly safe. Good job we've kept the place tidy and half empty for the viewings. It means they can just walk in and use it.'

He looked at her for a moment and she could see a flicker of doubt, then he seemed to shake whatever negative thought he'd had from his head. 'I suppose we'll just have to trust them,' he muttered, his attention no longer with her, his mind in the world he was creating for the new video game. But she had his agreement and that was all she needed.

She mentally rubbed her hands together, hardly able to contain her excitement. 'I'll get the ball rolling then.' He nodded, his fingers busy on his keyboard.

She almost started skipping with joy as she made her way to Alex's apartment. *It seems too good to be true.* That thought made her stop for a moment, a niggle of doubt burrowing into the back of her mind. Something about this whole arrangement was bothering her, despite not wanting to admit it to herself. She just couldn't put her finger on what it was.

5

NOW

The next morning, after the failed get-together, Maddie was up early and decided to call round and see Alex, to make sure she was okay to travel, because if she was still unwell, they were going to have to adjust their arrangements. She'd hardly slept, worrying about having to re-organise everything and although she'd sent Alex a message, there'd been no response. That little voice of doubt had grown louder in her head and she was hoping it was wrong. Whatever the situation, she had to go and find out for herself.

Tom was still sound asleep, so she slipped out of their room and hurried towards Alex and Ed's apartment. She'd thought Alex had said their flight was at 10 a.m., so she was hoping they'd still be there. She rang the buzzer for the ground floor apartment, shifting her weight from foot to foot, while she waited.

The apartment was in a lovely old building, with golden yellow stonework, and she tried to imagine how the evening sun might reflect on the walled terrace at the back. It opened out from the living room and was full of plants and climbers, not to mention the swimming pool, creating a green oasis that Maddie couldn't wait to enjoy.

Alex opened the door, looking surprised to see her. 'Oh hi, I thought...' She seemed flustered. 'I wasn't expecting you. I thought Ed had sorted everything out last night.'

'Yes, he gave us the keys, but he was in a rush to get back to you and I wasn't sure if you'd be travelling today. Because if you're not well enough, we'll have to sort out a room for ourselves at the hotel, you see. We're supposed to be out by tomorrow lunchtime.'

Alex glanced at her watch. 'I'm fine now, in fact I've got to head off very soon. And I couldn't call because the battery in my phone is refusing to charge.' She gave a tentative smile. 'I thought for a moment there you might have changed your mind and that would be horrendous because I'd be sleeping on Mum's floor, in a corner of her living room.'

Maddie understood now why Alex had looked nervous, worried that she and Tom were going to back out. 'No, it's all good. I just had a few questions about practicalities, like electricity and if it's on a meter. And what happens with rubbish. And if there's Wi-Fi in the apartment.'

'Come in.' Alex stood back to let Maddie past. 'I made a list for you but I can run through it quickly, if you like.' She checked her watch again. 'I'm so sorry, I don't want to rush you, and this feels so rude, but I've got a taxi arriving any minute.'

She walked over to the table and picked up an envelope, covered in neat columns of writing. 'Sorry, I couldn't find any paper so I had to use this. Looks like junk mail, so I think it's okay.' She dangled a keyring in front of Maddie. 'Here's the second set of keys. This big one is the front door, the small one is the patio door at the back. I've written instructions for the utilities and the contact number for the landlady if you have any problems. But other than that, it's pretty straightforward.' She waved the envelope before putting it on the dining table along with the keys. 'Anyway, it's all on there, including the Wi-Fi password.' Alex frowned and checked her watch again, clearly a bit agitated. 'Is there anything else?'

'No.' Maddie shook her head. 'No, I don't think so.'

It's done. No going back. And that's what she wanted, wasn't it? Not to go back to the life they'd left in London for a bit longer. She wanted to go forwards, do something that might bring the fun back into their lives.

Alex hooked her bag over her shoulder, clearly keen to go. 'Can you message me with anything I need to know about your apartment? I've run out of time.'

Maddie's heart was racing, her mind scrambling to work out what she needed to tell her temporary tenant. 'Okay, yes I'll do that because my mind's gone blank. The key with the dimples is for the main door of the block, then there's a Yale key for the apartment.'

Alex walked towards the hallway where her suitcase and carry-on bag stood ready by the door.

'We'll have to sort out what we're going to do in two weeks in terms of getting the keys back,' Maddie gabbled. 'But we've plenty of time to chat about that. Monday is bin day. We left everything switched on because we were only intending on being away two weeks. We've sort of half moved out so there should be plenty of empty drawer space you can use. Kath next door is brilliant and she'll help you with any problems. Best to go and introduce yourself.'

Alex had her hand on her suitcase handle and was glancing round, obviously checking she hadn't left anything.

'Oh, hang on a minute,' Maddie said, pulling her phone from

her pocket as she hurried towards Alex. She angled the camera to get them both in the shot. 'I just wanted to get a selfie because Tom hasn't met you and I've had to convince him you're not part of the mafia or something.'

Alex blinked, a startled look on her face.

'I can post things on to you if I find anything you've forgotten,' Maddie said. 'And you can message me with any questions.' She flapped a hand, feeling hot and flustered, everything happening too quickly for her to be able to think straight. 'You get off. I don't want to make you late.'

Alex gave a tight smile and pulled up the handle of her wheeled case. 'I'm sorry things have been such a rush, but you're a lifesaver, honestly I can't thank you enough.'

Maddie realised then, what was missing. 'Where's Ed?'

Alex's eyes dropped to the floor. 'Oh, he's already gone.' She picked up her carry-on bag and balanced it on top of her suitcase.

'Ah, right.' The way she said it, her voice all clipped and snippy, left Maddie thinking it was odd they weren't travelling together. But then again, maybe they couldn't get seats on the same flight. She changed the subject. 'And how's your mum doing?'

'My mum—?' Alex frowned, looking more flustered by the second. She opened the door. 'The same, I think. I don't know.' She checked outside. 'I'm sorry, my taxi's here. I really do have to go.' And with that, she left.

Maddie hurried after her, calling her goodbyes as she watched her climb into a waiting taxi, Alex giving her a little wave before she disappeared down the road and out of sight.

It had all happened so quickly, Maddie was in that weird headspace where you're not quite sure if things are real. It had been an awkward exchange with Alex, but she put it down to her friend's anxiety about her mum and the stress of having to pack up and go home so quickly.

She went back inside and closed the front door, her eyes scanning the space. *This is my home now.* It sounded almost ridiculous. *For two weeks, anyway.* She gazed around her, the excitement building. She wanted to put her head back and scream for joy. But she didn't, because that might scare the neighbours.

Now she was on her own, she could have a proper look at the place. The front door opened into a square hallway, with hooks for coats and a rack for shoes. A door off that opened into the living room, with an archway into the kitchen at one end, and a door into the bedroom and bathroom to the side.

The walls were all white, the floors tiled with a cream-coloured stone throughout. Nice and plain and simple with a few abstract pictures on the walls to add a touch of colour. The furniture was modern and minimal, a chestnut-brown sofa and a light oak dining table and chairs, like something you might find in IKEA. It felt spacious and light and the terrace at the back was a place where Maddie knew she'd be spending most of her time. There was an awning to provide shade, which would stop the living room becoming too warm, a table and chairs to sit out, and pots full of flowers which she would enjoy looking after. But the best bit was the pool, with the fabulous view out over the sea. Tom was going to love it.

The place was perfect. Absolutely perfect and if this was what her future had in store, Maddie would be delighted. She picked up the envelope and read the instructions, which all seemed straightforward enough, then turned it over to see if Alex had continued on the other side.

But she hadn't written more instructions. In someone else's angry handwriting were the words:

Don't you DARE back out now. Actions have consequences.
Ed

6

She dropped the envelope, recoiling as if it had attacked her.

It's not meant for you, she told herself, her hand pressed to her racing heart. This was a message for Alex, left by Ed. It made her wonder what was going on in their relationship but it was none of her business and it could refer to a myriad of things. Or had Alex wanted to back out of this arrangement? Surely not, because it was her mother's health that had caused them to leave early in the first place.

There was clearly a bit of tension in the relationship, a disagreement about something, which could explain why Ed had already left. In fact, thinking about it, Alex hadn't made proper eye contact for the whole of their conversation. She'd been agitated, but Maddie had thought that was because she was running late. Maybe that wasn't the reason at all. Maybe he'd just left her to make her own way to the airport and she was too embarrassed or upset to say. She'd definitely seemed distracted but along with her mum's cancer diagnosis, this message from her boyfriend was probably the last thing she needed.

It's none of your business, she reminded herself, pulling back from emotional involvement in Alex's drama. Even though she might feel sympathy for her situation, she didn't know what was really going on. That might be an old message left after a fight and they'd made up. There really was no telling and there was no point second guessing.

Leave it alone. It didn't affect their plans to stay in Croatia in any way, did it? She thought about that for a moment and decided it made no difference at all. She picked up the envelope and put it on the table, hiding the scrawled message on the other side, before walking over to the patio doors and stepping outside.

The terrace was bigger than she'd remembered, a hidden area wrapping round the side of the kitchen. It was in the shade and the coolness of the air was like a balm on her skin. A hammock was strung from two hooks in the walls and she sank into its embrace, relishing a few moments of calm.

The swinging sensation was instantly soothing and she closed her eyes, enjoying the sounds of the city, life going on outside the boundaries of this little oasis. A church bell chimed. A woman laughed. The ching of a bicycle bell. A group of people in muffled conversation passing on the other side of the wall, speaking a language she didn't understand yet. The background sounds of cars and people going about their daily business.

After a few minutes, a sense of wellbeing seeped through her, balance restored once more. She didn't have to worry about whatever was going on with Alex and Ed. All she had to do was concentrate on her and Tom and the different future they could build together. Thinking of Tom, she pulled up the selfie she'd taken with Alex and sent it to him with the caption:

The Getaway

> This is our house guest – Alex!

Her mind brought her back to the question that dominated her thoughts in quiet moments. Being in a long-term relationship didn't have to be all about having children, did it? In fact, she knew plenty of couples who'd ruled out having family, all of them citing different reasons. For some it was the financial commitment. Others wanted freedom to pursue their dreams. Another friend was adamant she'd never wanted children and had known that from when she was young. Others didn't want to bring a child into such a troubled world. It didn't make their partnerships weaker; in fact, they were the couples who seemed to be the strongest in their commitment to each other. They had fun together, went on adventures. Her friends with young children on the other hand, always told her how tough it was to be working parents.

Do I want my life to be tough? Or could I embrace a life of exploration?

Knots unravelled in her mind, the tension seeping from her body as the hammock gently swayed. *Isn't this lovely?* Her time was her own to use as she pleased. It wouldn't be like that if she had children. Then, she'd have to work round their schedules rather than her own. Was it wrong to enjoy being selfish?

Her boss, Nadia, didn't think so and had been very supportive of her plans when she'd spoken to her earlier.

'You can go to Timbuktu, darling, for all I care, as long as you give us what we need when we need it.' Nadia had laughed. 'In fact, it might give your creativity an extra boost if you're somewhere new, don't you think? I know you've been feeling a bit down and jaded. Anyway, if it's only for a couple of weeks, I'm happy for you to do it and let's see what difference it makes.'

Nadia was a great boss and they'd become friends over the decade they'd worked together. Unfortunately, Tom had taken a dislike to her, but then she was the sort of outgoing and confident woman he found a bit intimidating.

Her phone rang and she pulled it from her pocket, already knowing who it was by the ringtone. 'Talk of the devil,' she said. 'I was just thinking about you.'

'Let's not do it,' Tom said, no preamble, his voice urgent. 'I'm sorry, you know what I'm like. Sometimes it takes a little while for things to sink in with me. And I woke up in a right panic this morning thinking about strangers in our apartment.'

'What?' Maddie couldn't believe what she was hearing.

'I know I said yes, and I do like the idea of being digital nomads, but the apartment swap... I've got a bad feeling about the whole thing. It just seems... too convenient. Too perfect. You know... it could be a scam of some sort.'

Her good mood was shattered, his words hammering her daydreams into tiny pieces. He couldn't mean it, could he? Anger burned through her, making her teeth clamp together. 'Why would you say that?' she snapped. 'Why can't nice things happen to us after all the problems we've had? Life doesn't have to be all struggle, you know! There are lots of lovely people in the world and I think Alex is one of them.' She clambered out of the hammock.

'You only met her a week ago. That's not long, is it?' Tom insisted. 'You don't really know her at all. Or Ed.' She could hear his breathing, fast and ragged. He sounded in a right state. 'I'm telling you, something about this whole thing feels off. It's all happened too quickly.'

Despite her frustration with him, Tom's words were making Maddie uneasy. Hadn't she had the same thoughts herself? Her scalp seemed to shrink round her skull, the tightness making her wince. 'It's too late, Tom. If you didn't want to do it, you should have said sooner. She's gone. Ed's gone. They've got our keys, and it's a done deal, whether you like it or not.'

7

Maddie locked the apartment and stomped back to the hotel, furious with Tom. Firstly, for going back on an agreement. Secondly, for not paying enough attention when they were making the decision in the first place. And thirdly, because somewhere deep in her heart, she knew he had a point. At the same time, another part of her brain was telling her that being in the apartment just then had felt liberating, like she was at the start of something she needed in her life right now and she really wanted this arrangement to work.

Sometimes, Tom was the very definition of a spoilsport and it was infuriating when he went back on decisions like this. It wasn't the first time he'd done it to her. When they'd been looking at houses to buy, she'd get excited that they'd found one they both liked, and agreed they would go for it. He'd watch while she sent an email to the agent confirming their offer, only to wake up the next morning having changed his mind. And then she'd have the embarrassment of explaining they'd had a change of heart and apologise for wasting everyone's time.

It wasn't far to walk back to the hotel, but by the time she reached their room, her brain was fried and she was seething, slamming the door behind her. Tom wasn't sitting on the bed with his laptop on his knee as she'd expected, but was standing by the window, chewing on a fingernail. He looked agitated, unable to stay still.

'What on earth are you doing, Tom? I don't understand how you go from being happy about something to being sure we shouldn't do it in the space of an hour.'

He looked rattled. Nervous. His face pale.

She frowned as she walked towards him, worried now rather than angry. 'What's going on?' She'd never seen him in this state before and as she reached out to him for a hug, he backed away, unable to meet her eye. His hand rubbed the back of his neck.

'There's something I need to tell you.'

'Okay,' she said, carefully, watching him prowling round the room. 'You're scaring me now.'

'I'm sorry. I just— I don't know how to say this. I really don't.'

Maddie's pulse was racing, her mind scampering around looking for the most dreadful thing her long-term partner could say to her. Was he breaking up with her? Is that what this was about? Had he decided that she wasn't the woman he wanted to spend the rest of his life with because she couldn't give him a family?

Her legs threatened to go from under her, and she sank onto the bed, anxiety writhing in her belly. He continued to pace around the room and the nausea that swirled in the pit of her stomach grew stronger with every passing second. 'Just say it,' she pleaded, thinking she was going to be sick. 'Say something.'

There was a hitch in her voice, her emotions swelling like the incoming tide, threatening to engulf her. The waiting was unbearable, the narrative in her head telling her this was the end. She'd been waiting for it, expecting it to come ever since they'd had the test results and she couldn't blame him, not really. She wasn't going to stand in his way if he wanted a different future, but she needed to know.

A tear trickled down her cheek, followed by another.

Tom looked conflicted, torn. 'I didn't tell you because I didn't think it was important. And it hasn't been important. But now you need to know. Because then you might understand.'

'Understand what?' She thumped a fist on the mattress in frustration. 'You're not making any sense.'

'Oh, Maddie, I love you so much. You are my world, my whole universe and I never want to do anything to hurt you.'

A sob burst from her throat. There was a big 'but' coming. One that was going to change her life. She could feel it with every fibre of her being, her body tensing in readiness.

'It's Lexi.'

She frowned, puzzled. 'Who's Lexi?'

'I mean Alex. That's what she's calling herself now.'

'What about her?'

'She used to be— We were—' He looked her straight in the eye and swallowed. 'Married. She's my ex-wife.'

8

Maddie reeled, unable, for a moment, to comprehend what she'd just heard. *His ex-wife? Is that what he'd said?* But Tom had never mentioned being married before. Not once. Not ever.

She couldn't speak, no words forming in her mouth, while questions spun so fast in her brain, she couldn't catch hold of them and translate them into sentences. Her mouth opened and closed, her fingers twisted together so tightly it hurt.

'Look, I know it's a shock,' Tom said, walking towards her, then stopping, clearly unable to decide what to do for the best. 'I didn't mean to hide it from you but it was a long time ago and we were only married for a short while. Just a few months.' He was gabbling, his words rushing out in an unending stream. 'Honestly, it was a stupid impulsive thing we decided to do one night when we were drunk and then a few weeks later, it was done. Lexi organised it all and at that point, I couldn't pluck up the courage to tell her it wasn't what I wanted. We pulled a couple of witnesses off the street and it was all a bit of an anti-climax really. Then once we were married, we just argued, because I think we both realised it wasn't going to work and we blamed each other.'

Beads of sweat were visible on his brow, his chest rising and falling like he'd been running, his eyes fixed on her, pinning her to the spot.

'Bloody hell, Tom.' It didn't seem enough, but it was all she could muster, her thoughts paralysed by disbelief.

'I know, I know. I should have told you. But I felt ashamed that I'd been married and separated by the time I was twenty-three.' His chin wobbled. 'I didn't think you'd want me if you knew.'

Maddie felt light-headed, the nausea still there. She put her hands on her stomach hoping it would help to calm everything down, but somehow it made things worse and she jumped to her feet, managing to get to the bathroom before she vomited.

The shock of being sick seemed to exacerbate the shock of Tom's words. It felt like a betrayal, even though she and Alex… or Lexi… or whatever the hell her name was had never been in Tom's life at the same time. There wasn't a cross-over but she tried to do the maths in her head, to make sure. Maddie had known him close to four years now, which meant she must have met him maybe three years after he and Alex split up. That was a big gap. Long enough for a heart to heal, wasn't it? She would hate to think her relationship with him had been formed on the rebound.

A headache throbbed at her temples, questions buzzing in her brain like a swarm of angry wasps. She felt his hand on her back, the warmth of his touch seeping through her T-shirt. But she didn't want him near her and she shrugged him off, unable to speak, to tell him to go away and leave her alone.

He took a step back, still hovering in her space. Her eyes

were closed but she could feel his presence, could hear him breathing. 'I'm so sorry I didn't tell you.'

She grabbed some toilet tissue and wiped her mouth. 'I'm sorry too,' she said from between clenched teeth. She stood up straight, still feeling shaky, but at least the nausea had gone. 'How could you keep something like that a secret all this time? Is that why you're so against marriage?'

At this point, she couldn't even consider why and how Tom's ex-wife was back in his life and organising an apartment swap. She'd get to that later, but with a shock this huge, she only had the emotional capacity to address one thing at a time.

He closed the toilet lid and flushed while she leant over the sink and splashed cold water on her face, hoping it might wake up her brain. She felt blindsided, suspended in that place where reality hadn't quite met up with acceptance, robbed of the ability to express herself.

'I'll be honest, it's been eating away at me, but I thought the chances of bumping into Lexi, I mean Alex, were slim to zero. I told myself you didn't need to know.'

Maddie turned to face him, anger sitting like an unexploded bomb in her chest. 'Of course I needed to know. I thought I knew who you are as a person and what has shaped your life. But now I find out there's this big gap I know nothing about.' Tears pricked at her eyes, emotion swelling in her throat, making her voice squeaky and ridiculous. 'You didn't tell me you'd been married. *Married* for God's sake. It feels... deceitful. Like you've only shown me part of who you are and hidden the bits you don't want me to see. And yet...' Her voice cracked. 'You know everything there is to know about me.'

Perhaps that isn't completely true, Maddie thought, as soon as the words were out of her mouth. Had she really told him everything, or had she edited her own truth too?

9

'I didn't mean to hurt you,' Tom said, looking truly remorseful. His hands were moving like he wanted to reach out to her, but wasn't sure if that was the right thing to do. It felt claustrophobic in the bathroom, the smell of her vomit souring the air. She pushed past him into their room and opened the door to the balcony, stepping out into the fresh air, filling her lungs with big gulps of it while she tried to stop her tears.

She sensed him behind her and she turned, her back against the wrought iron railings that ran round the outdoor space. He looked distraught. 'It wasn't an intentional lie. More of an omission, but then as time went on, it became harder and harder to say anything because every day I'm with you I love you more. And I didn't want you to think any less of me.' He stumbled over his words. 'I was frightened to tell you in case— in case it broke us.'

Maddie burst into tears and Tom finally came over and wrapped her in a hug. She clung to him, not sure what his revelation meant in terms of her feelings. What would she have thought if he'd been upfront right from the start? Would the fact he'd been married and separated at twenty-three have made her wary of him? Would it make her doubt his long-term commitment? He kissed her, an urgency to his mouth on hers that she couldn't resist. Her thoughts stopped for a moment, her body responding while her mind stood back and watched. She felt distant, detached, confused and after a moment, she pulled away.

'I'm struggling to get my head round this. I mean... your ex-wife turns up and we end up swapping apartments with her. Is that... just a weird coincidence?' As she was saying it, Maddie could feel the hairs standing up on the back of her neck. Tom was staring at his feet, his hands on his head like he was trying to stop himself from launching into space. He was giving off a strange energy and she could tell something wasn't right. 'Is this a scam or something?' She frowned, growing more concerned by the second. 'What's going on?'

He looked up. 'I honestly have no idea. Coincidences do happen, don't they?' He didn't sound convinced and neither was she.

She glared at him. 'Are you even divorced?'

He looked alarmed. 'Yes, yes, I promise you we're definitely divorced.' He made a move towards her, but she backed away, wondering if there was unfinished business between Alex and Tom.

'I'm sorry, I just need...' She glanced over his shoulder at the door. 'I need a bit of space.'

She scooted round him into the room, grabbed her bag and stumbled out into the corridor, blinking back tears as she took the lift down to the lobby. She decided to go back to the apartment, where she wouldn't be disturbed. There would be no need to speak to anyone, or see anyone. And Tom didn't know where it was yet. He hadn't been there in person, just seen the pictures.

On her own, she could let her thoughts settle and really work out how she was feeling. Then she could decide what to do.

Everything was as she'd left it, welcoming and benign, the sun streaming through the kitchen window, the light playing on the surface of the swimming pool, the lounge cooled by the shade of the awning. She sank onto the sofa, leant back and closed her eyes. Already this felt better. *I could stay here on my own,* she thought, the idea of being in the hotel room with Tom making her feel panicky. She didn't know what to say to him and she definitely couldn't share a bed with him. Not until she'd worked this through in her mind.

How could you hide something like that from someone you love and not expect it to damage your relationship when the truth came out? Had the trust been broken?

Life had a way of revealing secrets. Chance meetings, altered plans, last-minute changes, overheard conversations. Inevitably, the truth forced its way to the surface, like air bubbles in water, casting ripples where stillness had been before.

What ripples would Tom's secrets cast?

That was the question Maddie was struggling to answer. She felt bruised and tearful and spent the rest of the morning dozing in the hammock, enjoying the warm breeze on her skin and the sounds of normal life going on around her. She let her mind wander, glad that she'd switched off her phone and nobody could bother her. By lunchtime, her stomach was rumbling and she'd come to a decision.

She turned on her phone, her heart sinking when she saw the nine missed messages from Tom. It was time to get this over with and face up to things rather than hiding away. She gave him a call, her body tense and rigid as she sat at the dining table, her fingers curling and uncurling as she tried to rein in her hurt and anger.

'Maddie, thank God.' There was a note of panic in his voice. 'I didn't know where you'd gone. I've been so worried.'

She sighed. 'I just needed some time to think about things.'

'Where are you?'

'I'm at the apartment. And I've decided I'm going to stay here on my own for a while so I've got space to think things through.'

'On your own? For a while?' His voice had gone up an octave. 'What do you mean?'

She thought her statement was pretty clear, but she repeated it slowly and evenly, so there could be no doubt. 'I mean I'm going to stay here, in the apartment, while I think about what you told me earlier and how it might affect our relationship.'

'Oh, Maddie, please come back to the hotel.' There was a tremor running through his words, a flush of emotion in his voice. 'Let me explain.'

She stopped herself from snapping an immediate reply, not wanting to say anything in anger she might later regret. She took a deep breath before she spoke, but it didn't work, the words flew out like angry bees. 'I don't think my reaction to the fact you've been married before and didn't tell me needs much explanation. I just wanted to ask you to leave the room for half an hour so I can come and collect my things.' Silence, apart from the sound of his breathing and she could almost hear him thinking, trying to work out how to persuade her to change her mind. 'Please don't say anything else, just give me a bit of space to think, okay?'

'Oh, Maddie, I can't because this isn't right. None of it.' The panic in his voice made her uneasy. 'There's more to this. Lexi turning up here. The apartment swap.' He made a sound that was somewhere between a whimper and a strangled scream. 'We need to go home. Urgently. There are things I need to tell you about Lexi... Then you'll understand.'

10

Tom's words made Maddie pause. What on earth might he need to tell her? He sounded so panicked, she couldn't dismiss his concerns, however much she didn't want to see him.

'Okay.' She dragged the word out, her reluctance clear. 'Give me half an hour. Let's meet at the café on the promenade.'

She didn't want to be in an enclosed room with him, given how furious she was. It would keep things civilised if they were in a public place and avoid their conversation degenerating into a shouting match. Her mind was already busy listing all the possible things he might be about to tell her, preparing herself for the worst. Although she was struggling to define what the worst might be. If she wanted them to fix this, to have a chance at repairing their relationship, she knew she had to give him the chance to explain.

But will I believe a word he says?

Maddie tapped her phone against her lips, an idea pushing to the front of her mind. If she wasn't going to believe what Tom might tell her, perhaps she should speak to Alex first? Then she could go into the conversation with Tom properly prepared. After all, there were two sides to every story.

If she spoke to Alex before she met up with Tom, she could compare their stories and then decide what she wanted to believe. Although she had to take into account that Alex had flat out lied to her, too, by not mentioning that she was Tom's ex-wife. She thought about that. How would Alex even know that Maddie's partner Tom was the same Tom she'd been married to? They hadn't met while they'd been on holiday because their arrangements had been scuppered several times either by Tom's work meetings, or Ed and Alex having to change plans, and finally, by Alex's illness.

Unless Alex hadn't really been ill. That was a possibility. She'd been fine earlier that day. A shiver of unease ran through Maddie's body, the urge to speak to Alex even stronger now.

The truth was not a stable thing, that was the problem. Everyone perceived the same thing differently. However, their stories should more or less match and it would be interesting to get Alex's take on things before hearing Tom's version.

What on earth had happened to end their marriage? It must have been really bad if they were together as man and wife for just a few months. Her stomach was tying itself in knots as her mind got busy second guessing everything she thought she knew about her life and Tom. What if his lies were worse than she'd thought? What if she decided she couldn't forgive him?

I don't want to be on my own.

She knew that with a searing certainty. Her life plan had always centred around finding a partner to share the ups and downs, and her heart ached with the hurt of betrayal. The sense that something precious had been broken, like a beautiful flower that had been trampled underfoot, with little she could do to make it good again. Except talk. Ask the questions and listen to the answers. And maybe she would find out that her assumptions were wrong, that her doomsday scenario was a fabrication of her insecurities. She would speak to Tom *and* Alex, try and stay objective, then decide what the truth might be.

Her heart thundered in her chest, panic rising. It felt like she was teetering on the edge of a cliff, the decisions she made now crucial as to whether she stayed on solid ground or she fell into the void.

Perhaps it's not as bad as I thought?

She sat with that idea for a moment.

Not telling me he was married before is pretty bad, a voice in her head scolded.

She'd been in relationships before Tom, one of them quite serious until they'd hit problems. She'd... fallen apart was probably the best way to describe it. They hadn't spoken since. Was it the same with Tom and Alex?

She decided to have a quick shower and freshen up before meeting Tom, and as she shampooed her hair, her mind drifted back to when they'd first met. At the zoo. Tom had been filming the monkeys, and she was curious as to what he was doing, so struck up a conversation. He'd explained it was research for his work, filming how they moved so he could translate that into his gaming models. He'd invited her for a coffee and they'd chatted for hours. It turned out they were both obsessed with Marvel films and that was Tom's cue to invite her to the latest release at the cinema the following week. It felt like she'd found a missing piece of herself when she'd met Tom, and it didn't take long before she couldn't imagine a life without him.

What about now, though? Could she imagine a life on her own?

She let out a weary sigh before finishing in the shower and getting herself dressed. It was time to go, but she decided to try calling Alex first. Her heart skipped a beat when she actually answered.

'Hi,' Maddie said, feeling awkward and unprepared. 'How was your trip?'

'Oh, it was fine. Bit noisy on the plane with a hen party and a crying baby, but thankfully, it wasn't too long a flight.'

Alex sounded absolutely normal, which threw Maddie now she'd been led to question her friend. She cleared her throat, unsure how to start the conversation. 'I was... er... just ringing to make sure everything is okay for you at the apartment.'

Silence for a moment. 'Yep, everything's fine. I've not been here long.'

'Good. That's good.' She took a deep breath, preparing herself for the big question, which was the whole point of the conversation after all. 'Look... I need to... Tom told me...' She swallowed, finding it hard to get the words out, but before she could speak, she heard a burst of coughing on the other end of the line and waited. Then banging, a muffled shout.

'I'm so sorry,' Alex said. 'There's someone at the door. I think it must be Ed. Look, I'll ring you back, okay?'

The line went dead.

Maddie waited. Five minutes, ten minutes, then she couldn't wait any longer and rang Alex back. But it went straight to voicemail. She left a message, asking Alex to call her, but she had a funny feeling that she wouldn't hear from her for a while. If Ed was there, did that mean they'd made up whatever falling out she thought they might have had? Or were they in the middle of a row? It could be either, but an alarm bell jangled in her brain, putting her on edge.

What is going on?

11

TOM

Tom paced around the hotel room, constantly checking the time as the seconds crawled by. He'd been gritting his teeth so hard his jaw was aching and he opened his mouth, stretching out the muscles. Why, oh why, hadn't he listened properly to what Maddie had been saying to him about Alex? Why hadn't he been more curious about her?

It wasn't the first time his failure to listen had caused problems. Maddie was always telling him off about it, the way he switched off mid-conversation, especially when he was engrossed in world-building for a new project. He couldn't help it, that's how his brain functioned. It wasn't that he was wilfully changing his focus, his brain just did that without him actually realising. Distracted by something like a cat chasing a butterfly. That was ADHD for you.

It had been a problem his whole life. School had been a nightmare for him, but luckily, he'd had a great form teacher who'd noticed the signs and mentioned it to his parents and then, once he'd been diagnosed, he'd been prescribed medication. It had helped at school, to keep him focused, but as with any medication, there was a downside. So when he became old enough to make his own choices, he'd decided he could manage without.

At that point, he'd been on the meds for so long, he didn't even know who he really was any more. He'd also become increasingly worried about long-term side effects. The fact that the doctors told him it was safe didn't mean it really was, did it? Who was motivated to research side effects of long-term medication on ADHD kids? Certainly not the pharmaceutical companies.

Once he'd been off the meds for a little while, he'd felt so much better in himself, more alert and actually 'in the room'. He liked that feeling and had decided, on balance, now that he had a well-rehearsed set of coping strategies, this was how he wanted to live his life.

Once he'd realised working for himself was the best way forward, he could please himself how he organised his time. He generally worked in creative spurts, and any distractions were often related to what he was doing anyway. His working pattern might seem chaotic to other people but he always got the job done in the end, even if the route to completion was a bit circuitous and apparently random. Sometimes, when he was really into a project and maybe up against a deadline, he'd become hyper-focused and get an enormous amount of work done to the exclusion of everything else. So, it sort of evened out.

The downside of not being medicated was switching off in the middle of conversations, when he really needed to listen. Like yesterday. He cursed himself again, hammering a fist against his forehead. Now he'd agreed to something he knew was a very bad idea.

When Maddie had been talking about her new friend Alex, he'd no inkling that it could be his ex-wife, Lexi. The two things didn't match up in his mind and maybe other people might have made that connection, with her full name being Alexandra, but he really hadn't. She'd only ever been Lexi to him and her family. Nobody, but nobody, had ever called her Alex.

Never in a million years had he expected her to turn up here and when Maddie had sent over the picture of the two of them, he'd started hyperventilating. In fact, he'd become so dizzy he'd had to lie down. He still felt light-headed now.

Oh God, what have we done?

He couldn't believe he'd been so careless after years of caution where Lexi was concerned. But he and Maddie had been chasing a dream... or were they running away from the sadness of their reality? Whatever it was, both of them had become excited about the digital nomad idea. So wrapped up in it that he hadn't done due diligence on the plan. He chewed at a nail, angry with himself for being so lax with a decision so big. But he'd wanted Maddie to be happy and her excitement had brought a sparkle to her eyes that had been missing for a while.

Okay, so he'd been just as excited. He shouldn't pin this whole decision on Maddie. That wasn't fair. In fact, he'd wanted to travel years ago when he'd first met Lexi, but she'd wanted to focus on her career and then... well, things had gone from bad to worse. Now he was definitely up for travelling and the suggestion of a different lifestyle had sparked a desire in him that had lain dormant for years.

On the surface, Maddie had hit on a really cool idea with the apartment swap, but now he knew they were swapping with Lexi, the whole plan took on a different complexion. It had disaster written all over it in great big capital letters. Obviously, Maddie had snatched at the idea because it was so convenient and financially, it worked. But wasn't it just a little too perfect?

As Maddie had said, Lexi turning up in Croatia seemed too much of a coincidence. Just thinking about it made him feel sick.

Of course, it had been wrong of him not to tell Maddie about being married to Lexi but there was so much about that period of his life he was ashamed of, so much he didn't want her to know. He hadn't wanted his past to ruin his present and Maddie was his soulmate. The one he wanted to be with for the rest of his life. Now he had a job on his hands to mend the trust. Was that even going to be possible? She'd sounded so mad and when Maddie was angry, she was as stubborn as a mule. Oh God, he hoped she'd believe what he was about to tell her.

He rapped his knuckles against his forehead. It was his own stupid fault for being immersed in his project and not giving Maddie the time she deserved. Sometimes he wanted to give himself a slap round the head for being so idiotic. For getting his priorities so drastically wrong. But unfortunately, that was part of his ADHD as well. Wonky executive function.

It suddenly dawned on him that there was only one person who could make sense of this situation. The person he least wanted to talk to, but this was an emergency and he had to man up. His phone was still clasped in his hand and he scrolled through his contact list until he found her number, hoping she'd kept it after all these years. His breath caught in his throat when she answered almost immediately.

'Hi, Tom. I wondered if you'd call.' Hearing the sound of her voice after so long made his heart skitter, a familiar anxiety rearing its head.

'What are you playing at?' he snapped, in no mood for games.

Silence for a moment.

'What do you mean?' She sounded so innocent, unsure, like

she hadn't a clue what he was talking about. It wound him up even more.

'You know what I mean. Why were you in Croatia? What's the game with the apartment swap?'

'Oh, Tom, why are you always so suspicious? There *is* no game, it was just a happy coincidence. And I can tell you, I was completely gobsmacked when I spotted you two together the other day. I slipped into a shop so neither of you would see me and I didn't say anything to Maddie. I hope that was the right thing to do?' He could hear a muffled conversation in the background, the sound of a car door slamming, then she came back on the line. 'This arrangement is perfect though, don't you think?'

Was that laughter in her voice or was he imagining it? His anger bubbled up like molten lava and he had to clamp his jaw shut to stop himself from yelling at her down the phone. But this was what she did to him. Every. Single. Time. He squeezed his eyes shut, as if that would put a lid on his rage. So much pent-up frustration with this woman it might take a lifetime to rid himself of it.

'Like I said, it was pure coincidence that I happened to be in Croatia at the same time as you,' she continued. 'Weird, I'll give you that, for us to both end up somewhere as random as Croatia, but life has a funny habit of doing this shit, doesn't it?' She laughed, that tinkling laugh of hers that always put him on edge. How he'd ever been with this woman, let alone ended up married to her, he honestly had no idea. But he wanted her to stay in the past and have no involvement with his future. He definitely hadn't forgiven her, that was for sure.

In the background, he could hear footsteps tapping, then the jingle of keys. When she spoke again, her voice was serious. 'Look, honestly, I wish you and Maddie nothing but the best. I really like her and I think it's great that we can help each other out. I can stay at your place while Mum's... not well and you get to try out being digital nomads. Where's the harm in that?'

Where is the harm in that?

He had no simple answer to that question, because it would mean delving into the dark recesses of his mind where he'd secured the memories, all the wrongs, all the hurt and fear and pain, not wanting to ever have to confront them again.

Tom ended the call without saying goodbye. Despite his reluctance to relive the past, his brain wasn't listening and he found his thoughts filled with the day he'd met Lexi.

12

THEN

Tom was sitting in the café, conveniently located on the ground floor of the office block where he worked for a firm of stockbrokers. The place was rammed now, although it had been quiet when he'd walked in. He'd learnt to be quick off the mark at lunchtime, if he wanted to avoid queuing and have a decent choice of food from the chiller.

'Is this seat taken?'

He looked up into a woman's big brown eyes, a wide, white smile lighting up an utterly gorgeous face. Her short, bleached hair contrasted with caramel skin, giving her a striking appearance. Immediately he felt a blush rushing to his cheeks. 'No, that's fine, I don't mind sharing.' He was mumbling, thrown by the presence of this lovely woman. Maybe because he'd never had any luck with girls. He was too shy, a bit geeky, so tongue tied he struggled to have a proper conversation at times. All those characteristics had been thrown at him as insults in the past and had severely dented his confidence.

'It's my first day,' the woman said, unloading a coffee and a toastie onto the table, sliding her tray against the wall beside her. 'I'm a bit all over the place.'

He smiled at her, and recognised her expression as the one he'd probably worn on his first day too. But at least he'd known his boss, which had made things easier. Uncle Trevor. Not a real uncle, but his dad's best friend who'd been very much a part of his life as he'd grown up. He'd felt protected as Uncle Trevor showed him round, introduced him to people and took him out to lunch. He couldn't imagine what it must feel like if you knew absolutely nobody. Pretty overwhelming, he guessed.

He gave her what he hoped was a reassuring smile. 'It's a lot, isn't it? You working at Johnson and Brown too?'

She nodded. 'That's right. I'm starting in trading. What about you?'

'I started in trading but I was terrible. I'm in compliance now.' He grimaced. 'Boring, but it pays the bills.'

'Well, it's good to know they let you move departments if it doesn't work out.' She gave a nervous laugh. 'I've no idea how I got this job at all.' He watched her take a small bite of her toastie, crumbs scattering over her plate and the table top, speaking while she chewed. 'I applied on a whim because I wasn't getting anywhere with any other job applications and someone I knew sent the advert to me. Told me to try something different.' She took another bite of her toastie. 'I did history at uni and now I'm like, what was I thinking? Why didn't I do something that led directly to a job, you know, like... architecture or something?'

Her comment struck a chord with him and he laughed with her. 'It's funny you saying that. The opposite happened to me. I did a degree in video and animation and wanted to get into gaming, which I could have done. I had the right qualifications and experience. But my dad said it wasn't a proper job. That's why I'm here. It wasn't by choice. My dad pushed me into it.' He could hear the bitterness in his voice and he wondered if that revelation made him sound lame. Like he wasn't in control of his own life. A blush warmed his cheeks and he wished he hadn't blurted out his truth.

She gave an eye roll. 'Pushy parents. The worst. At least I've been spared that. I just wish mine had cared enough to talk to me about the subjects I was choosing and where it might lead me in life. No guidance whatsoever and school was worse than useless.' She took a sip of her coffee. 'What are we like? Hopefully it'll all work out in the end.'

She carried on eating and he finished his mango smoothie, sad that he had no real excuse to linger. He was starting to relax now, liking the mellow sound of her voice and the way she moved her hands when she spoke. She was so expressive, he was mesmerised. And she leant towards him, like she really wanted to speak to him, and hear what he had to say, not just tolerating his presence, like most people did when he had to share a table. Before he knew it, his phone alarm was reminding him it was time to go back to work and they rode up in the lift together, still engrossed in conversation. Somehow, the afternoon didn't drag quite so much as normal and he caught himself daydreaming with a daft smile on his face as his mind went over and over their conversation.

Joining Lexi for lunch became part of his daily routine after that, and on the days when she wasn't there, he felt a pang of loss that took him by surprise. It made him realise that their time together was the highlight of his day, the thing that put a bounce in his step on the way to work and he had a sneaky suspicion he was falling in love. Which made him sad because he was sure he was firmly in the friend zone. A stunner like Lexi would never be interested in someone like him. Not when she turned heads wherever she went. He'd seen other men looking, following her with their eyes when he was with her.

It was Lexi who finally asked him out on a date.

They were waiting for the lift to get back to their respective offices, her on the seventh floor, him on the ninth. 'I don't suppose you fancy going out for something to eat after work sometime, do you? Or a drink? Or catch a movie or something?' She was looking up at him from under her lashes, giving him a shy smile, and he couldn't believe what he'd just heard.

'Like a date? Really?' He stared at her, open-mouthed, then laughed. 'You're messing about, aren't you?'

She looked away, seemed a little flustered. 'It's okay, you can say no. I won't be offended.'

'Wait a minute... That was a genuine question?' Their eyes met and his insides melted.

'Of course it was. I really like you and I thought it might be fun to get to know each other a bit better. Outside of work.' He realised she was being serious. Her voice faltered. 'But only if you want to.'

Part of him was reluctant to ruin their friendship with a date, his past experiences telling him this probably wasn't going to end well, but he couldn't stop himself from saying yes. And that was that. They were an item. At the age of twenty-two, he had a date with a woman he thought he was in love with. He could hardly contain his excitement, his mind flitting off in all directions that afternoon at work, a grin never far from his lips. It seemed to take weeks for it to be the following evening when they'd arranged to go out for dinner.

Given the way Lexi looked, he knew in his heart that it was

probably too good to be true, but he'd told himself to be positive and hope for the best. So that's what he did. The first date led to a second, then a third. On their fourth date she stayed over and then, somehow, for the first time in years, he had a proper girlfriend.

13

NOW

Tom sat on the bed in the hotel room, fidgeting with his phone. *Everything's fine,* he told himself. *You're catastrophising again.* But he had that hollow feeling in his stomach, the one that he got when he had a premonition of doom. Not that he was always right. It was about fifty-fifty, so he couldn't take this feeling as an omen.

Remember what Lexi did to you...

He threw his phone on the bed, covering his face with his hands. *Oh God, just imagine if...* His mind took off again, presenting him with a whole movie reel of what could go wrong this time. He couldn't bear to think about it because if the worst happened, he would be to blame. And he couldn't bear to imagine anything bad happening to Maddie.

Why the hell didn't I tell her about Lexi? If he'd done that, this whole situation wouldn't have arisen. He'd still have Maddie by his side, not holed up in some unknown apartment in an unfamiliar city, in a country that was totally foreign to him. He'd never felt so vulnerable in his life. Or maybe that wasn't quite true. He'd been through some pretty scary times after he'd broken up with Lexi, when he was on his own with nobody to help him.

He tried to shake all the doom-mongering thoughts out of his head, and stood up, pacing up and down, trying to clear his thinking.

Lexi had sounded fine on the phone. In fact, she'd been positively friendly, if he could ignore the fact he'd thought she was laughing at him. That could be his paranoia. Was her being here just a weird coincidence, like she'd said? Was he reading things into this situation that weren't actually there? He also had to take into account the fact she was with a boyfriend and they were living together. Positive signs that she'd moved on.

What he needed to do was get out of his own way and accept what she'd just told him as being the truth. It was probably past trauma causing him to overreact. *Yes, that's it.* The thought made sense and he nodded to himself, sure that he was right. Meanwhile, panic stirred in his belly and tension pulled at his shoulders, his body unwilling to accept his pep talk.

It was over two years since he'd last seen Lexi, longer than that since he'd actually spoken to her. It was not impossible to believe that she'd overcome the troubles of the past, just like he had. Mind you, his body wasn't behaving like he was over anything. There was a weird buzzing in his head, and he was sweating, his brain agitated. In fact, he was reacting like he was still in a terrible place. A place he'd thought he'd never escape at the time.

You're okay, he reassured himself, trying to calm his breathing as he ran his hands over his face. *It'll be fine.*

The alarm on his watch sounded. It was time to go and meet Maddie and tell her everything. Well... maybe not absolutely everything, but as much as she needed to know for now.

14

MADDIE

Maddie left the apartment and made her way towards the café to meet Tom, wondering what he had to tell her about Alex. And whether she'd even believe him. She wasn't sure she would.

This was the worst row they'd ever had, but then, this was the worst thing he'd ever done. Everything else was a minor niggle compared to this whopper. How did you get over the fact your long-term partner, who was dead set against marriage on principle, had been married before *and hadn't told you about it*? How?

Maddie was a great believer in talking things through, thinking it was best to have proper conversations, rather than shouting matches and playing the blame game. It was time to listen to her own advice, and make sure she heard what Tom had to say.

It was a shame her conversation with Alex had been cut short because she'd really like to hear her side of the story before she spoke to Tom. She stopped and leant against a wall in the shade while she pulled out her phone and called her again, glad when she answered on the second ring.

'Maddie, I'm so sorry, I said I'd call back, didn't I?' Alex sounded distracted. 'It's just been full-on since I got home. First Ed and now I'm at Mum's. She had her first chemo today and I think she's having a bad reaction. We're just waiting for an ambulance.'

'Oh no, I'm so sorry to hear that.' Maddie's agenda went out of the window. She couldn't be bothering Alex about past relationships when she was dealing with an emergency. She had to get off the phone and leave her to deal with whatever was happening. 'I'll ring back tomorrow and I hope your mum's okay.'

'No, it's all right. I'm stood outside waiting for the paramedics to turn up. Talking to you will keep me sane while I'm waiting.'

Maddie hesitated, thinking maybe she should end the call anyway, but then she pushed on. 'Tell me to mind my own business, but... I was just wondering are you and Ed okay? It's just... I saw that note he left you on the back of the envelope where you'd listed instructions for me and I wondered if you'd... well, I wasn't sure if...' She tailed off, uncertain how to put things in a diplomatic way. Really, it wasn't any of her business and she felt awkward now for even asking.

Alex sighed. 'We had a row, and I broke up with him. I was just so flustered with everything going on with Mum, I'm not really thinking straight. Anyway, that lasted for all of a day. That was him coming back to apologise earlier, so no need to worry, we're good. He's just a bit of a man-child sometimes and I lose patience. Then we have a bust-up and he storms off.' She laughed. 'But so far, he's always come back.'

'I'm glad to hear it. You're going to need a bit of support with your mum being poorly, aren't you?'

'Yep. You're not wrong there.' Alex sounded like she wasn't

really listening. 'Look, I'm sorry, I've got to go. The ambulance is here. Speak soon. Bye.'

With that, the line went dead, leaving Maddie feeling puzzled. And disappointed. She'd only been on her warm-up question and hadn't even got to the one she really wanted answering about Tom. It was an abrupt end to the conversation and there was something about the call that left her wondering if Alex was telling the truth.

If she'd been standing outside anywhere in London, there would have been noises in the background. Traffic at the very least. Maybe people. Sirens. Perhaps the rattle of wind. But there'd been nothing. It didn't sound like she was outside at all.

Was her mum really waiting for an ambulance or was that just an excuse to get Maddie off the line? A way to avoid the question she knew was coming about her marriage to Tom. She set off walking again, towards the café, thinking that the more she spoke to Alex, the less she trusted her and the more she was dreading what Tom had to say.

Who was this person she'd entrusted her apartment to? She was about to find out.

15

TOM

Tom arrived at the café first and picked a table right at the end of the row outside, where he hoped they would have a bit of privacy. It would have been better if Maddie had agreed to come back to the hotel room, where he could talk freely, without fear of being overheard. But if this was the compromise to get her to speak to him, he just had to make the best of it.

His body was heavy with disappointment and there was something else as well, a shiver of fear. Trepidation as to what the future now held for them. *I've screwed up so bad this time*, he thought as he pulled out a chair and plonked himself down. His eyes scanned the horizon, taking in the necklace of islands in the distance, his mind filled with Lexi and the past they'd shared.

Tom and Lexi had been seeing each other for just over a year when he got a call from her one evening. It was her Pilates night, and she always went out with the group for a drink afterwards, so he hadn't been expecting to hear from her. It was an evening he looked forward to because he stayed in for a night of gaming with his online mates. Sometimes, he did wonder what that said about his relationship, if this was his favourite night of the week.

She was crying down the phone.

He sat bolt upright. Immediately alert. 'Hey, Lexi, what's wrong?'

'I've got something I need to tell you,' she sobbed. 'Can you come round?'

He glanced at the screen, watched his character get annihilated and sighed. She rarely asked him to go to her apartment. In fact, in the year they'd been together, he'd only been a handful of times. And that was usually to collect things she needed to stay at his place, which accommodated the two of them more easily. Her apartment backed on to the railway lines at the rear and there was a main road at the front and it was so noisy, he found it impossible to sleep. It was convenient for transport, he'd give it that, but it was the only positive about the place.

'You don't want to come here?'

'I need you, Tom. Please.' She was sobbing so hard he couldn't bear it.

''Course I'll come.' His fingers twitched, desperately wanting to play another round of his game. But he knew that was it for him for tonight. He suppressed a sigh, wondering what drama was about to unfold this time. 'I'm on my way.'

When Lexi called, he answered. That's how their relationship worked, because it was easier that way. She had a fiery temper and a caustic tongue and he'd been sliced and diced by her harsh words more than once. He'd found it was better to obey when she was in this sort of mood.

He typed:

Gotta go. See you later guys.

And turned off his games console and made his way to Lexi's place, which was a three-stop Tube ride away.

When she opened the door, he was shocked to see her tear-stained face. Her make-up had run down her cheeks, black smears under her eyes.

'Oh my God, Lexi, what's happened?' Now he was worried, unable to think what might have upset her so much. Had she fallen out with her parents again? Or her sister? Or maybe she'd been assaulted. All the possibilities filled his mind as he waited for her to tell him what was wrong.

She led him into her apartment and pulled him onto the sofa to sit next to her. He passed her a tissue from the box on the coffee table. And did a double-take. Because there, next to the box of tissues was a long, thin plastic object. His breath caught in his throat, his heart sinking.

'Is that what I think it is?' he asked, staring at the stick, already aware of what the answer was going to be.

She nodded, her voice hesitant. 'I'm... pregnant.' Tears tracked down her cheeks. 'I don't know how, but I am.'

He felt light-headed and slumped back on the sofa, his eyes fixed on the ceiling, fingers pressing into his forehead. His brain was stuttering, like a car that had run out of fuel, and he found himself unable to string a coherent sentence together.

Pregnant. A baby.

That had not been in their thinking. Not at all. Which was why Lexi was on the pill. Their thinking had been to set off travelling for a year, going where the fancy took them. Neither of them were ready for a baby, were they? Not when they were barely adults themselves.

'But the worst thing is... my sister came round, just after I'd done the test and I'd left it on the sink in the bathroom, then forgot while I was talking to her and she went for a pee and saw it. So now my whole family will know.'

'But...' He was going to have to be very careful with his

phrasing here, terrified of saying the wrong thing. He put an arm round her shoulders, kissing her hair, not wanting her to see the expression on his face. 'What do you want to do?'

'Oh, it's gone way past that point. It's not about me any more, it's about my family.' She pulled another tissue from the box and swiped at the tears on her face. 'You know what they're like. They're staunch Catholics.' Her voice quivered. 'I have no choice but to have the baby, whether I want to or not. Otherwise, they'll never speak to me again.'

That was the day when Tom's life changed. The day that defined the turbulent years ahead.

If Lexi had no choice, it appeared he had no choice either. Lexi was having his baby and he could do one of two things. He could embrace it, or he could walk away. In his mind, walking away was not an option. He wasn't that person, couldn't desert her and his child with a clear conscience. They were in this together and maybe the turmoil that had beleaguered their relationship in recent weeks was down to hormones. He clung to that as an explanation for Lexi's erratic behaviour and embraced the idea of being a father. He could travel later. When he was older and had money and his family had grown, couldn't he?

Lexi's family sprang into action and two months later, they were married, before her pregnancy started to show. Her parents were a force to be reckoned with, her mother terrifying, in the mould of Margaret Thatcher, and he'd been swept along with the arrangements in a bemused daze.

He wasn't 100 per cent on board with it, and felt he was too young to get married, but who would abandon a woman he'd impregnated? Especially one as stunning as Lexi. If he said no, that would be the end of their relationship and he'd never have a chance like this again. Her family were wealthy, they'd help them out, wouldn't they? Make sure their grandchild didn't want for anything? Because Tom was going to struggle earning enough for a family of three. He could hardly cover his own expenses and the thought of it was guaranteed to send him into a spin.

He told himself he had to grow up and stop being so selfish. So what if his friends were planning foreign trips and had no stress in their lives apart from deciding which pub to go to on the weekend, or which video game they were going to buy next?

Looking back now, even at twenty-three, he was a child in a grown-up world, full of people and situations that freaked him out to the point where he couldn't say no.

16

Tom checked his watch. Maddie was late and he wondered if she'd changed her mind and wasn't coming. The thought stirred up his fears, even more than memories of Lexi had done. He shifted in his seat, looking down the promenade to see if he could see her.

Maddie was his rock, who tolerated his ADHD like nobody in his life had ever done. Not even his parents. He knew he'd driven them mad, and they were frustrated with his underperformance at school. There was a look they'd exchange that told him everything he needed to know. He was a disappointment and once he was an adult, they'd become increasingly distant. The only thing they approved of was his marriage to Lexi, because they knew her family, and were aware his in-laws had a wealth and status Tom would never achieve on his own. Consequently, they'd been devastated when his relationship with Lexi had ended and, once he'd started his relationship with Maddie, he made a conscious decision to keep them at a distance.

His parents were currently on a cruise somewhere and had not been specific with the details. He imagined they were relieved that he was no longer their responsibility and as far as they were concerned, they'd done their bit. Thankfully, Maddie came from a more supportive family, whose welcoming behaviour had shone a light on what he'd missed out on growing up. He was very grateful to have them in his life and if he lost Maddie, he would lose them as well. The thought of it was ripping him to pieces.

He pulled out his phone and called her.

She sounded out of breath. 'Sorry, I got held up. I'm on my way.' She hung up. Abrupt. Leaving him staring at his phone, his heart thumping in his chest. *Oh God, she's still mad at me.* But what did he expect?

He wiped his sweaty palms on his trousers, trying to decide how to phrase what he had to say to make it more palatable. Less scary. But it was hopeless. There was no good way to spin this, no perspective that might shed a positive light on their situation. He Googled flight times. The best he could do was be proactive, so at least he could prove he wasn't completely useless.

Bloody Lexi. Why the hell did she have to turn up again?

He'd thought he was safe, but it was inevitable that they'd let her out of the psychiatric unit at some point. He'd just hoped it wouldn't be quite so soon. The fact that she'd found him again was enough of a concern, but having her living in their apartment was terrifying.

17

He gazed out to sea, fingers drumming on the table while he waited for Maddie to arrive. Once Lexi had been incarcerated, life had been so much sweeter. It had been wonderful to feel free, lovely to not have to worry about her popping up at a random moments and causing trouble.

But I really should have told Maddie.

When he and Maddie had been together for over a year and he knew their relationship was serious, that he was in it for the long haul, that's when he'd decided to make a concerted effort to get Lexi off his back for good. He'd managed to hide her existence up to that point, but he was living on his nerves, constantly worried that one of his family would say something, or – more likely – Lexi herself would do something to undermine the foundations of his new relationship.

At that point, he'd gone to the police. Not once, or twice, but five times. Five times he'd had to report her before they took him seriously. In the meantime, he'd had to make up all sorts of stupid excuses to explain away phone calls from the police. Looking back, he could see that had been a mistake. He should have just come clean at that point and told Maddie the truth. But then why would she have stayed with him? He was sure she would leave and he couldn't bear the thought of that. So, he'd kept his secret. It had taken a herculean effort, involving a lot of guilt and deception, but at the time he was convinced it was his only option if he wanted Maddie in his life.

I'll tell her now. I'll tell her everything. Then they could decide what to do together.

A band of clouds had appeared on the horizon, hiding the speckle of islands from view. It looked like rain was on the way, after almost two weeks of wall-to-wall sunshine. Was it a sign? Don't be stupid, he told himself, wiping his palms again, surprised at how nervous he was feeling. It was like he was on a first date, not meeting up with his long-term partner after a tiff.

That's all it is. A tiff.

In his peripheral vision, a movement made him turn his head and there she was, walking towards him, her stride purposeful, eyes focused on the café, her face stern. His heart sank but he rose to greet her with a smile, hoping he was misreading things. He pulled her into a hug and gave her a kiss. But she didn't kiss him back and pushed him away before sitting opposite him at the table. She was all business, he could see that in the slight purse of her lips, the way she perched on the edge of her chair as if she was going to take off again at any minute.

Tom swallowed, everything he thought he was going to say disappearing from his mind, which was now completely blank.

'Shall we order?' he said, looking for the waiter.

She shook her head, one hand grasping the strap of the bag that hung across her body, the other clasping the edge of the table. 'I'm not stopping, Tom. I thought I would but now I'm here...' Her bottom lip quivered. 'I don't think I can.' He reached for her hand across the table, but she snatched it away, angry eyes meeting his. 'I can't get over the fact you lied to me. And seeing you now has just made me feel worse. I've put everything into this relationship. Everything. And you haven't been honest with me.'

'Oh, Maddie, sweetheart, I didn't lie to you. I just didn't tell you—' He snapped his mouth shut, knowing he was on to a loser as soon as he'd said it.

'Hiding the truth is almost worse than a lie,' she spat, her finger stabbing at the table as she spoke, clearly furious. 'I've been trying to work out why you wouldn't tell me you'd been married. And I had this thought...' She leant towards him, eyes boring into the inner workings of his mind. 'Are you still in love with her? Is that why you didn't want *us* to get married?'

He was so shocked by her conclusion that his throat clamped up like he was being strangled. 'No, no, no, what are you talking about?' he gabbled, when he finally managed to force out some words. 'You've got it all wrong. I haven't seen her for years. I mean, she hasn't been in my thoughts at all since—' He stopped himself, aware he was telling Maddie another lie. He let out a long breath, not sure what he could say to make things right.

Tell her the truth, shouted the voice in his head. *Just tell her.*

But he couldn't. Because who would want to be with someone whose ex-wife was a persistent stalker? Worse than that... A stalker whose behaviour was so threatening and dangerous, it had led to her being committed to a secure psychiatric unit.

18

Tom recognised the determined glint in Maddie's eyes and felt sick. This was not going well at all.

'The problem, Tom, is that I don't trust you now.' Tears glistened in her eyes and he wanted to reach out and give her a hug, do something to take the hurt away. But he couldn't, because she had an invisible forcefield around her that said, *do not even think about touching me*. He had to try and use words to cajole and persuade, which was not his strong point.

'Oh, Maddie, please don't say that. The reason I didn't tell you was because I felt ashamed that I'd married so young and got it wrong. I was separated by the time I was twenty-three! That's not something to be proud of.'

'No, it isn't.' Her eyes narrowed. 'So why *did* your marriage break down?'

'Because...' He dragged out the word, wondering how much to tell her. 'She wasn't honest with me.'

She rolled her eyes. 'How ironic.'

The fact that history was threatening to repeat itself in some way was not lost on Tom, but there was more to the story. Information that he really did not want to share. Because it couldn't possibly show him in a good light, and Maddie didn't need another reason not to trust him. He kept his mouth shut.

Her eyes hardened, her stare hawk-like in its intensity. 'Not because you didn't love her, then?' She leant towards him. 'I can't listen to any more of this, because there's no point. I don't believe a word that comes out of your mouth.' Her body language was enough to tell him how desperate she was feeling. 'This is your mess. You created this situation. I'm just trying to come to terms with the fact that my partner has been lying to me ever since I met him. Four years, Tom.' She slammed her hand on the table, making him jump, her face pink with rage. 'Four bloody years!'

Tom had never seen Maddie so angry. He tried to reach out to her again, but she batted his hand away. He ran his hands over his face, desperately trying to think of a way to retrieve the situation and make her understand. But he was conflicted, not wanting to make the situation worse. Given Maddie's reaction to being told he'd been married to Lexi, telling her about the baby would send her ballistic. Especially with everything they'd been through in recent years.

But she needs to know.

It would it be better to get everything out in the open, however difficult that experience was likely to be, so she couldn't accuse him of hiding anything else from her. But then, he reasoned, if he was going for full disclosure, he'd also have to tell her about the other problem with Lexi. And if she knew about that, his relationship would definitely be over.

One step at a time. Just tell her the essentials for now.

He took a deep breath, his hands finding each other on the

table, fingers clasping together as if that might give him strength. 'Let me explain about Lexi. And why she can't be in our apartment.'

19

MADDIE

Maddie was about to get up and leave when Tom threw in that last comment and now she needed to stay and hear him out. She'd promised herself she would listen, and anyway, she didn't feel Alex was being completely honest with her either.

'Why not?' she countered. 'Why can't she be in our apartment?' Her voice was prickly and defensive. The swap had been her idea, after all and she'd put a lot of effort into selling it to Tom. 'And let me remind you that it's actually *my* apartment, so it's up to me what I do with it.' She could hear how confrontational she sounded and softened her tone. Being argumentative was not going to get them anywhere and Tom was trying to tell her something important if only she'd listen. 'I just spoke to her before I came here. But I have to admit, what she told me about her mum didn't quite add up.'

He opened his mouth, about to speak, when her phone rang. She checked the screen. 'Talk of the devil. It's Alex again.' Her eyes met his. 'Shall I answer it?'

He gave a nod and she put her phone on the table between

them, on speaker, both of them leaning in so they could hear what was being said.

'Maddie, is that you?'

'Hi, Alex, is everything okay?'

She could hear the sound of clunking and scraping in the background. Men's murmured voices.

'Sorry I couldn't speak earlier,' Alex continued. 'They're keeping Mum in hospital overnight for observation. Apparently it's common to have a reaction to the first chemo, nothing to worry about.'

Well, that was quick, Maddie thought. It was not more than an hour since they'd spoken and from her experience you wouldn't even have seen a doctor in A&E in that time. Her suspicions were mounting that Alex was lying, but she had to pretend at this point that she believed her. The last thing she needed was for her to go on the defensive and clam up when she wanted answers.

'Oh, well I'm glad to hear that. How are *you* doing?'

'I'm fine. I've come back to your apartment to have a bit of a breather and grab some toiletries for Mum before I go back to the hospital. I just wanted to tell you that everything is okay here. I don't want you to worry and think you need to come home for any reason. And I want you to have a lovely stay in Croatia.' Her voice sounded forced, the tone a bit too jolly, considering the situation.

'Oh, right.' Maddie was thrown for a moment, not sure how to progress, but decided to press on and see if she could get an answer to her most urgent question.

'Look, I need to ask you—'

'No, Ed. No!' Alex's shout made her jump, her question stuck in her throat. There was a loud ripping noise and some maniacal laughter in the background. 'You're taking things too far now.'

The Getaway

Maddie's heart started to race. 'What's happening?'

'Nothing, it's okay, just Ed messing about with his friend. Honestly, it's like having a couple of toddlers to keep an eye on.'

Maddie didn't say anything, listening hard to see if she could work out what on earth might be happening. In her apartment. Their home. But it was quiet now and she finally asked the million-dollar question.

'Alex, why didn't you tell me you used to be married to Tom?'

She heard a gasp, then an incredulous whisper. 'He told you? He actually told you? What else has he said about me?'

'He just said you'd been married.' Maddie caught Tom's eye. He shifted in his seat, looking even more uncomfortable now and she was glad she hadn't stormed off because once this call was finished, she would make him tell her everything.

There was a long pause.

'Alex, are you still there?'

'I've got a message for your *partner*. The lovely Tom.' Her voice had a hard edge to it now, her words dripping with disdain. 'Tell him the game is on and we're moving up to the next level. He'll understand.'

The line went dead, leaving Maddie shaken. The vitriol in Alex's voice was not only unexpected but completely unnerving. Tom had gone very pale.

20

Maddie shivered. Was that a threat? And what was Ed up to? It had sounded like he was bouncing off the walls. And the ripping sound in the background... She imagined her lovely curtains being pulled from the rail as he grabbed at them, for a reason she couldn't quite work out. Their home swap guests seemed very different to the loved-up couple she'd met on holiday.

The unease that had been simmering deep in Maddie's chest rose to the boil, transforming into a terrible fear. Something was very, very wrong. She'd made a terrible mistake, getting carried away with the excitement of a new adventure without thinking about the practicalities and now she'd no idea what to do.

While she and Tom had been sitting under the awning outside the café, the storm clouds had edged closer and now they blotted out the sun. A rumble of thunder was followed by the crack and flash of lightning, at which point, the heavens opened and it started to rain. Not just ordinary rain, but torrential pellets of water bouncing off the promenade and pounding on the awning, so loud she couldn't hear herself think. The weather reflecting her mood.

Another boom of thunder made Maddie jump like a startled rabbit. She'd been frightened of storms, ever since their house had been hit by lightning when she was a child, putting a hole through the roof. Half her bedroom ceiling had fallen in and she was lucky not to have been hurt. To this day, she still had nightmares about it if she was feeling particularly stressed.

Tom stood up and hurried to her side of the table, putting a reassuring arm round her shoulders, knowing how storms affected her. 'Oh, you're shaking. Let's go inside, sweetheart.'

She nodded, too terrified to maintain her anger with him. He grasped her hand and guided her to a table at the back of the café where she would feel safer. 'Here, sit down, love.' He pulled out a chair and she sank into it, flinching as another rumble of thunder filled the air. It was busy inside the café, everyone having retreated from the outside tables. He looked around, then bent and rubbed her shoulder, his mouth close to her ear. 'I'll go and find a waiter and get us a coffee. Won't be a minute.'

Maddie shivered again, wishing she'd brought a jacket with her, not sure if it was the temperature that was the problem, or her concerns about Alex and Ed and what they might be doing to their apartment. What a stupid idea this swap had been. Obviously, she had to take some responsibility, but if Tom had been a bit more involved during the holiday, he would have met Alex earlier and this situation wouldn't have come about.

Tom arrived back at the table and sat next to her, gathering her to him, arms round her shoulders. 'I got you,' he mumbled into her hair as another bang of thunder, much louder this time, made her press herself into him. 'It's okay. We're safe here. Nothing to worry about, sweetheart.'

She was too frightened to think at that point, let alone speak, each new clap of thunder making her jolt, the flashes of lightning jarring through her brain. It seemed to go on and on for an eternity. It was a while before the waiter brought over their coffees and a couple of pastries and not long after that, the worst of the storm passed.

She peeled herself off Tom's chest, feeling a bit self-conscious. He held her hand and she wrapped her fingers round his, hoping they could find a way through this mess she'd created. But then, if she hadn't met Alex and become friends with her, she would never have known that Tom had been married before. And that felt like something she was going to struggle to get past.

She uncurled her fingers from his, picked up her coffee and took a sip, unsure how to start the conversation, waiting for Tom to speak.

'I'm so sorry about Lexi.' He rubbed at the back of his neck, looking uncomfortable. 'I can't believe what she just said.'

Maddie nodded. 'Yeah. I think I know what you wanted to tell me. Clearly Alex isn't what she seems, is she?'

Tom bowed his head, apparently struggling to find an answer.

Maddie nibbled at her pastry as she waited for him to get his thoughts together.

He took a gulp of his coffee. 'Okay, so the truth is that – some years ago – Lexi was diagnosed with a serious personality disorder. She has to be centre of attention or, in her mind, it's like she doesn't exist. External validation is vital to her. It's her oxygen. She's also terrified of abandonment. That's her worst fear and – in her head – that's what I did to her when I left. She believes I abandoned her and every bad thing that happens to her now stems from that. So... it's all my fault. Whatever happens in her life, whatever struggles she has, it's all my fault.' He paused. 'But with Lexi, what you have to understand is that every accusation is a confession. She twists things round.'

Maddie considered that for a moment and thought it made sense. 'But why exactly did you leave?'

Tom took a deep breath and started to talk.

21

TOM

Then

Tom remembered the moment, a couple of months after he and Lexi had been married, when he realised that Lexi had been lying to him. Not in a small way, but in a very big way. A way that had changed his life.

They were at a family get-together. A monthly ritual where Lexi, her sister and their respective partners were invited to their parents' house for Sunday lunch. He used to find the whole event overwhelming, not sure how he was supposed to behave in such a setting. His upbringing, as an only child of emotionally distant parents, hadn't prepared him for all the hugging and physical contact, the chatter and teasing and table manners. Everyone was nice enough, but he always had the feeling that he was on display, her family watching him, monitoring every move while they tried to work out if they liked him or not. Assessing if he was good enough. Sometimes, it felt like they were ganging up, making fun of him but he couldn't say anything because he was never quite sure. Was it joking or was there something more malevolent at play?

On that particular Sunday, he noticed that Lexi's sister, Pippa, was starting to look noticeably pregnant. You could see the curve of her belly, her face a little plumper. It had been a source of delight to their parents that both girls would be having children very close together, possibly only days apart, with endless conversations about how their children would be friends for life. More like siblings than cousins.

The thought horrified Tom because he wasn't too keen on Pippa, or her lawyer husband. She worked for a high-end estate agent in Chelsea and was a terrible snob. Her child would be attending private school, no doubt about that, whereas Tom and Lexi's child would definitely be going through the state system. Pippa's child would enjoy the luxury of a four-bedroom detached new-build with a large garden and would be ferried around in a Range Rover. Lexi's child would grow up in a two-bedroom apartment with not a blade of grass in sight, travelling on public transport.

He often found it hard to believe that the two women had been brought up by the same parents, although he'd increasingly noticed that Lexi did revert to type when she was at home on Sundays. That's when she had a tendency to make little digs at him, snide comments that had everyone quietly sniggering or rolling their eyes. He'd quizzed her about it and she'd laughed it off, telling him he was paranoid and an inverted snob himself.

There would be constant comparisons once the children were born and he knew he would be made to feel that he was letting his wife and child down. His father-in-law was one of the managing partners of the stockbroker firm where both he and Lexi worked. Turned out she hadn't been completely honest with him about how she'd got her job, but he'd let that pass, accepting her excuse that she wanted to be treated like a normal person, not the boss's daughter who'd got the job through nepotism.

Her dad was always going on at him about ambition, suggesting ways he could further his career. Ways that involved playing a round of golf with a CEO his father-in-law happened to be friends with, or going with him to his London club for lunch with some influential acquaintances. It was even suggested he should involve himself in dubious projects which definitely bent the rules. But nobody would know, would they? People with money didn't seem to care about the rules. That's what he'd learnt by spending time with his wife's family. Rules were for the little people and the wealthy weren't even worried about getting caught. Not when they had friends in the higher echelons of the police and the criminal justice system.

The thing that struck him as odd that day was the realisation that, compared to her sister, Lexi was not looking pregnant at all. And as soon as he'd allowed himself to think that, all his doubts about her pregnancy rushed to the front of his mind. He'd always been super careful about contraception and even though Lexi had been on the pill – at least she'd said she was – he used a condom as well. Two layers of protection. How could both of them have failed?

The other niggling doubt was the timing of it. He was a numbers type of guy and he liked to keep track of things. He knew when Lexi had her period, because she suffered from PMT and he could tell by her behaviour which part of her cycle she was in. He had his mother to thank for this awareness, because she'd always blamed her mood swings and flares of unreasonable behaviour on her reproductive cycle. It had made him super wary when he got together with Lexi, determined not to pick fights when hormones might blow up a slight disagreement into a relationship-ending row. To him, the timing of her pregnancy didn't add up. Now he'd seen her sister's growing bump, he was becoming more uneasy about the whole thing.

He didn't say anything until they were home that evening. 'I couldn't help noticing that Pippa's starting to look quite pregnant now, isn't she?'

Lexi was making them a cup of tea, her back towards him, and he noticed her hesitation, just for a couple of seconds before she finished pouring in the milk. She turned round, the two mugs in her hand, a smile pinned to her face. One of her fake smiles. He'd learnt to spot these as they could be a precursor to an argument. 'Yes, she is, isn't she?'

'And it made me think...' He took a deep breath and decided to just go for it. 'Lexi, I don't think you're pregnant, are you?'

She tipped forwards, dropping the mugs on the floor, hot tea splashing all over his legs. The heat was unbearable and he jumped up, trying to pull the material of his trousers away from his skin. He dashed to the bathroom and sat on the edge of the bath, legs under the tap as he ran soothing cold water over them, hoping he'd got there fast enough to prevent burns. His heart was racing. Had she done that on purpose, or was it a genuine accident? He waited but she didn't come to see how he was, or call out to ask if he was okay. There had been no apology and that wasn't normal, was it?

He went into the bedroom and changed into joggers before going back into the living room, his legs still smarting. Lexi was curled up in the corner of the sofa, her body heaving as she sobbed, her face in her hands. If there was anything that unravelled Tom, it was a crying woman; he just couldn't bear it and he dropped onto the sofa beside her, desperate to make things right.

'I'm sorry,' he murmured, rubbing her back before pulling

her into his chest. 'I didn't mean to upset you. But I've been thinking this for a while now.'

She raised a tear-stained face. 'I had a miscarriage.'

'What? When?'

'A couple of weeks ago.'

He was finding it hard to compute what she was saying. 'Why didn't you tell me?'

'Because I thought you'd regret marrying me if I wasn't able to carry your child.' She sobbed harder. 'It made me feel like a complete failure. And I couldn't face telling my family with Pippa being so happy about everything. I didn't want to spoil it for her.'

Her explanation did have a ring of truth about it and he held her in his arms while she sobbed, telling her that he didn't think she was a failure and of course he didn't regret marrying her.

That last bit was a lie. He definitely *did* regret marrying her.

He wasn't ready to be in a serious relationship. Not with someone as moody and unpredictable as Lexi. He hated the pressure from her family to up his game, so he could give Lexi a better life, like her sister's. And he hated their constant judgement. It was uncomfortable and demoralising and he'd preferred his life before. Although it was sad that Lexi had suffered a miscarriage, he was actually relieved. Did that make him a bad person?

Later, when he'd had a bit of time to think about things, he began to wonder if there'd ever been a pregnancy. She hadn't mentioned any of the little niggles women supposedly had when pregnant. He had a work colleague who'd fallen pregnant the previous year and, given that his desk was one of four pushed together, and the other three were occupied by women, he couldn't help listening to her regular updates on how sore her boobs were, how she was peeing all the time, her insatiable appetite and the overwhelming tiredness. Lexi hadn't mentioned any of those things. And yet, he'd allowed himself to believe her because he didn't want to face up to the possibility she would deceive him like that.

It was a foolishness, a cowardice that had cost him dearly.

When pressed, she eventually admitted that the pregnancy test she'd shown him had been her sister's and she'd never been pregnant at all. Once his eyes had been opened to that deception, their relationship quickly became untenable and it was only a matter of weeks before he told her that it was over and he wanted her to move out. It was his apartment, after all, and she had family she could stay with, unlike him. Plus the fact it was her lies that had caused their relationship to end.

And yet she'd argued against a divorce, because she didn't see her behaviour as being unreasonable. He'd even had to trick her into moving out, because it turned out she wouldn't be doing it willingly. He took a day off work and when she went out in the morning, the locksmith came and changed the locks.

He packed up her belongings and took them to her parents' house, making sure he apologised for being the shit husband they thought he was, but also making sure they heard the truth from his own lips. They must know what their daughter was like, mustn't they? They were non-committal, their expressions neutral, their manners impeccable. But he felt they'd be celebrating, once he was out of sight, happy to have their precious daughter home again and on her way to being free to marry a better match. Someone who might fit in.

As time went on, he realised Lexi's unwillingness to accept defeat was something he'd seriously underestimated. And that just about summed up his relationship with his ex-wife.

22

NOW

By the time he'd finished telling Maddie about the tragedy of his marriage to Lexi, Tom was exhausted. 'In her mind, being dishonest about her pregnancy wasn't a big deal. But I dared to leave her. That was the problem, because nobody in her family stood up to her. I'd actually had the gall to end the relationship, and she couldn't accept it was permanent.'

He sighed and gazed around the crowded café, wondering how everyone's life could be so normal when his was such a mess. 'What you have to understand, to make any sense of this— she thinks in a crazy upside-down way, and was convinced I'd thrown her out because she wasn't spending enough time with me. In her eyes, I was having a hissy fit. Attention-seeking. Making a point. She couldn't understand my intentions were real.' He took another gulp of his coffee, glad of the caffeine boost because this was one of the hardest conversations he'd ever had. 'Since then, she's hounded me. And it's been going on for years, with her tricks becoming more and more dangerous.'

Maddie frowned. 'What do you mean tricks? What sort of tricks?'

He fiddled with his teaspoon, not sure how much to tell her, because he didn't want to freak her out. But she deserved to know. Not least because he had to convince her that they should forget about staying in Croatia and head straight home.

'She messed with the brakes on my bike, causing me to crash. That's how I fractured my wrist.' He held it up. 'See, it's still a bit wonky. But that wasn't the worst thing. When we first broke up and I left my job, she started rumours that I'd been sacked for insider trading. She told work colleagues I'd been arrested and... rumours stick. It meant I could never work in the finance sector again.'

Maddie's mouth dropped open. 'Oh my God, that's terrible.'

'Yeah... But there's more. A lot more. She kept turning up drunk outside my apartment block, ringing all the buzzers until someone let her in, then hammering on my door, disturbing the neighbours. I felt so isolated, to the point where I hardly ventured out.' He finished the last mouthful of his pastry, remembering how lost and alone he'd felt at the time. 'Of course I went to the police, but as she was a nuisance rather than a threat, and I'm a man being hounded by a woman, they just had a word with her and left it at that.'

He hesitated, wondering whether to tell Maddie the next bit. It had been happening while they were together and he hadn't breathed a word about his troubles to her, managing to keep his problems hidden. Until now. He took a deep breath and decided he'd got this far, he might as well go for full disclosure in terms of Lexi's state of mind.

'Eventually, a couple of years ago, she had a meltdown at work and attacked a co-worker with a stapler and a pair of scissors. Due to the fact there were plenty of witnesses, she was actually arrested and charged.'

He glanced at Maddie who was carefully dabbing at her

pastry crumbs with her finger. 'When you say charged, you mean she was sent to prison?'

He hesitated for a second. 'No, not prison as such. Her father pulled some strings. Lexi was diagnosed as having a psychotic episode and instead of going to prison, she went to a secure psychiatric unit.'

Maddie nodded, clearly giving this some thought. 'And how long did she get?'

He shrugged. 'I honestly can't remember, and anyway it's different when there are mental health issues involved. But they must have decided she was fit to be released, because she's reappeared.'

Maddie's frown deepened. 'They would have told you she was coming out though, wouldn't they? You know... the probation service or somebody would have said something if she was put away because she was a danger to you.'

He gave another shrug, thinking he should know the answer to her questions and feeling awkward that he didn't. 'I honestly don't know. That's probably how it's supposed to work, but everyone is so overloaded, I don't think they always have time. And it wasn't me she attacked, it was a co-worker. I suppose, in their eyes, if she was fit to be released, she no longer posed a threat to anyone.'

Maddie stared at him and he could almost see her thoughts whirring in her brain. She wasn't happy, he could tell that much from the twist of her lips. 'I'm just trying to work out the timeline of all this... She was stalking you while we were together, and you didn't think to say anything to me about your dangerous ex-wife?'

His heart sank. It sounded really bad when she said it out loud.

'I'm so sorry.' He reached across the table for her hand but she snatched it away, folding her arms across her chest. 'I thought the problem was dealt with and she was out of the way. I changed all my socials and my phone number. And when I sold my apartment and moved in with you, I didn't think she'd be able to find me. In my mind, she was history. A past I wanted to forget.'

Maddie snorted. 'Yeah, how's that working out? It sounds like she's going to ramp things up, rather than leave us alone. Next level, she said. So, what might that mean?'

Tom stared at the table while he thought about his answer, fear tightening his shoulder muscles, making his heart race. *Should I tell her the rest?* He glanced up and could see from her face that he was skating on thin ice. If he wanted any chance at all of getting their relationship back on track, honesty was going to be the best policy. Better to get it all out in the open and deal with the fallout in one go.

He grimaced. 'I'm afraid there's more. I want you to know everything so you can't say I've been hiding things from you. And I'm sorry I haven't been as open with you as I should have been. I was frightened you wouldn't want to be with me.' He held up his hands. 'I know it was wrong and it was selfish.' His voice cracked. 'But I love you so much and I couldn't bear to be without you.'

She gazed at him, silently assessing, her eyes so full of disappointment he could hardly bear it.

'The reason they sent her to a psychiatric unit wasn't just because she'd attacked her co-worker. She also had a violent episode in the police station after she'd been arrested, and once her lawyer got involved, they decided she wasn't fit to be in prison. I heard that she also attacked a couple of the nurses on the psychiatric ward.'

It was a former colleague at the stockbroker's who'd told him this, when he'd bumped into her in a pub one night. He was sure she was a reliable source. 'Given Lexi's behaviour, I was certain she'd be held there for years yet. Her potential for violence was why I was so keen for us to buy a new place together. A belt and braces solution, just in case she'd found out your address. I thought we'd be safe if she didn't know where we lived.'

He could see the fear in Maddie's eyes, hear it in the shaking of her voice. 'But she definitely knows where we live now. She's in our apartment.'

23

MADDIE

Maddie couldn't believe what she was hearing. The woman she'd embraced as a friend was actually a violent, dangerous stalker with severe mental health issues? She just couldn't reconcile Tom's description of Lexi with Alex, the laid-back, fun woman she'd come to know on holiday.

Is Tom telling me the truth?

His revelations had not only laid bare hidden aspects of Alex's character but of Tom's character too. Lies by omission still counted as lies, didn't they? She gazed at him, trying to work out what her gut was telling her. Be careful, that's the message she was getting. A warning to treat everything he said with caution, and not accept it on face value.

Tom was hard to read. She studied his face, watched his body language... what could she see? He was fidgeting with his teaspoon again, spinning it over and over on the table. A sure sign of anxiety.

She thought about the last phone conversation with Alex, remembering the vitriol in her voice when she'd threatened to take things to the next level. There was something else that was bothering her as well... the comment that had caused Alex to explode.

'Why weren't you supposed to tell me that you and Alex had been married? That's what seemed to really shock her.'

The question seemed to shock Tom too. There was no doubting that flash of fear in his eyes. Maddie held her breath, waiting for the answer, wondering if this was going to be another bombshell that would rock her world.

'I... um. I'm not—'

Maddie slammed her hand down on the table, making Tom, and the people on the neighbouring tables, jump. But she didn't care about their shocked glances, their quiet mutterings. Her eyes were focused on her partner. 'Enough of your bullshit,' she snarled. 'I've run out of patience with your excuses. If you're not going to be straight with me, after everything you've told me so far, we are over. Done. Finished. You hear me?'

Tom glanced at the people sitting close by, giving them a nervous smile. 'It's okay, love. No need to get worked up. Let's not do this here. Why don't we go back to the hotel room, so we can talk in private.'

Alarm bells were going off in Maddie's head. What did he need to say to her in private that he couldn't say here? Most of these people didn't even speak English, but she could see the curious glances, hear the murmur of hushed conversations, and there was no doubt that she and Tom were the subject matter. A blush warmed her cheeks.

'Okay.' If it was going to get a truthful answer out of him, then she was happy to go along with his suggestion. She stood, hooking her bag over her shoulder. 'Let's go.'

The rain had stopped now, and Tom followed her outside, grabbing her hand as she marched up the road, as if he was worried she'd run off. She could hear her teeth grinding, all the anger about his lies bubbling to the surface. She'd really thought she could forgive him for the first lie, but now he'd told her that Alex was actually dangerous, she felt his failure to tell her the truth had potentially put her in harm's way. What might Alex have meant by 'next level'? Her heart raced as her mind provided a movie reel of answers, each more terrible than the last.

On top of all that, he now had another revelation. She could tell by his unwillingness to talk about it in public that it was not going to be good and she steeled herself, trying to stop her mind from guessing what it might be. They entered the lift together, the silence loaded, the atmosphere between them strained by the burden of things unsaid. Tom unlocked their hotel room and held the door open for her to enter first.

She went in and sat on the bed, Tom opting to stand rather than sit beside her. His hands were in the pockets of his shorts, jiggling the loose change he kept in there.

'Just spit it out,' she said. 'I'm not sure you can tell me anything that's worse than the stuff I already know. What can be worse than finding out a crazy stalker, who's already tried to harm you, and who is staying in our home, has now threatened to move things up to the next level?'

Tom sighed. 'The problem is, she's not stable. There is no recognisable logic in Lexi's view of the world. What wouldn't matter to you and me matters a lot to her. The reason she doesn't want me to tell anyone we were married is because of... well, image, I suppose. Firstly, she doesn't want anyone to know she's a divorcee, because in her mind that makes her a loser and less of a person. It makes her unattractive. And secondly, when she was arrested, it was under her married name – my surname. It took me years to get a divorce because she was very difficult about everything, and I couldn't afford much in the way of legal representation. But at this moment in time, I guess the important thing for her is that she has no criminal record against the name she is now using.' He sighed. 'The fact that she is vengeful in nature, makes her believe everybody is the same. I'm only guessing, but I would imagine she's worried I'll tarnish her reputation and image under her maiden name.'

He gave a weary sigh. 'You heard the language she used. To her this is a challenge, a crazy game of one-upmanship and destruction. She wants to wipe me out. Game over.'

The words struck terror in Maddie's heart. *Game over? As in... dead?*

Her eyes met his and his steady gaze suggested he was telling the truth. 'You're telling me she wants to... kill you?'

'No, no, I don't think she'll go that far. Meddling with the brakes on my bike was just to scare me. I suppose she means she wants to scare me some more, but I honestly don't know what "game over" would be in her mind. I have a feeling she might be wanting to split us up. Ruin our relationship. That's my guess.'

She blew out her cheeks. 'Christ, Tom. It would have been so much better if you'd been honest with me from the start.'

Tom leant against the wall, chewing at his lip. 'And then the really bad thing...'

Maddie felt the fear surging back after the initial relief. It was the way he said it. Like a little boy who is about to own up to flushing his goldfish down the toilet.

'Oh for God's sake, Tom.' She threw her hands up in frustration. 'Why is there always more? Let's just get this over with. Come on. Get everything out in the open and then at least we know where we stand. Or at least I will.'

He sat beside her on the bed, his fingers plucking at the duvet cover. 'Her dad paid me to do something. They sort of made it part of the deal for her agreeing to a divorce. He told me if I did him this one favour, then he'd talk Lexi round. And to be fair, he did.'

'What sort of a favour?'

'I just had to change a video. Do a bit of editing.'

'Change it?' She frowned, wondering how big a deal this was. 'How did you have to change it?'

'Oh, it was just a few little details. Nothing major.'

'Well...' she said, cautiously. 'That's not too bad then, is it?'

His lips were pressed into a thin line, his expression grim. His eyes locked onto hers and she could see the desperation, could feel it coming off him in waves. 'Maddie, can you forgive me? I know some of it's my fault, but you were the one pushing for the swap and I had no idea the Alex you'd met was actually Lexi. Can we pull together to get that woman out of our lives and get our home back?'

Maddie bit back her retort, his remarks making her feel instantly defensive, but she knew fighting wasn't going to solve anything. Tom was right. Two heads were better than one and once they'd got rid of Alex and reclaimed their home, then she could think about everything Tom had told her and decide how she felt about their relationship. It was a case of resolving one thing at a time and Tom was the one who knew Alex best.

'Okay,' she said, her mouth refusing to match his hopeful smile. 'You're right, I am partly to blame. I was impulsive and if I'm being really honest, I suspected you weren't really listening when I was telling you about the arrangement.' She wrapped her arms around her chest and hugged herself tight. 'I just wanted it so much. I wanted an adventure, to believe we had fun things to look forward to after all the heartache.'

Tom pulled her into a hug, his breath warm against her neck. 'I know this is a difficult situation, but together, we can do anything, can't we?' He kissed the top of her head, nuzzling her hair.

If he was hoping for her to respond in kind and show him affection, then he must have been disappointed when she pulled away. 'Hardly,' she snorted. 'Look, if she's dangerous, I vote we just call the police and tell them everything. Won't she be out on licence or something? And if she's threatening us, or doing things under false pretences, they'll recall her, won't they?' She nodded, sure this was the best solution. 'Then they can go and get her and Ed out of the apartment while we're on our way home. Our old flights weren't transferable anyway, right? And those are tomorrow morning, so by the time we get back to London, the problem should be sorted.'

Tom grimaced, a look of panic flashing in his eyes. 'No. No we can't get the police involved. Absolutely not.'

'But why? They know she's bothered you before.' It seemed like a no-brainer to Maddie.

'Yes, but I made that deal with her dad.'

Maddie wasn't sure she understood what the problem was. 'You gave him what he wanted, though so…'

'Yes, I did.' He hung his head. 'But it was illegal. What I did was against the law and it caused a lot of trouble at the time. I got away with it, but Lexi somehow found out about it. After she was committed, she sent me a message saying if I ever went to the police about her again, she'd report me for what I'd done.'

Maddie had to take a moment to process what he'd just said. She could feel her frustration building. 'But that would incriminate her dad as much as it would you.'

Tom gave a derisory snort. 'I wish. I mean, he's dead now but he was cunning. He organised it so if there was ever any comeback, it would be my name in the frame. That was the cost of breaking free from her and at the time, I was so desperate I wasn't really thinking about consequences. Or how things might pan out in the future.'

Maddie could feel herself deflating, like a heavy weight was squashing all the life out of her. She appeared to be running round a maze with every path reaching a dead end. There was no easy way out of this, no cavalry to call to fight their corner. *We're on our own.*

She wanted to scream. So, she did, letting all her feelings bubble to the surface and exit her body in a sudden burst of noise.

Tom looked shocked for a moment but he grabbed her hand and squeezed it so tight it shocked her into silence.

'I'm so sorry, Maddie. I can't tell you how much I regret not being open with you from the start but I never anticipated anything like this happening. I thought I was free of her.'

She could hear the sound of material ripping in her mind, that maniacal laugh she'd overheard when she'd been on the phone to Alex. 'They're obviously going to do something like... destroy our home! And we're stuck here.'

She burst into tears, covering her face with her hands. Never had she felt so powerless. And furious at the same time. A potent mix of emotions that threatened to make her resort to violence. She wanted to hit something. Or somebody. Needed a way to vent. The room felt too small, claustrophobic and she sprang to her feet.

'I can't be here with you a minute longer,' she snapped.

Tom grabbed her arm, stopping her from reaching the door. 'Maddie, no, don't go. Just hear me out. I'm determined to put this right.' He sounded fired up, his jaw set. 'While I was waiting for you to come to the café, I managed to book a seat on a flight at 4 p.m. today. You can fly back tomorrow, as originally planned. By which time, I'll hopefully have got our apartment back.'

'But what if they get awkward about it? We'll have nowhere to stay and we haven't got money for a hotel.' She peeled his fingers from her arm. 'I can't even speak to you any more.'

He checked his watch, a resolute glint in his eye. 'I've got to go or I'll miss my flight. I promise you, I'm going to sort this out.'

PART II
MADDIE: LONDON

24

Maddie was glad when her plane touched down on the Tarmac. She wasn't keen on flying and to make matters worse, she'd been surrounded by a group of rowdy men, returning from a stag weekend. They were shouting to each other and singing rival football songs, while slopping their drinks all over the place for large parts of the flight. The poor flight attendants did their best to keep them quiet, but after about ten minutes of calm, it would start up again. Then the couple in front of her had a massive row and a child was screaming. By the time the plane doors finally opened, her head was throbbing and she couldn't get off the plane fast enough.

Thankfully, her luggage appeared quickly and she was able to make her exit, escaping to the relative calm of the train. It was still going to take her the best part of an hour to get home and she yawned as she gazed out of the window, not sure how she felt about being back in London. It was a drab day and after the glorious scenery she'd left behind, it felt tatty and mundane. She'd fallen in love with Croatia and the lifestyle and was sad that the dream of staying there longer had proven to be so brief.

She couldn't just pin the blame on Tom, although that was tempting. There'd been a niggle at the back of her brain telling her it was too good to be true, but she'd chosen to ignore it. Because, for once, she wanted to win at life. She wanted to be the lucky person. So, she'd ignored that little voice, telling her to be careful.

Her heart was heavy with disappointment, and she hoped Alex wasn't going to be difficult about giving the apartment back to them. After that last phone call, and Tom's confessions, she'd had to have a complete rethink about who Alex was as a person. Dangerous. Unhinged. Someone to keep at a distance.

Is that going to be possible if she has her sights set on some sort of revenge though?

The thought made Maddie break out in a cold sweat and she tried not to focus on it too much. It was a possibility rather than a reality and she had to stay positive. All her dealings with Alex had been friendly, but had that been genuine or had she been putting on an act? On Maddie's part, she'd felt there was a real bond between them. If she hadn't, there was no way she would have even considered suggesting the swap. But she supposed that was testament to Alex's skills as a manipulator. However, Tom had lied too. It was hard to know what to believe, the truth distorted by a murky mess of disinformation.

Her thoughts fell silent, her mind filled with the clickety-clack of the train speeding along the tracks and the background hum of other people's conversations.

It's probably not as bad as it sounds, she reassured herself. Tom could have been exaggerating to make himself look better for walking away from his marriage, making it Alex's fault. It was possible all those things he'd said about her were lies. But what about not wanting the police involved? His reaction had been absolute horror so she thought the bit about his illegal activities and being set up might be true. Then again, he might not want the police involved because there was something else he hadn't told her.

She closed her eyes, despairing at the situation she'd found herself in. *Who the hell is the man I've been living with?* It was quite horrifying to think she'd had no idea about much of his history. And it was *her* apartment these people had the keys to.

I hope Tom's sorted everything out. Then she wouldn't have to face the woman. In fact, she would hopefully never have to see her again.

Tom had flown back the previous evening, while she'd kept to their original booking as planned. He'd insisted he wanted to go and confront Alex on his own, even when she'd suggested it might be better for them to present a united front. He said he wanted to make things right, but she had this sneaking suspicion there was more to this and he didn't want her there to hear whatever might be said.

Once he'd left, she was relieved to be on her own and have a bit of time to mull things over, because Tom had given her so much food for thought. To say there was a distance between them, not just geographically, but emotionally, would be a fair assessment and the hurt of betrayal burned in her heart. Forgiving him was going to be quite a task but that didn't stop her worrying about his safety.

She'd called him the previous evening, to check he'd got there and everything was okay. He hadn't said anything about trouble. In fact, he hadn't said much at all. He was in the pub, and there was a lot of background noise – she couldn't hear him and he couldn't hear her, so they'd given up and messaged instead. In a way, that was easier because trying to keep her anger at bay while speaking to him had not been easy. Trust was going to be an issue going forwards and her frustration with his behaviour was going to take a while to simmer down.

According to his messages the previous night, everything was fine.

She pulled her phone out of her bag, wanting to read their conversation again, to reassure herself that she wasn't walking into the middle of a conflict. It was still switched off after the flight and she turned it on, waiting for it to power up before scrolling back to the beginning of their recent chat.

She'd written:

> Hi, hope you had a good flight. Have you been able to get into the apartment yet? Any problems...?

He'd replied:

> I'm at the pub having something to eat. Nothing to worry about. Love you xxx

That's when she'd called him, but he'd said he couldn't hear and suggested they stick to messaging instead. She continued scrolling through.

> Was Alex okay about leaving the apartment? Please tell me she's gone.

He'd simply replied:

> Everything is fine. See you tomorrow. xxx

And that was that. *Fine. Everything is fine.* Which told her absolutely nothing. There hadn't seemed any point in messaging if she was just going to get meaningless platitudes, so she'd put her phone away the previous evening and went out for a last walk round Split, hoping that she could come back one day and pick up this dream. This was an interruption to her plans, not a full stop. Once they'd overcome this hurdle, she had to believe the future she wanted was possible. She'd gazed out to sea, her heart full of love for the place and the calm it instilled in her.

With or without Tom, I'm coming back.

It was a promise to herself, one she was determined to keep. It was merely the timeframe that needed a bit of a rethink, not the dream itself.

Earlier that morning, when the dawn was breaking, she'd messaged Tom before she got on the flight, not wanting to call because Tom was not a morning person and it was way too soon for him to make any sense at all. He'd replied a few hours later, when she was mid-flight so she hadn't seen his text until now.

> Morning sweetheart, looking forward to seeing you later. Love you xxx

Hmm. Nothing more about the apartment, but his dealings with Alex and Ed must have gone okay, otherwise he would have told her. It struck her as odd that his replies were so cursory and vague, which tied her stomach in knots. Because what if it wasn't all right and he just wasn't telling her? Hiding the truth from her again. There would always be that shadow of doubt now, whatever he said. What if she turned up to a heap of aggression?

She hated conflict at the best of times and would rather run away than fight. It had always struck her as being a survival instinct, although her peers had suggested, more than once, that she needed to learn to stand her ground. It was why her boss had never trusted her with negotiations, why she'd been happy to stay in a design role rather than aim for a management post. She was a compromiser, not an enforcer. Someone who could always see both sides of an argument.

With all the what ifs and maybes floating round her head, by the time she reached her stop, she was jittery and nervous. She rang Tom when she got off the train, to tell him she was only ten minutes away, but there was no answer. She tutted and left him a voice message. Again.

She reminded herself he was not good at answering his phone if his mind was focused on other things. He just didn't seem to hear it, but she would have thought he'd be waiting for her to call. She'd sent him her schedule and told him what time she expected to be home. Still, he was probably busy getting shopping or something. At least she hoped he was.

She trudged down the main road, then turned off onto their quieter street, lined with trees. The sound of children playing in the park opposite filled the air with their lively chatter, laughs and screams. The rumble and clack of skateboards. The whoosh of a bike speeding past. This is home, she thought, their low-rise block of apartments in sight now at the end of the street. It was only four storeys high, slotted into a corner, where there'd once been a factory, at the end of a row of Victorian terraces. She loved this street. The yellow of the brick, the different coloured doors on each house. The wheels of her suitcase bumped over the uneven paving stones and, as she looked around, absorbing the familiar atmosphere, she felt okay about being back in London.

It doesn't have to be forever, she reminded herself. It was obviously not the right time for their adventure to happen.

As she got closer to her apartment, the brief uplift in her mood started to deflate, the nerves churning in her stomach again. It was horrible not knowing what to expect. She stopped and pulled out her phone and rang Tom again. Still no answer. She sighed and put her shoulders back, thinking she really had to work on this fear of confrontation. She and Tom were in the right, it was a casual arrangement, and if things got nasty, there was always the police. Whatever Tom might want, she'd be ringing them straight away if she felt threatened.

She was about to carry on walking when she spotted someone hurrying out of the front door of the apartment block. A familiar figure. Close enough for Maddie to see the thunderous expression on Alex's face, her jaw set, her lips pressed together. She had her phone to her ear and it looked like she was going to walk towards Maddie, then she stopped and looked at her phone in a way that said she couldn't believe what she was hearing. From the expression on Alex's face, it was clear there was a problem.

Uh-oh. There was a choice to be made. Maddie could be brave and call out to her, confront this thing head on. Or she could turn around and go back the way she'd come, maybe head off down a side street for a few minutes, until Alex had gone and then carry on to the apartment.

What's it to be?

She only needed a second to decide, turning on her heel and hurrying back up the road before Alex spotted her.

25

Maddie's heart was pounding as she speed-walked up the road, chancing quick glances over her shoulder to see if Alex was following. Thankfully it appeared her presence had gone undetected. She walked round the block, deciding to stop at a coffee shop on the high street, to buy herself a bit more time.

Tom still wasn't answering his phone, which was annoying, so she messaged him instead, telling him Alex was outside, just in case he didn't already know. She lingered over her drink, waiting for him to reply, but her phone stayed silent. When she tried ringing him again, it went straight to voicemail.

Is it odd that he isn't answering?

She didn't need another thing to worry about, but his silence was starting to bother her. Maybe Alex had been hassling him and he'd turned his phone off? Yes, that was a possibility. He had a habit of doing that when he wasn't ready to face up to something. Or somebody.

Nervously, she exited the café, so preoccupied by her thoughts, eyes on the pavement, that she almost bumped into the woman in front of her. She looked up when she felt a hand grab her arm.

'Maddie, I can't believe you've come back already. I thought I saw you outside the apartments, then you shot off.'

'Um, yes, we had a change of plan.' Maddie tried to remember what excuse she'd used. 'Unexpected work stuff. Like I said in my message yesterday, we had no choice but to come back.'

Alex was shifting her weight from foot to foot like the pavement was burning her feet. She looked agitated with a capital A.

'What's going on?' Maddie asked, aware of the pressure on her arm where Alex had hold of her. 'You seem a bit... uneasy. Have you seen Tom? He came back yesterday evening.'

Alex frowned. 'No, I haven't seen Tom. I've been with Mum in hospital and I just went to the apartment to get something and...' She stopped mid-sentence, her mouth twisting to the side. 'At this moment in time, I can't explain it, but it's probably better if I show you.'

Alex tugged at her arm, steering her down the road at such a fast pace Maddie had to jog to keep up. 'I didn't want to disturb you in the café, so I thought I'd wait outside. And we can't talk with all these people around.'

Maddie was so surprised, she didn't resist at first. But once her thoughts caught up with what was going on, she slapped Alex's hand off her arm. 'What do you think you're doing?' she snapped, stopping her in her tracks.

Alex looked surprised, like she'd expected Maddie to trot along wherever she'd planned to drag her. 'I'm so sorry, I shouldn't have grabbed you like that, but... honestly, I'm freaking out. Something really... problematic has happened.'

Maddie realised Alex didn't just sound like she was freaking out, she looked like it too. Her eyes were wild, her face drawn, her words tumbling over each other. 'Wait a minute. What sort of problematic?' It sounded ominous and she had no intention of just walking into trouble. *It could be a trap.* The thought increased the unease that was sitting on her chest, heavy as a lump of lead. 'What's going on?'

'I really don't know, but... look, as I said, I need to show you. Come on, come with me.'

Alex tried to grab Maddie's arm again, but she pulled away, backing up a step. 'Stop doing that. You're making me nervous.' She stood her ground and folded her arms across her chest, thinking she wasn't going anywhere with Alex while she was so hyped up. Not without a proper explanation. 'You need to tell me what's going on before I go a step further.'

'Sorry, I don't mean to hassle you but...' She grimaced. 'You need to see for yourself and then we can work out what to do.' She started walking again, indicating for Maddie to follow, which she did, making sure there was a sufficient distance between them that Alex couldn't grab her again. All her senses were on high alert, not sure what was coming next.

After the stories Tom had told her, Maddie was reluctant to be anywhere private with Alex. Especially not an enclosed space, like their apartment. 'See what for myself?' she asked, cautiously, alarmed at the string of thoughts unravelling in her head. What exactly might she need to see, rather than be told? It could only be something horrible, couldn't it? Her heart raced, her mind racing faster. *Is it Tom? Has Alex hurt him? Or does she want to hurt me?*

Stop it, she warned herself.
Alex said she hasn't seen Tom.
But she could be lying.

Her heart beat faster, sweat dampening her T-shirt, making it stick to her skin.

'Did you break something?' she asked, hoping this might be the answer. Something that didn't really matter in the greater scheme of things. 'I thought I heard things ripping when you were on the phone the other day. You were telling Ed to stop. What did he ruin?' She braced herself for news that he'd pulled a curtain down. Not the end of the world, but a cost to replace that she couldn't afford.

Better than Tom being broken. However strained her relationship with her partner, she couldn't face the thought of him being hurt.

'Please, just come to the apartment,' Alex begged, on the verge of tears now, which was confusing. 'I don't know how it's happened and I'm not sure how to put it right.'

Now she was being cryptic and Maddie was getting annoyed. They turned the corner onto Maddie's street, the park in front of them. 'Shall we find a bench where we can sit and talk privately?' she said, sure she'd feel safer outside, with lots of people around should things take a turn she didn't like. She headed in that direction before Alex could reply, deciding she had to take control of the situation, make like she was in charge even though she was shaking like a leaf.

She's dangerous. That's what Tom had said and until it was proven otherwise, she was going to believe him and act accordingly. Her hand closed round the phone in her pocket. She could call the police if she felt threatened and that gave her some comfort.

'Why are you being so weird with me?' Alex asked. 'Is it because of what I said about Tom? Because I was just mad at the world at that point. Hormones, you know. I get very tetchy when I have my period. I didn't mean anything by it.'

Maddie didn't answer straight away but led them to a bench by the entrance to the park, opposite her apartment building on the other side of the road. She looked out at this spot, liked to watch people coming and going. The joggers and dog walkers. Mums and toddlers, dads taking kids to the skatepark. Friends having a stroll, laughing and chatting together. She could people watch for hours as she thought up her designs, noticing what colours they were wearing, taking inspiration from everyday life.

She glanced up at her apartment window, hoping to see Tom looking out. She could signal to him that she needed help, if she felt threatened. But there was nobody there. There was something about the window that didn't seem quite right, but she couldn't work out what it might be.

They sat, Maddie shuffling up the bench a little until she felt there was sufficient space between them. She decided to take the initiative and get her say in first, so Alex was under no illusion as to what she knew.

'Look, I'll be straight with you. Tom has told me you've been stalking him for years. I know you faked a pregnancy to get him to marry you. I know he walked away from your marriage when he found out. I also know you threatened to report him if he ever went to the police about you in the future.' She took a deep breath, thinking this next comment might provoke a reaction, but it had to be said. 'And I know you've been in a secure psychiatric hospital for a while.' She gave a slow shake of her head, still appalled that she'd been taken in by Alex's pretence of friendship. 'Obviously there's more, but you already know that. I don't need to tell you the rest. I just want you to be aware that Tom has shared everything with me now.'

Alex's face contorted into a mask of disbelief. 'He told you what?' Her mouth dropped open. 'I can't believe it. Bloody hell.'

She gave a frustrated grunt and stared at a line of trees in front of them, her jaw working from side to side.

Maddie was relieved her pre-emptive strike had hit its mark and felt a little of the tension seep out of her body. She decided to press her point home while she had the advantage. 'I was shocked when he laid it all out for me. I've always thought I'm a good judge of character but...' She sighed, her eyes dropping to her lap where her fingers fiddled with the zip of her jacket. 'I honestly thought of you as a friend, so I felt pretty betrayed. By both of you actually.'

Alex pushed herself to her feet, a note of regret in her voice. 'I'm not sure there's any point in this conversation. He's filled your head with lies, so you're not going to listen to me. I suppose that was the plan. But, I swear this is the truth... The apartment swap was my way of trying to protect you, while I tried to sort out... um... let's call it a *situation*. I found myself in a difficult place. Compromised, if you like. And I was trying to make it go away.' She swallowed, looking and sounding on the verge of tears again. 'I've been very misled. I've made a big mistake.' She grabbed Maddie's shoulder. 'I am genuinely your friend, and I need you to believe that.' Her eyes narrowed. 'And now you know something important. Tom tells lies.'

Maddie pushed Alex's hand off her shoulder and shrank back in her seat, uneasy about the fervour in her voice. It was like she was trying too hard to convince her she was her friend. Which made her believe that she wasn't.

They stared at each other for a long moment. Alex glanced at the apartment, an angry twist to her mouth. 'I'll let you see for yourself what I'm talking about in terms of the problem we have.' She started walking away, then stopped and called back over her shoulder, anger shaking through her voice. 'Call me when you're ready to have a proper chat, rather than throwing second-hand accusations at me. When you're willing to listen, then we can talk.'

Maddie watched Alex leave the park, a deep unease stirring in her belly. She glanced up at her apartment, wondering what she might find inside.

26

Maddie sat on the bench for a little while longer, becoming more reluctant by the minute to return to her home. Alex appeared to be genuinely shocked when Maddie had summarised all the things Tom had said about her. But was she shocked that Tom had told her everything? Or... was she shocked that Tom had told lies about her? That's what Alex seemed to be implying.

The weight of uncertainty pressed Maddie into the bench, making it impossible for her to move as her mind ran round in circles, reliving conversations with both Tom and Alex. Clearly one of them was telling the truth and one of them was lying. Or was there truth peppered in both of their perspectives? Until she'd worked out who she could trust, it felt like a very vulnerable and precarious place to be. Especially if Tom had been right, and Alex was prone to violent outbursts.

Hmm. She pondered that for a moment. Really, given everything Maddie had just said to Alex, which, let's be honest, reflected her in a very poor light, she'd taken it very well. It was a measured response, walking away to compose herself rather than going in to battle. Not the response of someone who was unhinged and mentally unstable.

Or is this all part of the game she's playing?

Maddie tried to call Tom again, but he still wasn't answering and she left her fifth message since she'd got off the plane, asking him to call her back.

Her fingers fiddled with her zipper, her gaze fixed on the trees ahead of her as she let her mind wander. Amidst all the lies, it was very odd that Tom seemed to have disappeared. And Alex had just come out of the apartment building where Tom was supposed to be.

Has she done something to him? Hurt him? Is that what she wanted me to see?

The thought didn't really fit with Alex's demeanour, she decided, although she appeared to be panicky about something. Something that she'd wanted to explain to Maddie. And she'd said they could work out what to do about it together, which was mysterious. If Alex had hurt Tom in some way, she wouldn't be wanting Maddie to go with her to the apartment together, would she? *Or maybe she would if it gave her some sick sense of satisfaction.*

Thoroughly frustrated with the way her thoughts were going round in circles, she finally jumped up from the bench and hurried towards the apartment block, while her mind went on a rampage, throwing up dramatic images that belonged in a horror movie. It was the downside of having a creative brain and she stopped in the foyer of the building while she took some deep breaths to calm down.

Her brain wasn't making sense. It just wasn't. If Alex wanted to show her something in the apartment, that meant Tom wasn't there, didn't it? Which could mean that he hadn't been able to get in. In which case he would have had to find somewhere else to stay. But... if that had happened, why had he told her everything was fine?

There was no point trying to ring him again. She'd left enough messages now and he often didn't answer his phone. How many arguments had that habit sparked? When she'd needed to speak to him, and he was lost in his own creative world with his weird and wonderful creatures. That's probably all it was. He had that new project to focus on now and she knew she'd lose him, in terms of being emotionally present, until he'd started making progress. It happened every time. He was probably in a hotel room somewhere, glued to his laptop, oblivious to what time it was. Or he could even still be asleep if he'd worked late into the night.

Calmed by her logic, she climbed the stairs. She loved her apartment. Loved the area, the community she lived in, and she wondered why she'd entrusted something she cared about so much to a stranger.

It had been impulsive and reckless, chasing a dream that wasn't hers. You couldn't borrow people's lives, even if you yearned for what they seemed to have. It was a mirage, something you could never hold and call your own. Nobody can give you a life you haven't created for yourself, however much you want to believe it's possible.

Maddie got to the top of the stairs, happy to see the door to her apartment. It was a well-kept block and the communal areas were always clean and tidy. The atmosphere was calm, she noted. Nice and normal. A positive sign.

'Tom—?' She called out as she opened the door, wheeling her bag into the hallway. 'I'm home.'

The air felt strange and echoey, but it was only when she got through to the lounge that she understood what Alex had meant about a problem. The room was empty. Absolutely empty. In fact, there was nothing in there, apart from Tom's hat on the floor. Not a stick of furniture. Not a single floor covering. No curtains or blinds or even light shades. The whole place had been stripped bare. Her heart skipped in her chest, panic making her breathing fast and shallow.

Given the size of her mortgage, it had taken her five years to manage to furnish the place how she wanted, and now everything – except what they had in storage – was gone. A wave of disbelief crashed over her as she wandered around, hardly able to comprehend what she was seeing. Or not seeing. Even the locked work room had been emptied, Tom's computers gone, together with all the work stuff she'd stored in there. The certificates she'd had framed on the walls, prizes she'd won for her work, pictures of campaigns she'd been especially proud of. The highlights of her life had been in that apartment, on the walls, in the bits and pieces of soft furnishings, little trinkets that held memories of special moments.

Her eyes scanned the living room and settled on Tom's hat, lying on the floor. He'd obviously been back, but his bag was nowhere to be seen. *Where is he?* And where was all their stuff? Her brain froze, not able to comprehend what had happened, let alone work out what she should do.

Is that what I heard when I was last talking to Alex on the phone? Were the bumps and bangs in the background the sound of Ed moving the furniture out? Was the ripping actually the sound of him pulling her curtains down?

Tears stung at her eyes, her limbs leaden and uncooperative as she walked over to the window, perching on the windowsill while she surveyed the sad and empty space. She pulled her phone from her pocket and tried to ring Tom yet again but still no answer. It seemed pointless to leave another message, but she did anyway. Having seen the empty apartment, and no sign of him, she was growing increasingly concerned about his welfare.

She picked up his baseball cap. It was the one he'd bought on holiday, having forgotten to pack any sort of sun hat and she clasped it to her chest. If anything untoward had happened to him she'd be devastated. Just because he'd lied to her, didn't mean she'd stopped loving him. Love didn't work like that. And she wanted to believe he'd lied for a reason she was yet to understand.

Bloody Alex.

This was her doing. Part of her vengeful game. *The next level.* This was what she'd wanted to show Maddie. The power she had over her and Tom. Was there an ultimatum coming? A demand of some sort? Because she couldn't imagine what the woman might want. All she could think about was finding Tom and their stuff and putting their life back together, whatever that might take. She dropped Tom's hat, pulled out her phone, found Alex's number and dialled.

27

'What have you done with all our stuff?' Maddie demanded as soon as Alex answered the phone. 'Where the hell is it? How could you do that? How *could* you? And where's Tom?' She was incandescent with rage, her voice shrill and screechy as she thought about the destruction that had been wreaked on her life. Not to mention her concerns for Tom's safety. She had a terrible sinking feeling in her belly, like she was being sucked underwater.

'Hey, hey, calm down.' Alex's voice was remarkably even, given the circumstances, which stoked Maddie's anger even more. *How dare she tell me to stay calm?* But she couldn't risk her hanging up, so she bit back her response, and waited for her to speak again. 'I knew you'd blow your top and that's why I wanted to show you, so I could explain and then you wouldn't be quite so worked up.'

'This better be good, Alex, because if it isn't, my next call is to the police.'

'Firstly, why would I know where Tom is? When you

messaged to say you were coming back, I thought that meant you were coming back together. I mean, why wouldn't you?'

'Because once Tom realised it was *you* we'd swapped with, he wanted to come straight home, so he came back yesterday. I kept our original booking.'

'Oh, he did? Yesterday?'

'Yes. He did. I've already told you this. But he's not here. His suitcase isn't here either. And he's not answering his phone.'

'Hmm. You're sure he came back?'

Alex sounded as puzzled as Maddie and frustration got the better of her. 'Yes, I'm bloody sure,' she snapped. 'I spoke to him last night and he said everything was fine and his hat's here. The one he bought on holiday.'

There was a moment's silence and all Maddie could hear was Alex's breath rattling down the phone in a heavy sigh. 'Look, the truth is... I have no idea what's happened to all your stuff.' Another sigh. 'To be honest, it even crossed my mind that you and Tom had emptied the apartment to spite me. For all I know, you could have already planned to move out and got that organised with a removal company and didn't tell me. It's just the sort of mean trick Tom would play.'

Maddie was so astounded she could hardly speak. 'That's a ridiculous suggestion. Tom's not like that. He's not vindictive.' She was puffing like a raging bull, her anger mounting with every word she spoke. 'You wanted to show me my cleared-out apartment, didn't you? Wanted to gloat. Enjoy a little power trip. Tom warned me about you and I didn't believe him because I thought you were a friend.' Her jaw tightened. 'Is this the game you were talking about in that phone call the other day? Is this what the next level means?'

Alex sighed. Again. Making Maddie wonder if her reaction

was genuine or if this was a performance and she was acting a part. It was something to bear in mind, but for now, she had no choice but to listen. 'None of this is my doing. You've got to believe me, I have no idea what's going on, I really don't.' Maddie heard a hitch in her voice, like she was close to tears. 'I've been in and out because Mum's home now and needed looking after. I just saw it today, when I came back to get some stuff.' She sniffed, her voice breaking. 'My things have gone too.' There was a pause while she blew her nose. 'I wanted to meet you face to face and show you the empty apartment, so I could see your reaction because I thought this might be down to you and Tom playing tricks.'

Maddie wasn't taking any of Alex's denials at face value. She was a liar, wasn't she? *But so is Tom,* said a voice in her head, which made her hesitate before she jumped on a weakness in Alex's explanation. 'Apart from me, you're the only person who has a key. Whoever took everything out of the apartment, you must have let them in.'

'That's not exactly true though, is it?' Alex countered. 'Tom has a key. And I assume your estate agent has one too.'

'Of course Tom has a key, but he was in Croatia, Alex, you know that. How could he possibly have anything to do with this?'

'He could have had a spare key cut for someone and got them to empty it out. Or got your estate agent to organise it.' Alex was sounding as fired up as Maddie now and their conversation had degenerated into a row.

'I've already told you that's not what has happened.' Maddie's voice was getting louder, her tone harsh, willing Alex to listen. 'The apartment is our home. My home. I bought it five years ago and although we did think we were moving out, the sale fell through, so we decided to stay put for the time being. We. Did. Not. Do. This. Do you hear me?'

'All right, all right, no need to yell at me,' Alex snapped.

'You're not listening.'

Alex's tone softened, her voice suddenly weary. 'I am, I promise you, I am. And I suppose I believe you, but if you're ruling Tom out, then... it must be Ed. We're not really speaking because we had a big bust-up. Another one.' She huffed. 'I can tell you, from the messages he's been sending me, I am not his favourite person, but I honestly wouldn't have him down to do something like this.'

Maddie remembered the note Ed had left Alex in the holiday apartment in Croatia and wondered if their bust-up related to that. 'Can you ring him?'

'Don't you think I might have tried that already?' Her voice was loaded with sarcasm.

'Sorry, yes, I'm sure you have.' She felt frustrated and helpless, not wanting to leave control of this disaster in Alex's hands. 'Why don't I try ringing him? Here, give me his number. It's worth a go.'

Alex read out his number, but when Maddie called it disconnected, it didn't even go to voicemail. 'He's not answering.'

'I left him a message, so I'm hoping he gets back to me soon.'

Soon. That could mean anything. Hours or days even. Maddie's heart sank. How were they ever going to get their belongings back if they couldn't even reach the person who'd most likely taken them?

She might be lying. That voice in her head again. How disconcerting to not be able to trust a word people said, to be second guessing their motives, working out whether they were trying to manipulate.

Maddie could hear Tom's voice in her mind, remembering the raw emotion when he'd been telling her about Alex and her reign of terror as she'd attempted to ruin his life. But then Alex had looked horrified at what Tom had said about her too.

'It's easy for you to pin it on Ed,' Maddie said, carefully. 'But Tom and I don't even know the guy. As far as I can see he has no reason to do something so malicious. This is on you, Alex. I'm ringing the police.'

Maddie was determined this would be her best course of action because something about Alex's story didn't ring true. It was time to call her bluff and it didn't take long to have the desired effect.

'No, no. Don't do that!' There was a note of panic in Alex's voice. 'I don't think that would be in Tom's best interests, do you?'

Maddie thought that was an odd thing to say and couldn't work out what she might mean. Then she remembered what Tom had said about Alex's threat to reveal what she knew about the illegal tape editing he'd done for her father. Was that what she was referring to?

Every accusation is a confession. She twists things round.

Tom had said that about Alex. And Maddie needed to heed his words, because she'd only known Alex for a couple of weeks whereas, Tom had been married to her. She had to see this for what it was. *Alex* didn't want the police involved, that was the truth of it.

'Look, I'll come back to the apartment,' Alex said. 'I'm just at the Tube station, so I won't be long. You stay there and let's see if we can sort out how to resolve this. Hopefully Ed will return my call and he might have the answer.'

'Right, see you soon, then,' Maddie snapped, jabbing at her phone to end the call.

She tapped her phone against her chin while she tried to think, but it was hard to gather her thoughts when she was so angry. Why did she have the distinct impression she was in the middle of some weird, twisted game? One where she didn't know the objective, let alone the rules. She had to trust her gut, follow her instincts. And her instincts were telling her that Alex knew more than she was letting on.

Maddie decided she'd let Alex have her say, but she would be looking out for inconsistencies, for signs that she was lying. Her eyes scanned the empty room, settling once again on Tom's hat, lying on the floor.

Quite apart from the fact that everything in their apartment had gone, she was more concerned that her partner had disappeared too.

28

While she was waiting for Alex to arrive, Maddie tried ringing Tom again, but this time, a message said the number could not be reached.

What? How could that be right? She'd called from her contacts list, the number she always rang for Tom. Why couldn't his number be reached? Now she was really worried. Had he lost his phone and somebody else had picked it up and changed the SIM? *Or has Tom done it himself?*

Alex's comment about Tom not wanting the police involved had jarred with her. But hadn't he told her himself that he would be in trouble if he involved the authorities? That illegal thing he'd done as a favour to Alex's father, on a promise that he'd get his daughter to agree to a divorce.

Oh God, what the hell is happening?

Maddie felt so helpless, her life ripped apart in front of her eyes and so much confusion about who and what to believe. She could feel the panic rising, fluttering in her chest like a trapped bird and paced the room in an effort to calm herself down. It felt like she was in one of the strategy games she and Tom sometimes enjoyed playing. Seemingly impossible situations with puzzles to solve and it took a bit of lateral thinking to move to the next level.

The next level. That's what Alex had said in her warning. *Hmm.* Maybe she needed to view this as a situation in one of those games, see if that helped her to work out what was going on.

Ten minutes later, she heard a key in the lock and Alex hurried through the door looking as troubled and flustered as Maddie felt.

'I feel so awful that this has happened,' she said, leaning against the wall on the opposite side of the room, as if she needed the safety of space around her. It was probably a good move because Maddie felt like wrapping her hands round her neck and choking the truth out of her lying mouth. 'I honestly don't know what Ed's playing at.' She looked around the room, eyes studying the ceiling, her fingers knotting themselves in the strap of her shoulder bag. 'But I need to tell you something. And I want you to hear me out.'

Maddie glared at her, understanding that whatever she was going to tell her was not going to be good.

'Go on.'

Alex grimaced. 'The truth is… I haven't actually known Ed long. Maybe three months? We met in a chatroom for people recovering from addictions.' She looked down. 'I got addicted to sleeping tablets after Tom left me and I keep going back to them when life gets rough. Ed said he was the same. Anyway… long story short, we got chatting and met up a few times. He was so easy to talk to and we had our struggles in common, we just seemed to click and started dating.

'Then he said he'd got a cheap deal for a holiday to Croatia and did I want to come along? He was paying. Well, I jumped at the chance. Who wouldn't? He was like the man of my dreams, at first anyway, whisking me away on a holiday by the Med. And I haven't had a holiday in years.' She walked over to the window, standing next to Maddie, gazing out over the park. Maddie felt an immediate spike in adrenaline, her body telling her to move, so she did, edging away to put a more comfortable distance between them.

Alex gave her a sideways glance, a rueful smile playing on her lips. 'You think I'm a crazy lunatic, I can tell.' She huffed. 'I can't even begin to describe what an awful experience that was.' There was such a note of bitterness in her voice Maddie could practically taste it. 'Anyway, an offer of a free holiday...' She shook her head. 'No such thing as a free lunch, as they say. But I wanted it so much, I couldn't say no, even though, at the back of my mind I sort of knew it was too good to be true. What can I say...? I was smitten with him.'

Maddie stared at Alex, trying to work out if she believed her. Whenever she'd seen them together, Alex had looked at Ed as though she was completely in love, she'd give her that. And Ed was a handsome man, very polite and charming, full of funny stories that made him endearing and fun to be around. She could imagine how it might have played out and although she was resisting, she felt herself edging towards the conclusion Alex was being straight with her.

There was more to the story though, that was obvious, things not quite adding up, and she tried to dig deeper. 'So, you weren't digital nomads?'

Alex bit her lip and looked at the floor. 'No, we were just on holiday.'

'Why did you lie?'

'Okay, God's honest truth...' Alex looked decidedly uncomfortable, her eyes flitting around the apartment, like a butterfly, unable to settle. 'The second day of our holiday, I spotted you and Tom, walking on the promenade and I couldn't believe it. Of all the places to see him, it seemed unreal and it sent me into a bit of a spin. Ed couldn't work out what was going on with me, so I had to tell him my full history with Tom, and how awful the last few years had been because of him.'

Maddie frowned, annoyed that Alex was making it sound like Tom was to blame for their break-up and everything that had happened afterwards. She was clearly somebody who avoided taking responsibility for her own actions and Maddie reminded herself to keep that in mind.

'Ed said, "Let's make him and his new woman jealous of us then," and we came up with this big cover story, pretending we'd been together ages and travelling all over the world.' She shrugged. 'I knew there'd been a time when that was what Tom wanted, but I wouldn't go along with it at the time.'

'And what about the apartment swap? Whose idea was that?'

Alex bowed her head. 'It was Ed's. The apartment in Croatia belongs to a friend of Ed's family. They rent it out on Airbnb. Apparently they'd had a last-minute cancellation for four weeks and offered it to us. It made no difference if you used it instead.' She shrugged, her hands gravitating to the pockets of her jeans. 'That's what he told me, anyway.'

Maddie realised she'd been played. She hesitated, before asking the other question that had been on her mind. 'Your mum. Does she really have cancer or is that a lie too?'

Alex's silence and her refusal to meet Maddie's eye told her the answer.

She couldn't believe they'd been taken in so badly. *Me. It was me,* she reminded herself. *I was taken in.* She couldn't blame Tom for accepting the arrangement, because she'd been the one pushing for it. After Alex had pretended to be her friend for almost two weeks.

She rued the day she'd met this woman. But, in a way, she'd been just like Alex with the offer of a free holiday. She'd wanted something so badly, she didn't want to think there was anything suspicious about good fortune landing in her lap. How could she judge her actions when she herself had acted in the same way? *I didn't ruin anyone's life, though. I didn't steal their possessions and rip their home apart.* But it wasn't just possessions that had been taken. It was their history and their means to make a living as well.

They settled into a loaded silence, the two women staring at each other like they'd no idea what to say or do next, until Alex's phone started to beep.

'Ed!' Alex exclaimed when she answered it. 'What the hell—' She stopped talking, chewing at her lip as she listened to him speak. 'You're kidding me,' she said, after a few moments, then silence again while Ed carried on speaking. 'Oh, thank God we know what happened now... Yep, yep, I'll tell Maddie. Thanks for calling... Okay... Bye.'

She beamed at Maddie. 'Mystery solved. I think I told you Ed's family are into property rentals? Well, it turns out they also have a house clearance business.' She shrugged, all the worry erased from her face. 'I had no idea, you see, that's how well I know the guy. Anyway, there was a mix-up with addresses in the office. Ed had written this address on a notepad to remind himself where we were staying and put it on his desk along with the spare key he'd had cut and the admin person thought it was a property to be emptied.' She beamed at Maddie, clearly relieved. 'The good news is everything is in a storage unit. Ed sends his sincere apologies and says he's organised for the guys

The Getaway

to bring it all back tomorrow. Apparently it's too late to organise it today because the guys are out on other jobs.'

'Tomorrow? What am I supposed to do until then? Where am I supposed to stay?'

Alex shrugged, looking very uncomfortable. 'I don't know. Have you got a friend you can stay with? Or see where Tom's staying?'

'I don't know where Tom's staying, do I?' she snapped, beyond frustrated at the turn of events. And furious that Ed had cut a spare key for himself without even asking. 'He's not answering my calls. If he was at the pub, maybe he ran into someone he knows and he's staying with them. Or he got a hotel room.'

The fact that Tom wasn't contactable was a major source of annoyance now, but there was nothing she could do. She had to think about herself and where she was going to stay. Most of her friendship group had started families and their homes were already bursting at the seams. It was hard to think of anyone who might have some space.

'You can come and stay at Mum's tonight, if you want? I mean it'll be a squeeze but I feel bad about leaving you in this mess.' Alex gave her a sheepish smile. 'I'm so, so sorry this has happened. Honestly, I'd really like to help out if I can. It's a shame my sister moved to Dubai because you could have stayed with her, but... nah, that wouldn't have worked.' She gave a hollow laugh. 'No way would I be asking that bitch for a favour, not after...' She flapped a dismissive hand. 'Sorry, you don't need to hear my family history. But you can come back with me if you really have no alternative.'

Maddie's head was telling her she couldn't afford a hotel room, but her gut urged caution. She gave a tight smile. 'I have a couple of work friends I can try. But if I'm stuck, I'll give you a ring.'

'Okay. Well, the offer's there.' Alex checked the time on her phone. 'Look I've got to go. Mum's expecting me. I'll ring you later, shall I?'

Maddie forced another smile. 'Okay, thank you.'

She watched Alex walk away, heard the door close. The apartment was silent, an unnerving quietness that amplified the sound of her thoughts. At least she knew where their belongings were now and felt reassured they would be returned. It was an administrative error, simple as that. She was almost ready to accept Alex's story until that doubting voice piped up in her head. *Or... is this just part of the game?*

29

Maddie sank to the floor, exhausted by her early start, the travelling and the shock of finding their apartment cleaned out. Not to mention the tense and awkward conversation with Alex. There was so much to process and it was stuck in a glutinous mass in her brain, sitting there like a lump of overcooked noodles. She put her head in her hands, not sure where she could turn for support, but yearning for someone to talk to, who could help her find a way out of this predicament.

Her phone rang and she snatched it up, glancing at the screen, hoping to see Tom's name. It was her mum.

'Hello, love. How was your holiday?'

Her mum's cheery voice brought a lump to Maddie's throat. What would she give for a hug from her right now? But she couldn't burden her poor mum with her problems. Not when she had her dad to look after. He was recovering from a heart attack and Maddie was sure she couldn't tell her mum anything, because she was a natural over-sharer, and would blurt it out to her dad. That was the last thing he needed right now. As a protective father, he would want to come and help and the fact that he couldn't, would surely increase his blood pressure, which could spell disaster in terms of his recovery. Anyway, she'd given them enough stress with her baby woes over the last few years. No, she couldn't dump this on them as well.

She swallowed hard, having to clear her throat before she could speak. 'Croatia was lovely. It's a beautiful place. I've just got back, actually.' Although her words sounded good, her voice was dull and made them into a lie.

'You sound a bit tired.' There was a note of concern and Maddie knew she wasn't fooling her mum.

'Yeah, it was an early start. Ridiculously early, and travelling is so tiring, isn't it?' She gave a pretend yawn. 'I'm just about to go back to bed for a bit.'

'Oh, okay.' Her mum sounded disappointed. 'Can we... chat later then?'

'Yes, of course we can, you won't get much sense out of me now, honestly I'm dead on my feet.' Maddie felt guilty about fobbing her off, but knew that the longer she spoke to her mum, the more likely it was that she'd break down and everything would come rushing out. It was hard to keep her voice from cracking. 'How's Dad doing? Is he okay?'

'Yes, yes, he's doing well, but I've missed our chats while you've been away.'

Maddie was aware she was an important part of her mum's support network, and she told her things that she probably didn't feel she could share with friends. She couldn't just walk away from her mum's troubles because her own life had been upended. 'Tell you what... I'm just going to get my head down for a little while, then I'll give you a call when I feel a bit more human.'

'Okay, that would be lovely. I want to hear all about your holiday, and I'll put you on speaker so your dad can hear as well.

He'd like that. Give him something else to think about. He's awfully maudlin today, so hopefully that'll give him a boost.'

Whatever her mum had said, it sounded like her parents were struggling and Maddie's heart went out to them. 'I promise I'll call later. This evening, just in case I sleep for a while, okay? Love you, Mum.'

They said their goodbyes and Maddie disconnected. There were a few things she had to address before she could think about talking to her mum, because she had a way of wheedling her troubles out of her however much Maddie wanted to keep them hidden. Finding Tom was top of her list of priorities.

His hat being on the floor was evidence that he'd been here. So he'd come home, found the place empty and then what? If it'd been her, she doubted her first reaction would have been to go for a pint on her own. Nor would she have said everything was fine when it clearly wasn't, and still wouldn't be fine the following day. It really was a mystery.

She let the possibilities circle round her head for a bit, realising that lots of things could have happened. There was no point making up scenarios in her head. He could have lost his phone and that's why he wasn't answering. There was no need to be concerned just yet, and she was sure that's what the police would tell her if she tried to report him missing. It was probably best to stay put for a while, just in case he turned up. If he hadn't arrived back by this evening, then she'd start to worry.

Whatever happened, with or without Tom, she needed somewhere to stay for the night. She couldn't stay in the apartment with no furniture and she couldn't go back to her parents. Nor could she afford to stay in a hotel, given the precarious state of her finances. After deliberating for a few moments, wondering whether she could push herself onto any of her friends for a night, she singled out Bernie from work as her only option. She'd just moved into a new apartment after a relationship break-up and Maddie was sure she would have a sofa she could sleep on. Unfortunately, when she called, Bernie told her that her sister was staying, so that was a no.

Having ruled out all her options, she rang her boss, Nadia, who over the years, had also become a good friend. Maddie knew she wouldn't be able to stay with her, because she protected her personal space ferociously, but she was the only person who might be able to help her come up with a solution.

Nadia sounded upbeat when she answered her phone. 'Hi, Maddie, how's the digital nomad life going?'

Maddie cringed, already embarrassed that her plans had been such an instant flop. 'Ah, yes, well I've hit a snag. A very big snag as it happens.' She took a deep breath. 'I don't suppose you've got time for a coffee, have you? I could really do with a chat.'

'What's happened?' Maddie could hear the frown in Nadia's voice. 'Are you home already? Is everything okay?'

'I'll tell you when I see you, but if you could possibly make time today that would be so helpful.'

'Hmm, let me look.' She could hear the clicking of computer keys as Nadia checked her diary. 'I've got a gap at lunch if that works? 1 p.m.? I've had a client cancel on me, which is handy. Why don't you come to the office, and we can go and find somewhere quiet.'

Maddie felt her whole body sag. Just telling someone about her situation was going to make her feel better. And Nadia was a wise and resourceful woman. You didn't get to run a business turning over millions of pounds a year without problem-solving skills. 'Perfect. Thanks, Nads. You're a star.'

'I know I am, darling, I just wish more people realised.' Nadia laughed. 'Anyway, see you soon. And whatever's bothering you, I'm sure we can sort it out. Two heads are better than one, aren't they?'

They ended the call and Maddie checked the time. She had an hour to spare and decided she'd walk to the office, which was only twenty minutes away. She didn't want to stay in the empty apartment a minute longer and walking always helped her to think. There was a little notebook in her handbag that she carried around for jotting down ideas and she tore out a page, scribbling a note for Tom, which she left in the middle of the empty lounge, next to his hat.

Where have you been? Give me a call asap. Ed's bringing the furniture back tomorrow – crazy admin error, apparently. Gone to lunch with Nads. Back later.
Maddie Xxx

Once outside, as she walked towards the office, she made a mental checklist of the main issues she was struggling with, ready to give Nadia a quick summary. Unfortunately, by the time she reached her destination, she understood that none of what she thought to be true might be real. Tom had lied to her and now he'd disappeared. Alex had definitely lied and had willingly deceived her on holiday, which was pretty unforgiveable in terms of a continuing friendship. Ed was a virtual stranger to Alex, had cut himself a spare key without asking and they only had his word that he'd taken their furniture, which may or may not have been the admin error he'd claimed it was. Also, whether everything was really going to be delivered back in the morning was up for speculation.

In fact, now her mind was on Alex and her lies, what proof did she have that the phone call she'd answered was actually from Ed? She could have made the whole thing up. Maddie did have Ed's number though and she pulled out her phone, deciding she'd call. Then at least she'd know if that conversation had been real. But it disconnected again, so she couldn't even leave a message.

She had a bit of time while she was waiting for Nadia, and while she sat in the reception area of the office, she pulled out her laptop and started to Google Tom's ex-wife. Perhaps, with a bit of research, she could find out for herself what the truth might be.

How naïve she'd been, she thought, as she scrolled through the search findings and reality was revealed to her in black and white, her heart breaking a little bit more with each revelation.

30

'Maddie, there you are.' Nadia burst into the reception area with her usual aplomb and swooped in to give Maddie a hug and a kiss. 'Put that laptop away. I'm starving.' She was already halfway to the door. 'Come on, darling, chop, chop, I'm on a tight schedule today.' She clapped her hands together. 'Let's go.'

Maddie snapped her laptop shut and put it back in her bag, which she hooked over her shoulder. 'Can I leave my suitcase here?'

Nadia frowned, looking puzzled, not having noticed Maddie's case propped in the corner. 'Haven't you been home yet? You've come straight from the airport?' She sounded confused.

'No, I've been home, but…' Maddie flapped a hand, clambering to her feet, not wanting to keep Nadia waiting when she'd been kind enough to make space for her in her busy day. 'It's a long story. I'll tell you on the way.'

Nadia linked her arm through Maddie's. 'Hmm, mysterious. I can't wait to hear. But come on, Lucy booked us into the Mexican round the corner.' She pulled open the glass door and led Maddie into the street, giving her arm a squeeze as soon as they were out of the building. She leant her head towards Maddie's. 'Okay, spit it out. You know me, I want all the details.'

Maddie began with her first meeting with Alex and let it flow from there, carrying on talking, while they entered the restaurant and were shown to their seats. She was only interrupted when the waiter came to take their drinks order, then again when he came back to take their meal order and she was just finishing the whole tale when their lunch arrived.

Nadia looked pensive as she studied her plate of food. She'd gone for chicken enchiladas while Maddie had plumped for the chilli. Her thinking being that the spiciness might turbocharge her brain and allow her to make sense of the mess she found herself in.

'And you say Tom's gone missing, as well as all your stuff?' Nadia pulled a face like she couldn't believe what she was hearing. 'But according to this Alex girl, your stuff is on its way back?'

'Yes. Though now I'm getting worried about both those things. Because I only have Alex's word that it was a mix-up with Ed's house clearance business, and I can't get through to him on the number she gave me. And I haven't heard from Tom at all today. He must have found the apartment empty when he arrived yesterday, mustn't he? But I spoke to him last night and he said everything was fine. We couldn't really talk because he was out at the pub and it was a bit noisy.'

'And you didn't hear from him again?'

'We sent a couple of messages, and he repeated everything was fine and that was about it.' She sighed. 'The truth is, I'm still angry with him for not telling me he'd been married to Alex.'

'I'm not surprised you're angry about that. Hurt and upset too I would imagine.' Nadia took a big bite of enchilada and chewed, her expression saying she was in thinking mode. 'Look,

I'm just firing possibilities here, but you don't think Alex could be right and this could be something to do with Tom? Could he be in trouble, and he's not told you? And did he say who he was drinking with last night?'

Maddie started to eat, the heat of the chilli setting fire to her mouth, making her take a cooling gulp of water. 'Honestly, I'm not sure I know anything any more. He didn't say he was with anyone last night and I didn't think to ask. I just thought he was at the pub to get something to eat and kill some time.' She sighed. 'The thing is... I did a bit of research while I was waiting for you and now I'm more confused than ever.' She took another gulp of water. 'Tom said to me that every accusation from Alex is a confession. But what if that's projection and he's actually talking about himself? While I was sitting in reception, Googling, I found some things out that made me realise I don't know Tom at all. Nothing I thought was true actually is. Honestly, it's like I'm walking on sinking sand and daren't move in case the ground sucks me under.'

Nadia frowned. 'You're going to have to explain, darling. You're talking in riddles.'

'Tom said Alex was put away for her crimes. Apparently she attacked some people. But actually, it turns out *Tom* is the one who's been in prison. Can you believe that? Another whopping lie by omission. I couldn't find any criminal records against Alex. Nothing at all. So that made me think that Alex could have been telling the truth and Tom is the liar. Which made me even more confused.'

'No way! How devastating.'

'He was accused of aiding and abetting insider trading, when he was working for a stockbroker. He told me Alex had spread a false rumour about that and he'd had to change profession, but it seems it was the truth after all. You know he never said anything about working for a stockbroker to me. Not a peep. My mind is completely blown.' She shook her head, frustrated and annoyed with the way he'd kept things from her. 'The report said he was in the compliance department and he'd forged documents. He got four years, so I suppose he would have served two or something like that.'

'Oh my God.' Nadia had stopped eating, looking at her wide-eyed and open-mouthed. 'Tom always struck me as one of the good guys. A bit quiet, admittedly, but a gentle soul. That's how he comes over.'

'I know, that's why I'm so shocked at the moment. But... here's the thing that's got me worried... it's not the only time he's apparently broken the law. He told me he'd altered some video footage for Alex's dad as part of a deal to get her to agree to a divorce. He said what he'd done was illegal and Alex had threatened to report him if he ever tried to get the police on her case again.'

Nadia's frown deepened. 'And do you think that's true?'

Hmm, that's the million-dollar question.

'Well, it might be. Neither Alex nor Tom wants the police involved in their affairs. And Tom was very clear that she wouldn't want the police involved, because she might get sent back to the secure unit where she was being held.' She rubbed at her forehead, her thoughts tied in knots. 'Now I'm doubting if she's ever been convicted of anything and it might be Tom projecting.' She puffed out her cheeks, more confused than ever. 'I think she had a mental health crisis, because she sort of admitted she'd been in a psychiatric unit, but that doesn't mean she's done anything criminal.' She sighed. 'Help me, Nads, I just don't know what to believe. It feels like I'm in the middle of this game and the people around me are making moves but I haven't a clue what the rules are.'

'Like you say, there's obviously something going on here that you don't fully understand yet.' She thought for a moment. 'Let's break this down, see if that makes things easier to understand. It sounds like the apartment being emptied was just human error. That's what you're being told, isn't it?' Maddie nodded. 'So, if we accept that at face value for now; for me, the big question is... why is Tom avoiding you? Why has he disappeared?'

'You think that's what he's doing, avoiding me? You think it's deliberate?' The thought hadn't crossed her mind and it was yet another possibility to add to the mix. 'Not that he's in some sort of trouble?'

'Well, it could be either of those two options. It could be something simple, like he drank too much, and got himself in trouble at the pub.' She shrugged. 'I mean, for all we know he might have got himself in a fight and has been sleeping it off in a police cell.'

Maddie hadn't thought of that either. Her theory had been foul play, because of everything Tom had said to her about Alex. Painting her as a she-devil out for his blood. But given his lies, she had to question his narrative. The thought of him being at a police station was actually quite comforting. 'I suppose anything is possible. And I could ring round the local stations, see if they know anything.'

'That might be a good move. But I'd save that for a little while and do a bit more digging. In lieu of being able to speak to Tom, if you want to probe a bit more into what really went on with him and Alex, I'd be keeping in touch with her while you still have that connection. Now she knows what Tom has told you about her – and it sounds like she wasn't impressed with his version of events – she might like to give her side of the story.'

Maddie thought about that for a moment and decided it wasn't a bad suggestion. 'The only problem is I don't know how much of what she says to believe. They both lied to me, didn't they? And then there was her comment about the game and going up to the next level. Do you think that's some sort of code between them? Is this a battle they're involved in with its roots in their past connection?'

'Yes, I get your point. But she might have proof that she's telling the truth if you ask. The problem is, you know now that Tom has lied a few times. Not about small things, but about major incidents. Things you have a right to know about as his partner. So how are you ever going to carry on a normal relationship with him going forwards? You'll be questioning every word he says from now on. I know you probably won't want to hear this, but you can't build a solid partnership on that. Believe me, I've tried to overlook a partner's lies and I can tell you it only leads to heartache. Which is why I'm happily single. So, my suggestion would actually be to take the opportunity to see what Alex has to say, see if she has any proof that she's telling the truth and then you'll have a better idea of how much Tom has lied. She might know something that will help you find him.'

It wasn't what Maddie had wanted to hear, and she fell silent, concentrating on eating her meal while Nadia did the same. It was only when she'd finished the last mouthful that she spoke again. 'Alex actually offered to let me stay with her. What do you think? Should I go?'

Nadia looked horrified. 'Good God, no. Look, we have a corporate rate at the hotel next to the office, so why don't we book you a room there. We can put it on expenses for now and sort it out later if that helps? And then you could invite her to the hotel for a chat, don't you think that's best?'

Maddie felt the weight on her shoulders lighten. She'd ploughed all her spare money for the month into the holiday and it was a few days until she got paid, which was why she'd been struggling to afford a hotel room. At least she didn't have to work out where she was going to sleep now, which was a great relief. 'Thank you so much, Nads. I can't tell you how much I appreciate your help.'

She reached across the table and their hands met. A squeeze of solidarity that meant the world to Maddie. She wasn't on her own in this and that made her resolve harden, determined to get to the bottom of what was going on. 'That's not a bad idea, meeting Alex at the hotel. I mean, she was very apologetic when we met up earlier and seemed genuinely concerned about what had happened with the apartment. Apparently, some of her things had been taken too. And she was visibly cross when I told her Tom's version of events.' She nodded to herself. 'You're right, there *is* more to learn from her about the past.'

'Exactly. And remember, the one thing you *do* know for certain is that she was married to Tom. So start from there and see where it leads you, no prompting her with what Tom's told you. Just let her talk and listen. Then you can see if and how their stories match up. The more you know, the easier it'll be to make a decision about your future.' She gave Maddie's hand a final squeeze before letting go. 'If you come back to the office, I'll get Lucy to book you in to that hotel for a couple of nights, to give you a chance to get your apartment sorted out. Assuming that phone call was genuine about your stuff being returned and not another lie.'

Nadia finished her drink and called for the bill. 'I'm so sorry, but I've got to dash. I'll call you tonight though, shall I? After you've had a chance to speak to Alex.'

Maddie flashed her a grateful smile. 'Perfect and thank you for listening. I know it's a lot to dump on anyone.'

'I'm just glad I could help.' She stood and shrugged her bag over her shoulder, linking arms with Maddie as they walked back to the office to sort out a hotel reservation.

Maddie waited in the reception area, staring into space, feeling shellshocked and more than a little overwhelmed. One thing she did know for sure though: she was determined to find out what Tom might have been hiding from her. There was a chance it might break her world completely, but wasn't that better than living a lie?

31

A little while later, Maddie made her way to the hotel, glad to see they had a dining room and decent-sized bar where she could meet up with Alex, if she agreed. Once she'd got herself settled in her room, she took a deep breath and gave her a call.

'Maddie, you rang.' Alex gave a little laugh. 'I'd convinced myself that you wouldn't want to speak to me again.' Maddie had almost convinced herself of the same thing, but she trusted Nadia's take on things and in her heart, she knew she was right. If she didn't know the truth about her husband's past, or at least Alex's version for the sake of comparison, nothing would be resolved.

'Well, I'll be honest, I'm pretty hurt that you lied to me like that on holiday. You used me to get to Tom and that doesn't feel good.'

'No, I know. I can't say I'm proud of my behaviour. Especially now that…' She halted mid-sentence and Maddie wondered what she'd been about to say. 'I'm so sorry. I didn't think we'd connect like we did. Honestly, I was prepared to hate you. But I didn't. Not at all; in fact, I liked us being friends.'

Alex sounded genuine and really, she was the only potential clue Maddie had as to what might have happened to Tom. She'd rung around the hospitals, but he wasn't in any of the local ones, so that was a relief. She'd held off from ringing the police, because they might want her to go further and report him as missing, and she wasn't ready to do that yet. She might as well wait and see what she could glean from Alex first.

She decided on a measured response, one that was contrary to the way she was feeling. 'Yes, well… it's all water under the bridge now.' Hard for Maddie to say because it was a lie. She still resented Alex, but for the sake of her own future, she had to pretend. 'Look, Tom still hasn't been in touch and I'm worried. I just wondered if you have any ideas where he might be? Any friends he might be staying with who I don't know about?'

Alex hesitated before she answered. 'I'm not sure I'm the best person to ask about that. I mean it's years since we knew each other. Feels like a different lifetime to be honest. And once he left the office, he dumped all those friends and reinvented himself.'

'What about Ed, then? Do you think he might know anything?'

'Hmm, I don't see why he would. I'm not really sure how they might have come across each other before the holiday.'

Another dead end and Maddie was frustrated with the way the conversation was going. 'Well, please can you check I've got the right number for Ed, because it just disconnects when I try to call.' She sounded snippy now.

'Oh, yes, of course. He's Ed Garvey. I'll message you his number instead of saying it, then you know you've got it right.'

Maddie heard the ping of a message on her phone, happy to see Ed's details. She checked them against the number she'd been ringing. 'Dammit, that's the number I've been ringing. But why is he blanking me?'

'He's got a lot on at the moment. But I'll message him, ask if he'll give you a call if you like?'

Maddie sighed. It was the best she could hope for. 'Thank you, that would be helpful.'

'No worries.' Alex was quiet for a moment before she said, 'I was wondering... if you still need somewhere to stay?' She sounded hopeful. 'Honestly, I'd welcome the company, so don't think you'd be imposing or anything like that.'

Maddie had to stop herself from laughing. There was trusting and then there was stupid, and she'd been stupid enough already by trusting the wrong people. From now on, she was only going to trust herself and try not to be quite so gullible. Given that she believed Alex had lied about her mum having cancer, Maddie had no idea what her current living arrangements might be. Did her mum live in a tiny one-bedroomed apartment? Maddie somehow doubted it.

'Thanks for the offer,' she gushed, deciding it was time to turn on the charm. 'That's really kind of you, but I've got a hotel room sorted now. I did wonder if you wanted to come over for a drink though, then we could chat some more. I've found out a few things about Tom and I wanted to run them past you, because it seems he's told me a bunch of lies.'

'Well... um, yes, I can do a drink. Maybe this evening. Say 8 p.m.?'

'Perfect, I'll see you then. I'm sending you the hotel details now and I'll be in the bar.'

Maddie rang off, nervous about her next encounter with Alex, but determined to get some answers to her questions.

32

Maddie was sitting at the bar, already on her second gin and tonic when Alex turned up on the dot of eight. She looked like she'd just stepped out of the shower, her face perfectly made up, dressed in a smart pair of jeans with designer boots and a neat suede jacket over a cream cashmere jumper. She definitely wasn't short of money, if her wardrobe was anything to go by.

'How's your mum?' Maddie asked, wondering if Alex would admit now that the cancer story had been a lie.

'Oh... um... better.' She flashed Maddie a quick smile as she climbed onto the bar stool next to her. 'Much better, thanks. They think she'll be out of hospital tomorrow.'

Hmm. Seems she was going to persist with the story. Perhaps it was true after all. But then, hadn't Alex said she was back home earlier? Maddie decided to press a little more, unable to help herself. 'So, what happened? Was it a bad reaction to the cancer treatment?'

'Um... yes, something like that. Apparently, it happens a lot during the first round of chemo.'

Very vague and inconsistent, Maddie decided. This meeting

was probably a complete waste of time but she might as well persist now that Alex was here. She ordered drinks, an awkward silence sitting between them. Maddie decided she just had to steer the conversation where she wanted it to go, and decide what to believe afterwards. There was nothing to lose.

'Look, I saw how shocked you were when I repeated the things Tom had told me about you and I wanted to hear your side of the story. There appears to be a lot he hasn't told me about his past and I'm wondering if that's connected to him going AWOL. Because it's out of character. He's always been Mr Reliable. He's never stood me up. Never not been there when we've arranged to meet. Always bang on time or early. I just don't understand where he's gone or why he isn't answering my calls.'

Alex took a sip of her drink, looking at Maddie over the rim of her glass. 'That's very fair-minded of you, after everything that's happened. Wanting to hear what I've got to say.' She gave a little laugh, a note of bitterness in her voice. 'Quite refreshing actually, because once you've been branded as mentally ill, you seem to lose your right to have an opinion. Or even to be believed. Everyone thinks you're just making things up, even when they're true.' She gave a derisive snort. 'That's the power people can exert, when they make up a load of lies about you, create evidence, then swear it's true. It makes you powerless. Especially if you're a woman and they're a man.'

There was a force of emotion running through Alex's words that took Maddie by surprise. And it sounded to her like Alex had just made a very damning accusation against Tom, even if it had been coded in general terms, with no names mentioned.

Maddie could completely relate to what her companion was saying. Hadn't she, herself, experienced a similar thing at school, when she'd been bullied and manipulated? Made out to be the bad guy to cover the actions of others. It had been the most terrible period of her life, and it almost broke her. Thankfully, she had very supportive parents who helped her through. Every cloud has a silver lining, as her mum used to say. What doesn't break you makes you stronger. And that ordeal, looking back, had been the making of Maddie. She'd found an inner strength and resolve she'd never known she possessed and rather than being overwhelmed by the bullies she'd finally stood up to them, called them out officially, gathered hard evidence and they'd been expelled.

They'd messed with the wrong girl. And now she was a woman, nobody was going to mess up her life again.

Maddie took another sip of her drink and filed Alex's comments away to peruse later. There were other things she wanted to discuss first. She put her drink back down on the bar. 'I think it's only right to have both sides of the story. There are things Tom has been hiding that he should have told me. Finding out he'd been married was a major shock in itself, because he's always been adamant he doesn't believe in marriage. Then today, I also found out he's been to prison.'

Alex's eyes widened. She clearly hadn't been expecting Maddie to know that, but she hid her discomfort with a shrug, her eyes sliding away, her focus on her drink. 'If you already know his darkest secret, I'm not sure how much more I can tell you. It ruined our marriage.'

'So... you didn't trick him into marrying you by pretending to be pregnant?'

'I did not! Tom pursued me for months before I agreed to go out with him and then I sort of got locked into the relationship. He was the cute nerdy guy, and I felt sorry for him. I can't explain it, but he played on my empathy and in the end, he broke me. I... well I tried to end my life and Tom had me committed to a secure unit.' She shuddered. 'Honestly, I don't want to drag all that up again.'

Once again, Maddie was shocked, Tom's version of events being totally at odds with Alex's version of the truth. So wildly different there was no way to tell which was right. Alex sounded so genuine, but the best liars always did. Tom had sounded genuine too. In fact, he'd sounded properly scared when he'd talked about Alex and her stalking. How she'd tried to kill *him*, not herself.

She glanced at her companion who was hunched over the bar, staring into her drink. Alex's body language didn't say confident or threatening. It said beaten and downtrodden, which fitted with her version of things. Maddie was going to have to delve a little deeper.

'So... you didn't tell him you were pregnant when you actually weren't.'

'No. That's a lie. I've never wanted children, not when I struggle to look after myself.'

'Okay, so what happened when you messed with the brakes on his bike?'

Alex laughed. 'Honestly, Maddie. That's pure fantasy. It didn't happen. That's Tom trying to scare you away from me, making you distrust anything I say, because he's frightened I'll tell you everything I know about him. And once you find out what sort of person he really is, then you won't want to be with him.' She turned her head and caught Maddie's eye. 'His greatest fear is abandonment.'

What? Isn't that what Tom said about Alex?

'It's difficult,' Maddie said, carefully. 'When the two of you are telling me two very different things. Do you have any evidence that would help me to believe your version? Anything that would discredit what he's told me?'

'Evidence? Ha! How do I prove I didn't sabotage his brakes? Or that I wasn't pregnant. How do you prove a negative?' Alex sat up straight, the muscles in her jaw tensing, obviously annoyed at being doubted. She gave a frustrated sigh, her fingers fiddling with her beer mat. 'It's okay though. Don't feel bad about calling me a liar. I'm used to it now. It's not your fault. It's Tom, filling your head with rubbish.'

Maddie felt really bad now, and she squirmed on her seat not sure how much more time she could spend with this woman. Alex was making her question everything she knew about her partner and that felt like the rug being ripped from under her, sending her tumbling to the ground. It could be a hard landing once she'd accepted the truth. But to do that she'd need to see evidence. She'd been fooled once by Alex, and she wasn't going to let it happen again.

'I'm so sorry to ask you, and I don't mean to offend, but I would really like to see something that would confirm it's you I should believe. I'm sure you can understand after the whole Croatia thing.'

Alex nodded, picked up her drink and downed the rest of it in one gulp. She slid off her seat. 'I'll see what I can do. I'm just going to find the loo, then I'll head off. It's been a stressful day.'

'Okay, well thanks for coming.' It was an abrupt end to their chat, but Maddie was quite glad it was over. She'd had quite a day too and the thought of being able to go and lie down on a comfy bed was enticing.

But what about Tom? Can I really sleep if I don't know he's okay?

Alex gave her a tight smile. 'No worries. After the apartment debacle, it's the least I could do. But I'm happy you've got a room for the night. Much comfier than staying at Mum's apartment.' Her smile faded. 'I'll be in touch, yeah?'

Maddie nodded and watched her stride purposefully to the

toilets in the corner of the room. There were so many contradictions, her head was scrambled, and she needed to mull things over. Maybe she should ring Nadia and give her an update. See if she had any ideas.

A few minutes later, Alex hurried back towards her, looking perplexed. 'I just had a call. I've found out where Tom is.' She grabbed Alex's arm and started steering her out of the bar. 'Something's happened, we need to go and get him.'

33

After everything Maddie had discovered about Tom, her world had been shaken to its foundations. But the news that he'd been found overrode any doubts regarding her feelings towards her partner. If he was in trouble, she had to go and help.

She dashed up to her room and grabbed her coat, changed into trainers and met Alex in the foyer. They set off at a brisk walk, Maddie still confused as to what the situation might be.

'Alex, slow down. Can we talk about what just happened? How did you find out where he is?'

Alex didn't slow down, and Maddie trotted along beside her, trying to catch her breath. 'Oh, didn't I say? Ed was meeting a friend in the pub down the road from your apartment. The Rose and Crown, is it? And who should walk in but Tom.'

The Rose and Crown was their local, and it made sense that he might turn up there. 'Perhaps he'd been back to the apartment and saw my note. Thank God he's okay.'

'Apparently, he was plastered and wasn't making much sense. Ed told him you were looking for him and explained about the apartment being cleared out by mistake. Anyway, long story short, Ed's taken him back to his place. I told you he's staying in one of his sister's rentals, didn't I?'

Maddie frowned, not sure if Alex had told her that or not.

'Is Tom okay?'

'Ed said he's a bit worse for wear but he'll be fine. He lost his phone, reckons he was mugged and they took all his valuables as well. You know, his wallet and passport and all that stuff. Anyway, Ed's looking after him.'

Maddie felt weak with relief, grateful that at least Tom had turned up, although what happened next with their relationship was a moot point. Nothing she had to work out now, though. That could all wait. Her priority was to retrieve him and take him back to her hotel. Then they could talk.

Alex gave her a reassuring smile. 'It's going to be okay. Promise.'

34

By the time they got to the Tube station, Maddie was totally out of breath, but excited to be reunited with Tom. Even after all her uncertainties and the knowledge of his lies, there was love in her heart and she decided to go with that for now and not overcomplicate things.

Her phone rang just as they were entering the station, and she turned away from Alex so her conversation could be more private.

'Hi, Mum, I'm so sorry. I forgot to ring, didn't I? There's such a lot going on.' She briefly explained what had happened with the apartment and Tom going missing. 'I'm just on my way to get him now. He's with my friend Alex's partner in Kentish Town somewhere. I've got Alex with me to show me the way.'

Her mum was quiet for a moment. 'That's quite a story, but Maddie... just be careful. You don't know these people and you're so trusting. That's why I worry about you being in London.'

'Mum, I've lived here for ten years,' Maddie said, firmly. 'Honestly, don't worry. I mean it's a pain in the backside having to go and get him, and it sounds like he's had a bit of a beating, but I'm sure it'll be fine. I'll call you in the morning, okay? Promise I will. Give my love to Dad.'

She ended the call and followed Alex into the station, reaching the platform as the train pulled up alongside. It was only a few stops and ten minutes later, they were there. Maddie's heart was still racing from their speedwalk, and she was a bit nervous about seeing Tom now, wondering how she'd feel when she actually saw him. She supposed if he'd been mugged and everything stolen, that explained him not being able to call her. But where had he been for the best part of a day? And why was he plastered and why was he not looking for her? Wouldn't he have gone back to the apartment ages ago?

It didn't make sense. Another puzzle at the end of a very confusing day and Maddie couldn't ignore the concern she'd heard in her mother's voice. *Am I being gullible?*

It was a tough question, because it wasn't something you wanted to admit to yourself, but somewhere, in her heart, she knew the question was valid. The feeling that she was being played, sucked into a game she didn't understand, was still there at the back of her mind, especially now Tom had magically reappeared.

Be careful. Her skin prickled, her senses on high alert.

'I've only been there once,' Alex said when they emerged up the steps from the station, the air suddenly cold after the heat of the underground. 'But I think I can remember the way. Down here. First right, second left, and then I'm pretty sure the house itself is painted blue. On the right-hand side, I think. Anyway, I can call Ed if we're not sure.'

They hurried down the road and ended up in front of a Victorian terraced house, surrounded by similar properties. Some of them had been updated and changed into apartments but this one looked like it was still in its original condition and was pretty run down. The paint was peeling on the door and window frames, and a gutter had come loose from its fixing on the roof. There was a tiny front garden and steps running down to a basement. A dim glow shone in one of the front windows, so at least somebody was home.

The street was deserted, just a few lights glowing in some of the properties. The house next door had boarded up windows and looked like it was in the process of being refurbished, a half-filled skip sitting outside on the road. The plot on the other side of the house was empty, where a building had been demolished. Further up the street, it had felt more lived in and alive, but here, it felt desolate and unloved. It was strange how a few hundred yards could make the difference between welcoming and unfriendly.

Nerves stirred in her belly, and she glanced back up the road, wondering if Alex had got the right house. 'Are you sure this is it?'

'I know it doesn't look great, but Ed's sister is doing it up to rent. That's what he told me. He's only here while he finds something more permanent.'

Alex squeezed her arm and walked her up the path to the front door. She gave three hard raps, then they waited. After a moment, the thud of footsteps could be heard from inside the house, the clunk of a bolt being pulled back, the click of the lock turning. The door swung open to reveal the shape of a man in the shadows, wearing a baseball cap.

'Hi, Alex. You got here. Come on in,' he said, disappearing into the gloom as he pulled the door open wide.

'After you,' Alex said, standing aside to let Maddie go ahead of her. She took a step forwards but something made her hesitate. It didn't feel right. Her gut instinct was to turn and run. But before she could do that, she felt a shove from behind and stumbled up the stone step, landing in a heap on the hallway floor. She was too shocked to move for a moment, unable to respond when a hand grabbed her wrist. She heard a click as a handcuff fastened, then another as her wrists were secured together behind her back.

PART III
TOM: LONDON

35

ONE DAY AGO

Tom sat on the plane, gazing out of the window at the endless cushion of clouds, thinking about all the pain Lexi had caused him over the years and wondering if this might be the start of a new onslaught. Initially, she'd sounded quite normal on the phone. And then she'd issued that threat when she was talking to Maddie. When she was having one of her 'episodes' or whatever the accepted term should be, there was no mistaking it. Her voice changed, becoming sharp and snappy. Her mannerisms changed, too, and she became restless and agitated, like a pan of water gradually coming to the boil. But once she'd reached boiling point, there was no telling what she'd do.

The Lexi he remembered had never been happy in herself, too worried about other people's opinions. She was like a chameleon, always changing her appearance, cutting her hair, colouring it, growing it, whatever she thought it might take to be accepted and wanted. That went for the way she dressed, too, constantly changing her wardrobe as she found a new influencer to follow and tried to copy their style. It was as though she was always looking for herself through somebody else. Sometimes, she even changed the way she spoke, picking up other people's idiosyncrasies, affectations and accents. Initially, he'd found it entertaining, interesting, intriguing. Later, when he'd been around her more, he found it unnerving and downright annoying.

Is she playing a part now?

It was too hard to tell, but he knew one thing for sure: He didn't trust her. He'd never trust her after the turmoil they'd been through.

He gazed out of the window, the sun starting to dip in the sky, colouring the clouds a glorious pink. It was a shame Maddie wasn't travelling with him. Despite the fact their relationship was going through a rocky patch, she was an indelible part of him, making up for everything he wasn't. He felt incomplete sitting here on his own without her. Quite lost and vulnerable. Unfortunately, he felt they might not be on the same page in terms of what they wanted for their future together, but he couldn't find the right words to start a conversation about it. That didn't diminish his love or respect for her though. It was just something they needed to work through, if only he could work out how.

It was a shame that Lexi turning up had meant he'd had to confess his past to Maddie. It made him nervous about their future, and taking this earlier flight was the best he could do to try and remedy the situation. Hopefully, actions spoke louder than words and she'd realise he was trying his hardest to make things right.

Really, he'd had no choice. If he wanted to have any chance of a future with Maddie, he had to sort things out with Lexi. Not just because the apartment was technically Maddie's, but because he couldn't have Lexi mouthing off in front of her. Who knew what else she might say?

A row with Lexi was inevitable, given the tone of her message at the end of her earlier phone call. A shiver of unease ran through his body as he remembered her words. A warning or a threat? The game is on, and she was taking it to the next level.

Those were the words of an angry person. A vengeful person. And although he wasn't sure what she had in mind, it could only mean trouble. Hopefully, he could nip things in the bud. Though quite how he'd encourage her and Ed to leave the apartment if they didn't want to go was another matter.

Poor Maddie didn't deserve this hassle, and he wished he'd been braver when they'd first met. At the point when he knew he loved her and was sure that she'd loved him back, that's when he should have told her everything. She was right that he'd misled her. She hadn't entered into their relationship fully informed, and that was wrong. Maddie was such a loving and generous person, always thinking the best of people, and now, the dark shadows of his past were blotting out everything that had been good about their relationship. It had already tainted things, the atmosphere between them strained, to say the least. Maddie hated liars, having been bullied and tormented at school, and now she knew he was one. Would she ever trust him again? It was his greatest fear that she might not.

He took comfort from the fact that she was still talking to him. They were communicating, even if it was only about practical stuff, rather than all the unsaid emotional issues they were going to have to wade through at some point. He set about drafting her an apology, finding it easier to write his feelings down than to vocalise them, and he hoped she'd understand that his words were genuine. That he'd only hidden his past because he couldn't bear the thought of living without her. That she was the centre of his world. The love of his life.

When he'd finished writing, he read his words back, but knew he hadn't got it quite right. It was something he'd have to work on before he pressed send, a bit more thought was needed. He put down his phone and closed his eyes, letting his mind wander.

If Maddie had the urge to travel and work in different places, then he'd follow her round the globe indefinitely. He would. Whatever it took to make her happy, he'd be up for it. After the crushing disappointment of not being able to have children naturally, and her reluctance to consider IVF or adoption, he hoped that he'd still be enough for her. That doubt was always there, sitting at the back of his mind, that one day she'd tell him she was bored, fed up of his annoying little quirks, and walk away.

He checked her last message now to make sure he'd got the time right for tomorrow.

> See you back at home about 11 a.m. I'll make my own way from the airport. Love you xxx

Love you. There, that was hopeful, wasn't it? And kisses. He hoped that meant there was a path that would lead them back to how they used to be. Or was their relationship now ruined?

He couldn't bear to consider that might be the case and focused his mind on the task ahead of him. Sorting out this apartment swap situation. His pulse picked up, wondering what Lexi was going to throw at him, either literally or metaphorically. *You've just gotta be brave,* he told himself. *Tackle the thing head on.*

It was getting dark by the time he got back to the apartment, and he could see there were no lights on. Which was encouraging. If Lexi and Ed were out, he could nip in there, gather up their stuff, put it outside and lock himself in. Even get an emergency locksmith to come and change the lock. Now *that* would be a win.

He trudged up the stairs to the first floor, fumbling his keys out of his pocket.

A sound made him turn and the door of the apartment opposite opened and a woman he didn't recognise came out, pushing a buggy containing a sleeping toddler. She gave him a quick smile. 'Can I help you?'

He didn't recognise her, deciding she must have moved in while they'd been away. Had Maddie said something about the neighbour moving? He had a vague recollection but wasn't too sure. People were always coming and going in the apartments, most of them owned by landlords, and it was hard to keep track of who lived where.

He returned her smile.

'Are you moving in?' She angled her head towards their apartment door. 'I saw some comings and goings and wondered what was happening.'

'No, we've just been away on holiday for a couple of weeks.'

She gave him a puzzled look, before closing the door behind her. 'I'm Saffy, by the way. And I'll apologise now for this one screaming. She's a bit of a handful at the moment.' She rolled her eyes. 'They weren't kidding when they called it the terrible twos.'

He gave her a tight smile. 'Oh, right, thanks for the warning. I'm Tom and my partner is Maddie. She'll be back tomorrow. I'm sure she'll pop over and say hello.'

She gave him a proper smile then. 'That would be lovely. I'm on my own, so adult company is always welcome. Anyway, I'd better go, I'm meeting up with my sister and she hates me being late.' He stepped to one side to let her pass and pushed the lift button for her, giving her a wave as the doors closed.

Alone now, he was feeling distinctly nervous, not sure if anyone was in the apartment or not. Would it be okay for him to just walk in? His hands were sweaty, his keys clasped in his fist. However much he didn't want a confrontation with Lexi, he'd come to a point where it appeared he had no choice. He just hoped Ed wasn't home, because two against one would make things difficult. He stood in the corridor, listening until he was sure he could hear no sounds. Nobody home.

He took a deep breath and put his key in the lock, letting the door swing back against the wall so he could wheel his luggage through. He noticed the mirror that usually hung in the hallway had gone. All that remained was a grubby outline on the patch of wall where it should be. He frowned. *Did they break it?*

The air felt still, but he couldn't be sure he was alone so he called out. 'Hello? Anyone home?' He stood and listened, emboldened when all he could hear was silence. Good. He was alone, and there was no time to lose to make sure it stayed that way.

He opened the lounge door, his mouth dropping open as he stared into the room. The place was empty, stripped of everything, his footsteps echoing on the bare floor.

What the heck?

A spurt of adrenaline sent him dashing round the rest of the apartment, horrified to find the same story in every room. The place had been completely cleaned out. Even his locked office had been emptied. Everything was gone.

36

Tom could hear himself hyperventilating and he slid down the wall, until he was sitting on the floor. If Maddie saw the place like this it would destroy her. She loved this apartment, and she'd taken such delight in finding the furniture, curtains and rugs, cushions, throws and pictures that made it into a home.

Not just that though, their personal possessions had gone too. No clothes nor shoes, apart from what they had in their suitcases. No coats. All their paperwork, his computers, his hard drive. All his work. And Maddie's. She had files full of ideas. Stacks of reference material. Everything gone. His heart seemed to have lost its rhythm, making him clasp at his chest. *And it's my fault.*

Never, for one minute, did he think this would be Lexi's game plan. He'd thought next level might be refusing to get out of the apartment or damaging it. Overstaying their welcome. Making things awkward, uncomfortable, like her previous tricks. This, however, was extreme and he was at a loss to know what his next move should be. It was catastrophic with a capital C. His heart was racing, his brain misfiring because when Maddie saw this, their relationship would surely be over.

He pulled his cap off his head and slapped it on the floor in frustration. If he'd paid more attention and carried out a bit of due diligence in terms of who they were swapping apartments with, he would have seen that Alex was actually Lexi and he could have stopped the whole thing. Instead, here he was, back in the middle of one of her games. And apart from trying to do him physical harm, this was the worst thing she could have possibly done.

Hats off to her, she'd spotted a weakness and exploited it with skilled precision. He thought about that for a moment. How on earth had they emptied the place in such a short time? They'd only come back this morning, which meant… they must have had help lined up and ready to go. *The whole thing was planned.* Christ, she was just as devious as ever, even if she'd pretended that she'd moved on.

Is this the end of it? He swallowed, dreading to think this might just be the beginning. There might be more now she'd found him again.

He scanned the empty apartment, certain that meeting Lexi in Croatia had been no coincidence. She'd engineered the whole thing and Maddie had fallen for her lies before Tom could step in. The question was how to put it right? How was *he* going to take things to the next level? It was imperative to get his head into game mode, imagine that he was on a quest, and get himself thinking outside the box.

He banged his fists on the floor, a frustrated drumbeat, accompanied by a grunt of despair. How on earth could he hide this from Maddie? Even if he could find all their stuff, it would take days to put the apartment back together and make it feel like home again.

What if Lexi's thrown it all away? Or sold it?

His mouth was dry as sawdust, the horror of the situation intensifying, the more he thought about it. He tried to put himself in Maddie's shoes. Tried to imagine how he might react and that made him feel a whole lot worse. There was no positive spin to put on this.

I can't lose Maddie. I can't.

He checked his phone. No new messages.

He steadied his panicked breathing, and rang Lexi's number. He would have to speak to her. This was the only way, however unpalatable the option might be. It went straight to voicemail. Panic turned his brain into a spinning top. He couldn't think. He could not string a single sensible thought together and he bowed his head, covering his face with his hands.

He'd been like that for a while when the sound of a key in the lock made his head jerk up and he scrambled to his feet, his heart jumping in his chest as he stared at the opening door.

37

Tom stood in the doorway to the lounge, watching the front door swing open, a mixture of fear and anger fixing his feet to the ground.

'Oh, hello,' Ed said, wheeling a suitcase into the hallway, an empty-looking holdall slung over his shoulder. He stopped and frowned. 'We weren't expecting you back for a couple of weeks. Is everything okay?'

Tom couldn't believe the demeanour of the man, how relaxed he seemed, and stood there for a moment completely flummoxed. In his mind, he'd been expecting Lexi. But either way, Ed was complicit.

'What's going on?' Tom demanded, his hand clasping the door frame to keep himself steady. He was consumed by rage, but he knew he had to keep himself under control because flying off the handle had never worked in the past and it wasn't going to work now. Shouting was not the answer, but his voice had a hard edge to it that left no doubt he was riled. 'What have you done?'

Ed's frown deepened, and he looked confused. 'I'm not sure

what you mean, mate.' He shrugged off his coat and went to hang it on the wall where the coat hooks used to be. Even they'd been removed. He stopped and frowned, then looked about him. 'Where's the—'

Tom watched him, eyes narrowed. 'Don't tell me you didn't know?'

'Didn't know what?' Ed was starting to sound impatient. 'You're not making sense, mate. Is Alex here?'

'No, she isn't,' Tom snapped. 'The place is empty. Totally empty. As in, it's been cleared out.' He stood to one side to let Ed into the living room. Watched him turn in a circle, his mouth dropping open as he surveyed the room.

'What the hell has she done? Where is everything?' Ed dashed into the bedroom, coming back with an expression that suggested he was just as astounded as Tom.

'You're trying to tell me you didn't know she'd had the place emptied?'

'Does it look like I bloody knew?' Ed's hands clasped his head, his anguished expression telling Tom that he wasn't a part of whatever had gone on here. This was all Lexi. 'I just came back to get the rest of my stuff, but it's all gone.'

Tom leant against the wall, sliding down until he was sitting on the floor again. Things had just gone to a new level of weird. It looked like Lexi had done the dirty on Ed too. He shook his head. 'I honestly have no idea what's going on.'

'You and me both.' Ed sighed and walked over to the window, one hand rubbing the back of his neck as he stared outside. 'She's gone too far this time. Christ, I wish I'd never met her, I honestly do.' He turned, leaning against the windowsill, his eyes travelling round the bare room. 'I can't believe she's even taken the curtains. I mean, why would she do that?'

Tom heaved a sigh that seem to travel from his toes all the

way up through his body. 'Did she tell you we were married? That she's my ex-wife?'

Ed blinked a couple of times, clearly surprised. 'You and Alex? You're kidding me.'

'She called herself Lexi then, but yes. We were married, just for a few months, but when I left, she took it badly. The divorce was a nightmare, and she hounded me. Right up until I moved in here with Maddie and she couldn't find me.' He gave a snort. 'There's a lot of history, I can tell you and it looks like she's started a new chapter of harassment.'

Ed looked dumfounded. 'Married and divorced? She never mentioned any of that. Not a word. I mean, she said she'd had previous relationships. Well, who hasn't when they hit thirty? But we didn't really delve into the past. We were more interested in the future.'

Tom realised why he'd been feeling confused about Ed. 'Wait a minute, I thought you two were living together here?'

Ed grimaced. 'Yeah, that was the plan, but we had a big bust-up. The latest in a series of fights and I just decided I'd had enough of her nonsense. I can't take it any more. There is no logic.' He looked up and caught Tom's eye. 'But if you were married to her, you'll know all about that.'

Tom huffed. 'God, yeah. And the rest.'

'Thankfully, my sister and her husband have a couple of rental properties and one of them was available while they redecorate before renting it out again. I've moved in there for the time being in return for doing a bit of the labouring work for them.' He stuffed his hands in his pockets, looking thoroughly fed up. 'I just came back to collect the rest of my stuff, but it looks like Alex has thrown everything out.' His shoulders slumped. 'It's not like I have many things. What with travelling for a while, you learn to keep it to the minimum. I'd whittled it down to my most important possessions, but it looks like a lot of that's gone.' His lips curled, eyes burning with anger. 'What a bitch.'

Tom nodded. 'Yeah, that sort of sums it up.'

Ed sighed and leant against the windowsill. 'Looks like we're both in the shit.'

'Yep. And Maddie will be home tomorrow morning, and she's going to be devastated. And angry. No, scrub that. She'll be furious.' He grimaced. 'I hadn't told her I'd been married, so that's put a spanner in the works. This could be the end for us. But maybe that's Lexi's aim. To break us up.'

Silence settled around them, Tom sitting on the bare floor, Ed leaning against the windowsill, the room echoey and unwelcoming.

'I'm going to call her.' Ed pulled out his phone and found her number. He listened, then left a message. 'Alex, what the hell are you playing at? I'm at the apartment. The empty apartment. You can't do this. It's not funny. Ring me back or I'm going to the police.' He disconnected and stuffed his phone back in his pocket. 'Straight to voicemail.' He grimaced. 'That's not good, is it?'

'I was going to say there's no point. I've already tried and if she's played a stunt like this, she's not going to be answering calls from either of us, is she?' Tom clambered to his feet, brushing the dust off his trousers.

'Look mate, I know this won't solve the problem,' Ed said, pushing off the windowsill. 'But do you fancy a pint? We can drown our sorrows together and maybe work out what we can do to get our stuff back.'

Tom managed a smile. 'Sounds like a plan. I've had a long day with the travelling, and I could do with something to eat as well.'

'There's a good pub down the road. My cousin lives over this way and we usually go there. I think it does food if you fancy?' He laughed. 'But you know that, this is your stomping ground, isn't it?'

Tom nodded. It *was* his stomping ground, and he wasn't going to give it up for his stupid ex and her ridiculous games. He grabbed his case and slung his backpack over his shoulder. 'You mean The Rose and Crown? Not far to walk. Then I'll have to see about getting a hotel for the night.'

Ed flapped a hand. 'Nah, mate. You can crash at mine. Like I said, I've got a whole house. I mean it's a bit basic, because they started clearing it out for doing a revamp, but there's everything we need. Then you're not spending extra money.'

Tom considered his offer for a moment. After booking a last-minute flight yesterday, his bank balance was in dire straits and a hotel room might take him over his credit limit. He grinned. 'That's decent of you. Yeah, I'll take you up on that offer and thanks for the help. Let's get a drink and see if we can work out how to get hold of Lexi.'

He grabbed the handle of his suitcase and followed Ed to the door, not feeling hopeful there was a simple answer to the problem. Maddie would want to go to the police, but what evidence did he actually have that Lexi had done this? She could claim she knew nothing, that criminals had broken in and done it. He honestly didn't think it was the route to go down. And anyway, given his experience with the police in the past, he wasn't sure they'd even be any help.

But if Lexi wasn't answering her phone, how was he ever going to find her?

38

Tom woke with a dry mouth and a banging headache. The sun was shining directly into his eyes, through a gap in the ill-fitting curtains, and he winced, scrunching his eyelids closed against the light. The sound of traffic rumbled through his head, the room shaking when a large vehicle went past. He rubbed at his temples, trying to ease the pain, not sure exactly where he was.

He squinted, peering round the room until he managed to drag something from the recesses of his mind. Ed. That was it. He was staying with Ed at his sister's place because... *Oh my God, the apartment.* He groaned at the memory. Lexi had cleared it out. Taken everything. The memory of the empty space, the shell of their home, squashed him like an elephant was sitting on his chest. There was all that to sort out and he had no idea how he was going to make it right.

He pushed the thought out of his head, unable to deal with it at that moment; just getting his eyes to open properly was a hard enough task. As he glanced round the room, he could see that Ed had been right about it needing decorating. The walls were a standard magnolia, a rushed paint job that allowed the darker blue underneath to show through in places. Perhaps it was just a first coat. But maybe not, because he could see shadows on the walls where pictures had hung, a damp patch below the windowsill. It didn't smell of fresh paint. It smelt of stale food and sweaty feet.

He could see that the bed was the only piece of furniture in the room, the mattress lumpy and uncomfortable, creaking when he moved as the springs shifted beneath his weight. On first glance, it looked like a typical student rental, the sort of room he and his uni friends lived in when they'd shared a house. It was clearly an older property, that hadn't been updated in many years and needed a bit of maintenance. The carpet was a nondescript grey, with splashes of what could be coffee stains. There were deep indentations where furniture had stood, lines of fluff against the skirting boards. It wasn't a room that had been loved – or even cleaned recently – that was for sure.

He was glad he was only staying there for one night, but that brought his mind back to the problem with their empty apartment. *What if I can't get in touch with Lexi and we can't get our stuff back?* The idea made him feel sick and he shifted his thoughts away from the problem. It was too much, way too much to deal with when he had a hangover. The throbbing in his head was getting stronger, the pain at the point where it was almost unbearable. *How much did I drink?* It must have been quite a bit, but he couldn't for the life of him remember.

In fact, he couldn't remember much about the previous evening at all, just random images flashing through his brain, coming and going too fast for him to make much sense of them. They'd had a meal. Him and Ed. He could remember that. Then what? Shots. He thought they might have gone on to shots. Maybe after a couple of pints, but he couldn't be sure.

He groaned as his headache banged harder on the inside of

his skull. It was a long time since he'd been this wrecked and now he knew why he didn't go on benders any more. His stomach heaved. *Oh God, no, not that.* How mortifying would that be, if he'd puked all over the floor?

He swung his legs out of bed, sitting up too quickly. Then he had to wait for the room to stop spinning before he dared stand up and stagger to the door. He had no memory of this place. None at all. Which showed how drunk he must have been. He didn't even know where he was, although it couldn't be too far from the apartment because they'd walked. Or at least they'd walked to the pub. He couldn't recall how he'd got back here.

His stomach heaved again, and he opened the door, peering into the hallway, his hand covering his mouth. The house was quiet, no sounds of anyone moving around. Ed must still be asleep.

He glanced down the hallway, seeing a door ajar at the end. Surely the bathroom. He dashed towards it, managing to make it to the toilet before he was sick. He stood for a moment, making sure his stomach had finished heaving, before he tidied himself up, splashing water over his face, drinking from the tap to freshen his mouth, then spitting it out again. The water didn't taste good. It had a metallic tang to it, like it might have been sitting in the pipes for a while.

He was fully awake now and shivered in the cool air. He was only wearing boxers, and his state of undress made him nervous about venturing out of the bathroom. He didn't want to meet someone he hardly knew when he was half naked.

This whole awkward situation reminded him how he hated staying over at other people's houses. He always had, ever since he was a child and had walked in on a friend's father sitting on the loo. He'd been mortified, although the father had laughed it off, but it had left a lasting impression and he'd never gone for a sleepover again. Even as an adult, he'd always preferred to make his way home after a night out, however much it might cost to get a cab. He'd only taken Ed up on his offer because he'd really had no alternative, given the state of his finances. And he'd also thought, through Ed, he might have more of a chance of getting in touch with Lexi.

His ears strained to hear signs of movement, hoping he'd be able to dash back to his bedroom without being seen. He assumed Ed was living here on his own, given he'd just broken up with Lexi, but he really didn't know if that was the case. Quietly, he opened the door and listened. Nothing. The coast was clear. He scuttled down the hall, trying to be as quiet as possible.

Once he was back in the bedroom, he closed the door and leant against it for a moment, his headache worse now he was up and moving about. It felt like there was a jackhammer going at his brain and he wiped his hands over his face, feeling nauseous all over again.

Then he remembered.

Maddie. This morning, Maddie's coming home. Christ, what time is it?

He scanned the bedroom looking for his case and his clothes but couldn't see signs of either. Neither could he see his phone. Panic surged through his body, speeding his movements into a flustered search. He looked under the duvet and the pillow, ran a hand under the bed in case his phone had slipped underneath. But it wasn't there.

Did I get undressed downstairs? He must have done, though quite why he would have done that was beyond him. Perhaps it had been raining and he was wet, or he'd spilt something on himself. It wasn't beyond the realms of possibility. He'd been known to do any number of stupid things when inebriated.

Including getting naked on one occasion. He blushed, his cheeks burning, hoping he hadn't embarrassed himself in front of relative strangers.

There was no choice but to go downstairs in his boxers. Hopefully he was still alone, and nobody would be the wiser, but he grabbed the duvet and wrapped that round himself for good measure. He crept downstairs, ready to dash back up if he heard anyone else moving around, but luckily, he still appeared to be the only person up and about.

The standard of decoration downstairs was the same as his bedroom, all the walls suffering from the same slapdash magnolia treatment. There was an unloved living room, with nothing but a ring-stained coffee table in the middle of a 1970s brown patterned carpet. Two wooden chairs stood either side, one with a stained seat, like someone might have peed themselves while they were sitting on it. A sour smell lingered in the air. His stomach heaved and he had to wait for a moment to make sure he wasn't going to be sick again.

He exited the lounge and moved across the hallway that bisected the downstairs, through a doorway into the kitchen/dining room. Another tatty space. The cupboard doors were dated and wonky. The appliances had been removed. No fridge, freezer nor washing machine. Just grubby, empty spaces where they used to be, marked with piles of detritus on the floor. It smelt of blocked drains. There was a kettle on the worktop, a couple of mugs on the drainer, a carton of milk, a box of tea bags, a bag of sugar and a small jar of coffee. These were the only signs the place was inhabited. Ed hadn't been kidding when he'd said the living accommodation was basic. Even for student digs, this was a dive.

He returned to the hallway, a battered wooden front door to the right, the stairs going up to his left. A row of metal coat hooks were fastened on the wall and that was it. Nothing else to see. But one thing was very clear to Tom. His suitcase and clothes weren't here. And neither was his phone.

Clutching at straws, he wondered if he'd left his things in Ed's room for some reason. Things were put in peculiar places when you were drunk, for reasons that defied logic when you were sober, but had seemed eminently sensible at the time. Pulling the duvet tighter round his body, he trudged back upstairs, reluctant to use the sticky handrail to haul himself up. There were only two bedrooms. He knocked on the door closest to the bathroom, assuming that was the room where Ed was sleeping.

No reply. He put his ear to the door but couldn't hear anything, so he gently pushed it open. The room was empty, apart from a bed that had clearly been slept in at some point. Ed wasn't here. Neither were Tom's clothes, his case, nor his phone. He was alone.

39

Tom staggered back to his bedroom, sure he must be missing something obvious. Was his drink-addled brain failing to see what must be in front of his eyes? But nothing had changed. It was still an empty room with just a single bed and pillow. He sat on the mattress, wrapped in the duvet, at a loss to know what to do. Oh God, he felt sick again and he had to focus all his attention on keeping the contents of his stomach down, rather than puking all over the floor. He bowed his head, thankful when the feeling finally passed. He was never drinking again. Never, ever, ever.

Minutes ticked past and as his stomach started to settle, his brain began to function again. What on earth was he supposed to do, stuck here with no clothes? If he went out dressed just in his boxers, he'd be arrested.

I'll just have to wait for Ed to come back.

At last his brain had come up with a rational idea instead of running around like a headless chicken, thinking the sky was falling in. It looked like Ed *had* slept in the other bedroom. He'd probably gone out to get food or something. Tom nodded to himself, panic loosening its grip on his scalp. That made perfect sense. Hopefully, he wouldn't be too long and, in the meantime, Tom decided he'd go and make himself a coffee. His body needed liquid, but the water tasted foul, and a caffeine hit might help him feel more human.

There was clearly a gap in Tom's memories, and it seemed pointless trying to guess what had happened. Truth was often stranger than fiction and there would be an explanation. Maybe not a logical one, but there was a reason he'd ended up here like this. A sequence of events, with decisions made that had led him to this point. Perhaps Ed knew where Tom's stuff was, and he'd gone to retrieve it. That was a possibility. If they were drunk, it would be easy to leave possessions in a cab, wouldn't it? Or even at the pub where they'd been drinking. A blurry memory floated into his mind. Did he tuck his suitcase in a corner by the bar where the bartender said he'd keep an eye on it? Or was that another time and another place? He hated feeling like this. So helpless, grasping at blurry memories which faded as fast as they came.

But my clothes. Why wouldn't I be wearing clothes?

He couldn't come up with an answer to that one. It made no sense at all. Neither did not having his phone. And without it, he didn't know what time it was.

I wonder if Maddie is back home yet.

The thought made his stomach lurch again, bile stinging the back of his throat. He could imagine her horrified face when she saw their empty apartment, could feel her anger from where he was sitting. She was going to be raging. Not just because of what had happened to their things, but because he wasn't there, and she couldn't contact him.

Oh God, I've messed up big time. Again.

Understatement of the year. He covered his face with his

hands, dread weighing his shoulders down. On top of their recent troubles, this was going to be a hard thing for their relationship to get through. She'd already caught him in a huge lie, so what would she make of this terrible situation? Would she think he was avoiding her because he couldn't face up to what had happened to the apartment?

He hoped she'd be more worried by his absence than angry. But if he wasn't there to guide her through this, she might go to the police. It was the logical thing to do, but getting the police involved wasn't a good move as far as he was concerned.

Not with his history.

A history Maddie knew nothing about.

40

Tom hadn't managed to get himself to move off the bed and go and make his coffee when a door banged shut downstairs. He jumped to his feet, relieved that Ed had returned. At least now he could get himself back to the apartment and Maddie, even if it meant borrowing some clothes. He waddled down the hallway, the duvet getting under his feet as he tried to hurry.

Tom was halfway down the stairs when Ed poked his head out of the kitchen door, a grin on his face. 'I got bacon baps for breakfast, if you fancy?'

Bacon baps. What could be more normal than that?

Ed looked the same as usual, the same cheerful smile. And he was behaving as though it was the morning after a lads' night out. Tom's body relaxed, letting go of the terrible tension that had held him like an iron fist. It was going to be okay. Difficult, but okay. He edged his way downstairs, his legs wobbly, having to focus hard on not tripping over the duvet that was wrapped round him like a cocoon. He must look a real sight, like a giant walking maggot. *What an idiot.*

'How are you feeling?' Ed asked, handing him a paper bag

with a warm bap inside. The smell was surprisingly enticing, given how nauseous he'd been feeling, but maybe food was what he needed to settle his stomach.

Ed pointed to the lounge. 'We'll have to sit in there. I know it's a bit grim, but beggars can't be choosers, can they?' He had two steaming mugs in his other hand and led the way into the room, putting their drinks on the coffee table. Tom waddled behind him, plonking himself on the chair with the stained seat, glad there was a duvet between his flesh and that stain. Whatever it was.

Something about the house was giving him the creeps. Was it the smell, or the shabbiness or just some sort of malevolent aura? He didn't normally subscribe to anything remotely woo-woo, unlike Maddie, but something felt distinctly off. He gave a shiver and wrapped the duvet more tightly around him, one hand poking out, holding his bap. He'd eat his breakfast, find his clothes, then he'd be on his way. Hopefully it wasn't too late, and he could still get back to the apartment before Maddie arrived.

As they ate, Ed kept up a cheerful monologue about the planned renovations to the property and where he was going to start. His words drifted over Tom, who'd wolfed his bap down and was now gulping his tea, keen to be gone. Ed was a nice enough bloke, but whatever he was planning for this house was of no interest to Tom. He just wanted their own apartment put back together and Ed and Lexi out of his life, then hopefully he and Maddie could get back to normal. As if this stupid apartment swap had never happened.

There was just one problem.

He frowned at Ed. 'This is going to sound odd, but do you know where my clothes and suitcase are? And I can't seem to find my phone.'

Ed burst out laughing, his hand slapping his leg like he'd

just been told the funniest joke ever. 'I wondered when you were going to mention that. Honestly mate, you were completely wrecked last night. I think we did too many shots. But anyway, you were hilarious. I went up to the loo when we got in and when I got back downstairs, I couldn't find you. Then I hear you banging about in the cellar and found you standing there in your boxers looking very confused.' He finished his tea. 'You thought it was the bedroom. You blacked out at that point, and I pretty much had to carry you upstairs.'

'Really?' Tom's jaw dropped. He was appalled. But it sounded feasible. 'God, I'm so sorry. I don't drink much these days and it must have gone to my head.'

Ed waved a hand, dismissing Tom's concerns. 'No worries. It was pretty funny. But that's where your things are. In the cellar. After I'd carried you upstairs, I was knackered. I mean, you're not a light weight, are you? Anyway, I didn't have the energy to come back down and carry your stuff up there as well, so I thought it could wait until the morning.'

Tom gave an embarrassed laugh. 'At least that mystery's solved. I can't remember a thing about it. I woke up very confused, I can tell you.' He laughed again, then stopped, the sound hurting his brain. He was feeling a bit weird again and wasn't sure breakfast had been such a good idea after all.

Ed finished his tea and stood. 'Come on, let's go and get your things, then you can get dressed and go and meet Maddie.'

Tom jumped to his feet, eager to get away from the place. But he must have got up too quickly because his head was spinning, his legs so weak he thought he might fall. He staggered, dropping the duvet that had been clutched to his chest, needing his hands to steady himself against the back of the chair.

'You okay?' Ed asked, concern crumpling his brow. He took a step towards him. 'Need some help, mate?'

Tom tried to speak but his tongue seemed to have a life of its own and wouldn't form the words he wanted, turning his speech into a sloppy, incomprehensible mumble.

Ed came and put his shoulder under Tom's armpit, his arm round his waist as he half walked him, half carried him through to the kitchen. There was a door at the far end and he opened it, switching a light on the wall.

'These stairs are a bit tricky,' Ed said, his voice echoey now. Tom was seeing double, finding it hard to focus and his legs weren't working properly any more. But that didn't seem to matter because Ed was practically carrying him now, down the stairs and into the room below. He lowered him into a chair.

Oh, he felt heavy, so very, very heavy. His eyelids refused to stay open, his world spinning before the blackness descended.

PART IV

MADDIE AND TOM: LONDON

41

MADDIE

Now

The front door banged shut and Maddie was hauled up off the floor by one of her arms. She cried out, the metal handcuffs biting into her wrists, stunned at the rapid turn of events. 'What are you doing? Alex, help me!'

The hall light came on and she squinted against the brightness of the light. Alex was leaning against the wall, arms folded across her chest, a smug look on her face. Her lips curled in a wry smile as she looked over Maddie's shoulder at the man gripping her arm. 'You see, Ed. I told you I could do it.'

He laughed, his breath hot on the back of Maddie's neck, his grip on her arm tightening. 'Never doubted you, my love. Not for a minute.'

Maddie screamed inside her head, furious that Alex had played her like a fool. *Tom told you what she's like. He bloody told you and you didn't listen.* Her gut instincts had well and truly let her down. She gritted her teeth, letting out a growl as she tried to wriggle from Ed's grasp. 'Get. Off. Me!'

'Oh, we've got a feisty one here,' Ed said, his fingers digging into her flesh as she writhed and squirmed like a fish on a line.

Alex frowned, at last showing a bit of concern and Maddie allowed herself to hope that she might intervene after all. 'Don't be too rough with her, Ed. None of this is actually Maddie's fault.'

Ed laughed. 'What do you mean don't be too rough? Get with the programme, babe. This is all about rough and I haven't even started.' There was a sinister tone to his voice and Maddie knew, with a terrible certainty, he meant every single word.

Adrenaline fired through her body, but although she yanked and tugged at her arm, Ed's grip held firm. When that didn't work, she stomped on his foot, but she was wearing trainers, which proved completely ineffective against his work boots. She squirmed harder, tried kicking at his shins, but he'd got the measure of her by now and made sure she couldn't hit her target. With her hands cuffed, she couldn't use her elbows or fists as weapons, and had to accept she'd run out of options.

'You finished?' he snarled. She panted with frustration, her body limp with exhaustion.

Alex pushed off the wall and Maddie tried to catch her eye, wanting to plead with her, beg for mercy, but she was staring straight at Ed. 'You promised not to hurt her.'

Ed gave a dismissive grunt. 'We are going to get justice, remember? You and me. That's what we agreed. We're both going to get payback for what that bastard has done to us. For all the pain he's caused. For ruining our lives.'

'I know but...' Alex grimaced. 'Tom not Maddie. I don't want to be involved in—'

'Christ, you can't wimp out on me now,' Ed snapped, clearly exasperated. 'Look, if you don't want to see, why don't you make yourself useful and go and get us something to eat. I haven't had anything since breakfast.'

Alex's hands gravitated to her hips, her frown deepening. 'What's got into you? I'm not your lackey. I don't like the way you're talking to me.' She gave him a defiant glare. 'My thinking is... if I don't see, then I can't know. And if I don't know... if anything goes wrong, I can't tell anyone what's happened. So... I actually think it's better like that.' She emphasised her point with a sharp nod of the head.

'I'm not following your logic.' He sounded impatient. 'There won't be anyone to snitch if we both keep quiet. Nobody's going to find out. I've thought it all through. I mean, I've been planning Tom's demise for years, remember?'

Tom's demise. Maddie's heart flipped. *So... does that mean he's here?*

It was a relief to know she wasn't alone in this situation, but the word 'demise' had a horrible ring to it. A finality that made her blood run cold. She started to shake, her whole body trembling, her mind unable to find a single positive to grasp onto.

They're going to hurt me. And Tom. Of that she was certain.
Or at least they're going to try.

She gritted her teeth, the will to fight burning inside her. There was still a chance she could work out a way to get free, but at the moment, her options weren't obvious. If this was some twisted sort of game they were playing, she thought she'd maybe have a chance. Because she was good at strategy games. The trick was to get her mind into gameplaying mode and allow her lateral thinking to have free rein.

If this was the next level that Alex had alluded to, Maddie had to give it to her, she'd played a blinder. She'd been so convincing, persuading Maddie to come with her, but all of it had been a con. She even looked different now. A hard edge to her jaw, a flinty look in her eye. She was just as culpable as Ed, and it sounded like she was making sure she was covered if things didn't go according to plan. A wise move, in the circumstances, but Maddie could guarantee that Alex didn't have the measure of her. She didn't know what she'd fought her way through in life.

At school, when she was being relentlessly bullied, she'd gone through the proper procedures, and her bullies had been hauled in front of the headmistress and expelled. Had that worked? No, of course not. It had made things worse because a bully cannot stand to be humiliated. On her way home from school, she'd been jumped by three girls, who'd dragged her off onto a patch of wasteland where nobody could see what was happening. Maddie had honestly believed they were going to kill her, and in that moment, she found something within herself that she didn't know was there. Nerves of steel and a cunning that allowed her to pretend to submit before launching her attack. They'd thought they'd won, so weren't prepared. Didn't realise she had a broken brick in her hand.

Two girls had broken facial bones and one a broken hand. Maddie left them and ran away, determined to deny ever being there. The funny thing was... she later heard they'd been ambushed by a group of boys. Why the lie? Maddie had asked herself later. It was obviously to cover their shame that little Maddie had beaten them up. She'd never told a soul, but held it in her heart as proof that she could survive in any situation when the odds were not in her favour. She drew on that secret now, telling herself this was no different. The key was to use her brain.

She watched Alex, and could see she was considering what Ed had been saying about planning Tom's demise. Her mouth twisted from side to side, the tip of her toe prodding at a tear in the lino. Then she squared her shoulders and looked Ed in the eye, a small smile on her lips. 'Yeah, I know and I'm in.' She'd clearly done a calculation, deciding to play along with Ed for now. 'I'll go to the Chinese round the corner, shall I?'

'Yeah, get me the usual.' He pulled a couple of bank notes from his back pocket and slapped them into her outstretched hand. 'Don't be too long.' He chuckled and shoved Maddie towards the kitchen. 'I've got a long night ahead of me and I need some fuel in the tank.'

Maddie's stomach churned. Despite her internal pep talk, the awful reality of her situation hit home. There was no way she could fight against Ed, and self-doubt took all the strength out of her legs. Ed yanked her up as she crumpled towards the floor. 'Don't be a bitch about this, or I'll make it worse for you, okay? You play nice, and I play nice. That's how it works.'

He pushed her forwards, through the kitchen towards a door in the corner. 'I've got someone here who will be very happy to see you.' He opened the door, flicking on a light. 'Careful of the steps,' he said, shoving her downwards. He was mocking her, no concern for her wellbeing at all as she skidded on the narrow steps, the musty smell of the basement filling her nostrils. It was all Maddie could do not to burst into tears. Emotion swelled in her chest and she knew she couldn't speak. Not now. She couldn't beg or plead, or even reason with her captor, the shock and fear rendering her mute.

Do not show them weakness, she cautioned. *Stay strong. It's not over yet, this is just the beginning.*

At the bottom of the steps, Ed pushed her round the corner, into a narrow room. Her breath hitched in her throat when she saw Tom, sitting on a chair against the far wall, wearing only a pair of boxer shorts, his head slumped on his chest.

Oh God, what have they done to him?

The walls of the basement had once been whitewashed but were now peeling and patchy with black mould. The ceiling was low, making the windowless room claustrophobic. A bare lightbulb cast a harsh light round the space, the concrete floor pitted and uneven and dirty. She stumbled as Ed pushed her forwards towards another chair, on the opposite side of the room to Tom. It was fixed to the wall with a chain.

Fear writhed inside her, like a mass of snakes, hissing and striking out, making her wriggle and squirm, determined not to make this easy for him. Wanting to believe there could be a chance, however slight, that she could get away.

Ed tried to push her into the chair, but she made her body rigid, like a plank, determined not to co-operate. 'Have it your own way,' he snarled, kicking her behind her knees, making her legs buckle and her hip smack against the edge of the chair. He slapped her across the face and the shock of his assault made her go limp, allowing him to push her onto the chair and attach her upper arms to the chain with cable ties.

He stood back, a hardness in his eyes, a satisfied grin on his face.

'There you go. Enjoy your room. I hope you'll be comfortable, and I'll see you later.' His grin widened. 'I'm sure Tom will be awake soon. And then the fun can start.'

He turned and walked up the stairs, bolting the door behind him, leaving Maddie shaking in her chair.

42

TOM

Tom heard voices and didn't know if it was a dream or reality. His head felt heavy, so heavy he knew he couldn't lift it, and there was a pain in his neck, like he'd been in the same position for so long, his muscles had frozen in place. His chest was damp, a stream of drool hanging from his mouth.

The sound of Ed's voice made him force his eyelids open and he was astounded to see Maddie being manhandled into a chair on the opposite side of the room. A room that looked and smelt like a cellar.

He couldn't seem to keep his eyes open, and he rested for a moment, trying to work out his new reality. He had no recollection of coming down here. None at all. The last memory he could dredge out of his brain was eating breakfast with Ed and, judging by the gnawing pain in his belly, that was a while ago now. This was confirmed by the damp patch on his chest where he'd dribbled in his sleep, and the crick in his neck. He must have been out cold for quite a while.

His head throbbed, a steady drumbeat playing on the inside

of his skull, and it was hard to think, hard to grasp that this was really happening.

He could hear Ed's words. Something about the fun starting. Then he heard footsteps, the bang of a door, the clunk of a bolt being driven home.

What on earth is he talking about and why is Maddie—?

The thought of her being forced into the chair opposite made him try again to lift his head, his muscles resisting, sending shards of pain down his neck as he managed to move. He blinked in the harsh light of the naked bulb, shocked to see a red welt across her cheek.

'Maddie?' he croaked, still unsure if this was part of the dream he'd been having.

'Tom,' she gasped. 'Oh, Tom, are you okay? I was frightened you might be—' She stopped what she was saying and gazed at him. 'What has he done to you?'

He didn't know the answer to that, but his arms were locked in a strange position, something digging into his skin, a tight band round his biceps. As he tried to get more comfortable, he heard a jangle. A chain.

I'm tied up?

He squirmed on his chair, testing out his bonds, but it was no use, it only caused him pain. He was fixed to the wall, his hands in handcuffs behind his back. He stared at Maddie, and as his focus became clearer, he realised she was tied up in the same way.

We're prisoners. He had to repeat that again in his head to convince himself it was true.

Oh my God. This is the next level Alex was talking about. Ed must be her accomplice. Doing her dirty work.

Fear squeezed the air from his lungs, freezing the blood in his veins. He didn't want to imagine what might be in store for them, but if you tied people up in a cellar... He swallowed, a scream of anguish filling his head.

'Tom?'

He gave himself a mental shake. *Poor Maddie.* It was his fault she was involved in this horror show and he had to stay strong for her. He cleared his throat, his voice hoarse and croaky. 'I'm... yeah, okay, I think.' He frowned. 'The last thing I remember is Ed getting us breakfast, so I ate that, had a cup of tea.' It dawned on him then. 'Oh God... I think Ed must have put something in my drink to knock me out.' It sounded fanciful but he could find no other explanation. All that faux friendship was just a ruse to make it easier for Ed to get him down here without a fuss. But why? And what was Maddie doing here?

'I don't even know what time it is, or how long I've been down here.' He shivered, the chattering of his teeth rattling in his skull. Now that he was fully awake, he realised he was chilled to the bone.

'What's going on Tom? Who *is* Ed and why didn't you tell me you knew him?' Maddie sounded frantic, scared, a shrill note of panic in her voice.

Which made Tom feel scared too. And very confused. 'I *don't* know him. The first time I ever met the guy was in Croatia.'

She shook her head, lips pressed together, fury in her eyes. 'You're lying. I know you are. He was talking to Alex upstairs, and he said he'd been planning your "demise" for years. That's what he said. Verbatim.' Her voice was getting louder, anger piercing through her words. 'Do you know what demise means, Tom? Do you? Death. That's what it means.' She leant towards him as far as her bindings would allow. 'They're going to kill us. And he said it was going to be a long night. In fact, he said it was going to be "fun".' She stifled a sob. 'Whatever he has planned is for his entertainment. And at a guess, slow and painful.' Her voice cracked. 'And it's because of you. It's payback for ruining both their lives. That's what Ed said. So what did you do, Tom? What the hell did you do?'

Tom was even more confused now. So, Lexi was definitely involved in this as well. He supposed that figured. To be fair, he could understand Lexi's desire to get back at him. He'd always understood that he'd wronged her when he'd got her sectioned. But it was a means to an end, a way to free himself of the past. It was amazing how a man's word held more weight than a woman's, especially when she was having a mental health episode. He'd admit he'd exaggerated things, made up some stuff so the doctors would take him seriously. And he'd stalked her for a while, making her so on edge she'd had a breakdown at work. But Ed? He honestly had no recollection of ever meeting the guy before Croatia.

Tom's heart was racing, his body convulsing in waves of uncontrollable shivers, caused by a mixture of cold and fear now he'd begun to understand the danger they were in. And it *was* his fault. Maddie was right about that. Somehow, he'd caused this, and all that apartment swap nonsense had just been part of a trap, a way of getting them to this basement. A place where terrible things could happen and nobody would know.

Fear gripped his throat in a strangle hold, his breath rasping as he desperately tried to drag air into his body.

Maddie glared at him, clearly infuriated by his silence. 'You're a liar,' she snarled, eyes narrowed, looking more ferocious than he'd ever seen her. 'You told me Alex was the liar but really, it's you, isn't it? What did you do to these people to make them want you dead? I know you've been to prison, and you didn't tell me that, did you?'

He winced like he'd been slapped. How did she find that out? Did Lexi tell her? In which case, what else might she have let slip? His world was tilting on its axis, his life crumbling before his eyes and he was helpless to do anything about it.

Maddie was seething at him, teeth clenched. 'I can't believe a word that comes out of your mouth. They're going to kill us, Tom, and I—' She gulped, her voice a plaintive wail. 'I don't want to die.'

His heart felt like it was being yanked from his chest. It was unbearable to see Maddie beside herself like this and it overrode fears about his own safety. His brain kicked into action.

Perhaps Maddie was being melodramatic and there was no danger of them dying at all. This could be scare tactics. A way of getting something from them, though what that might be, Tom had no idea, as yet. They appeared to have stolen all their possessions, so he was at a loss to know what else they might want. It wasn't as though they were wealthy so he couldn't imagine this was about money. He had to calm Maddie down, get her thinking straight and between them they might be able to work out how to escape.

He cleared his throat. 'We're not going to die, love. We're not. We'll think of something.' It was nothing but a meaningless platitude but it stopped him having to address her comment about his lies.

'Oh, get real. We're both tied up. They can do whatever they want, and we can't fight back, can we? Even if they don't kill us, they're going to hurt us, I'd put money on that.'

Is she right? Tom was the sort of person who couldn't just accept what he was told. He assessed things, had to make up his own mind. He rocked backwards and forwards on his chair, testing out the fastenings, quickly confirming that they were secure and with his hands behind his back, he was pretty much helpless. He couldn't even stand up. And the handcuffs were fastened so tight, there was no wiggle room. They had their feet free, but that was it, and considering he had no shoes on, he couldn't think how that was going to help.

Panic reared inside him. They really were prisoners. Nobody knew where they were and Lexi had a monstrous injustice to avenge, should she wish to. Maybe Ed was tagging on to her grievance, wanting to hurt Tom and Maddie in return for her love.

He felt like sobbing, but held it back, wanting to be strong for his partner. Wanting to give her hope that there might be a way out of this.

Can I ask Ed to spare Maddie? Will he listen?

The situation felt hopeless. Absolutely, completely hopeless.

43

MADDIE

Maddie couldn't even look at Tom. She was furious, panicked and terrified all at the same time. A potent cocktail of emotions that made her want to scream. She was here because of him and something he'd done. Something so terrible it made people want to imprison him and quite possibly murder him. But not just him, her as well, which seemed completely unjust. One thing she knew for certain, she wasn't going to wait for Tom to have a bright idea. She was going to have to work on a solution to this life and death game herself.

Calm. She had to try and stay calm and then she'd be able to think. Her eyes scanned the room, and she noticed that the plaster had crumbled off the wall in places. Big scales of it had dropped off, leaving patches of brickwork exposed. Maybe the fastenings weren't as secure as she'd thought. She copied Tom's actions from earlier, rocking her chair, straining against the chain, pulling in different directions to see if she could detect any weakness. But the fastenings held firm, dousing her hopes. It was never going to be that easy, was it?

The handcuffs had been fastened so tightly round her wrists, one of her hands was going numb, her fingers tingling. It was an unnatural position, sitting with her hands tied behind her back and she struggled to find a position that was comfortable. This was torture, but she supposed that was the point.

She wondered who might realise she was missing. Who might try and find her. Her mum wouldn't start to worry until the morning, when she'd promised to ring. Even so, she probably wouldn't do anything for a few hours. Unfortunately, that wasn't going to be any help because Ed would be finished with them by then. Nadia was too busy to even notice if Maddie hadn't been in touch, and they didn't fix a time when they might meet or speak again. And apart from those two people, there was nobody else. She had no client meetings booked for a few days, no conversations organised with work colleagues until the following week.

Her spirits sank to a new low when she realised nobody was going to be looking for her. At least not soon enough to save her. A surge of panic squeezed the air out of her lungs. She didn't want to die, not here, not now and not because of something Tom had done.

Although resentment and hurt at his lies had hardened her heart, she couldn't help feeling sorry for him. He cut a pathetic figure, sitting there in his boxers, his body shaking with cold. It was chilly in the cellar, and she was cold fully dressed, so she couldn't imagine how Tom was feeling. Getting close to hypothermic, possibly. He did look very pale, and he'd gone quiet, his head sunk down onto his chest again, his body language telling her he'd given up.

If only she understood what this was all about, she might be able to find a way to reason with Ed. At least buy them some time until her mum reported her missing the following day. It seemed like a long shot. A very long shot. Because it sounded like Ed and Alex had been planning this moment for quite some time. Now it was here, the grand finale Ed had apparently been working himself up to, she doubted he'd be persuaded to give up.

Her best chance might be to appeal to Alex if she reappeared because she *had* asked Ed not to hurt Maddie. When he'd rebuffed her, she'd seen a glint of something in Alex's eyes, an expression of defiance sliding across her face for a second. Had she imagined it? No, she didn't think so. It was just a tiny sliver of hope, but it was all she had and was better than nothing.

The echo of footsteps clumping across the kitchen floor above her head made Maddie tense, every nerve in her body on edge as she strained to hear. The cellar door opened, a shaft of light flooding the stairs to her left, a shadow moving on the wall as a figure slowly descended, carrying something. She held her breath, the terror of anticipation making her shake.

Ed appeared at the bottom of the stairs, carrying a cardboard box, and a folding stool, his jaw set and a deep groove between his eyebrows. It was the face of a man on a mission. Footsteps moved about above her head, so it seemed Alex was still upstairs. They must have just finished eating and she wished her life could be ordinary again. Wished that she was the one tidying up after a takeaway.

'This is where the fun starts.' Ed grinned at her, but his eyes were cold. He stood in front of her chair, opening up the stool and setting it on the floor before resting the box on top. He frowned when he noticed Tom slumped in his chair and walked over, giving him a slap so hard and sudden it made Maddie jump. Tom grunted, but didn't react as she would have expected, his head swaying about before slumping onto his chest again. His lack of alertness was worrying, and she wondered again if he was hypothermic.

'You need to wake up,' Ed snarled. 'Or it'll be twice as bad.' He leant towards Tom, his face only inches away. 'And that's a promise.'

'Why are you doing this?' Tom mumbled. 'Leave Maddie alone.'

'Oh, I can't leave Maddie alone. Nope. She has to be part of this if you are going to understand what you've done.'

Tom managed to raise his head then. 'But I don't understand. I don't even know you.'

'Really?' Ed gave a derisive snort. 'Okay. I thought you'd see the resemblance.' He pointed to his face. Tom frowned, no spark of recognition in his eyes at all. 'No? That's weird because people say I'm the spitting image of my dad.'

He moved away from Tom and leant against the wall, where he could see both of them. He folded his arms across his chest. Then unfolded them and started pacing the floor. 'Well, we have time. I don't suppose there's really any hurry. Let me see if I can jog your memory.'

44

Ed pursed his lips, silent for a moment. 'Cast your mind back five years, Tom. Do you remember a little favour you did for Alex's dad? Hmm? Changing a video image?' Ed stopped pacing, bending to study Tom's face. Maddie shifted in her seat, trying to see round Ed's body, which was blocking her view, wondering where on earth this was going. Tom had mentioned this story in passing, but no real details other than a comment that what he did was illegal.

Tom didn't say anything but as Ed started pacing again, Maddie could see he was a bit more alert now and paying attention, his eyes glancing over to her and back to Ed. He adjusted his body position in the chair, sat up a bit straighter.

'You could have said no,' Ed continued. 'But you didn't, did you, because you wanted the money? And Alex tells me it was rather a lot of money. And that money helped you to buy a nicer apartment. Gave you enough for a big deposit. Lucky you, eh?'

Maddie was already confused. Tom had told her he'd had an inheritance from his grandma which had helped him to buy his apartment. Money they'd recently put aside to help them buy their future home together now that Tom's apartment had been sold. And although he'd admitted to doing something illegal with some video footage, he said he'd been coerced into it. A favour to get Alex to agree to a divorce and out of his life. She gritted her teeth. *More lies. More bloody lies.*

Ed straightened up and turned towards her. 'Has he told you any of this, Maddie?'

She shook her head, deciding it was better to stay silent as much as possible.

'Tom, you're a lying bastard, aren't you?' Ed walked up to him and gave him another swipe across the face. So hard this time, Tom's head bounced off the wall with a sickening thwack. Maddie gasped. Tom cried out, a trickle of blood snaking from his temple and down his face.

'But we know this.' Ed glanced at Maddie. 'We all know this now, don't we? That Tom's a liar?' He stared at her, apparently waiting for a response and she nodded, her throat so tight she could hardly breathe let alone speak. 'What you may not be aware of is the consequences of those lies.'

He glared at Tom who looked like he was about to cry. He was blinking furiously and she could hear him sniffing. Blood trickled down his face and started dripping off his chin, landing on his thigh. Ed paced up and down between them and it was clear his emotions were building, his hands curling into fists at his sides. He stopped in front of Tom, his back towards Maddie, and she heard a grunt as he punched Tom in the stomach. He turned and smiled at Maddie for a second before walking towards her. She shrank back in her chair terrified she was going to get the same treatment as Tom.

'Let me enlighten you,' he said, crouching in front of her so their eyes were level. There was a manic air about him, something unhinged that ramped up her fear another notch.

I could kick him, she thought, imagining him falling back. Maybe banging his head, but then what? There was no doubt it would be satisfying, but it wouldn't help her get free and would anger him more.

He must have read her mind because he leant his hands on her knees, pressing down so his weight rooted her feet to the floor. She could smell the garlic on his breath as he stared at her. A tear escaped and rolled down her cheek, followed by another and he tutted, reaching out and brushing them away. 'There, there. Crying's not going to help.' He pushed himself up to standing and glanced over his shoulder at Tom. 'See what you're doing to your partner? The woman you love. What's about to happen is all down to you.'

He walked in a slow circle. 'So, Tom. The man you set up for a fall in that video you tampered with was my father. A successful stockbroker. In fact, he was a partner in the firm with Alex's father, wasn't he? And the video was altered by you, so it appeared to show him taking a bribe.' He spun on his heel and stood in front of Tom. 'Don't deny it. I'll admit, it's taken me a very long time to pin this on you, but I finally worked it out when I was checking through all the past employees, thinking it must have been somebody in the firm. Then I saw what you did for a job now and the penny dropped. Especially once I'd worked out the connection between you and Alex's dad.'

Tom's eyes widened, guilt written all over his face.

Ed gave a satisfied nod. 'You did a good job. Very professional and you know what really stank about the whole thing? His partners, the people he worked with, his friends and even his wife – my mother – all of them believed the video and not my dad. I was the only one who didn't believe he'd do such a thing. The only one.'

He took a deep breath, fingers pinching the bridge of his

nose, head tilted to look at the ceiling before continuing. 'And you want to know what happened then?' He lowered his head, blinking furiously as his emotions forced their way to the surface. 'He was sacked from his job in disgrace. He was unemployable with that accusation hanging over him and the possibility of a police investigation. My mum said she could never trust him again and he'd let her down. She divorced him. The house had to be sold. It broke up my family. Everyone shunned him. Even his own parents. It broke him and I'll never forget the trauma of watching this once proud man crumple in front of my eyes.' His chest heaved as he took a deep breath, the sadness in his voice palpable. 'He was completely diminished and felt he'd let everyone down. He wouldn't even see me any more. In fact, he said my life would be better without him. Can you imagine how I felt?'

The question was still hanging in the air when Ed walked over to Tom and, without warning, stamped on both of his bare feet. Ed was wearing work boots, which looked like they might have steel toecaps. Tom screamed. An ear-splitting explosion of sound that tore through Maddie as she watched on in horror. Ed stepped back, giving a thoughtful nod. 'I think I broke something. There was a definite crunch, wasn't there?' He turned and gave Maddie a smile. 'Anyway, where was I? Ah yes, coming to the end of my story.' He lashed out at Tom with his foot, catching him on the shin. Tom screamed again. 'My dad...' He kicked Tom's other shin. 'My wonderful, lovely, kind dad. He took his own life.'

Maddie gasped.

Ed turned and walked towards her, his lips clamped together, eyes burning with hate. 'That's right. Shocking, isn't it? That his life was ruined. Taken from him, really. And my life was ruined too. All because Tom here fancied a nice big lump of cash.' He stood in front of Maddie and she was so frightened she thought she might pass out. 'Tom's life got better because he ruined somebody else's. And Maddie, I've got to say, you have benefitted from his actions too. Otherwise, how could you possibly have been looking to buy that lovely new-build property without the big lump of money from the sale of Tom's apartment? Hmm? Shame it fell through.'

He put a finger to his chin, looking up in a theatrical way. 'Now, I wonder why your buyers pulled out at the last minute? Did they say?' He laughed, leading Maddie to believe he had something to do with it. Which explained a lot because they'd been so keen and had spent money on surveys and organising their mortgage, not to mention legal fees. They'd never given a detailed explanation as to why they'd pulled out so suddenly, just a comment that they'd changed their minds. Perhaps Ed had changed their minds for them. He gave her a knowing smile. 'Maybe they weren't real buyers at all.' He tutted. 'So many timewasters about these days.'

It was obvious now how deep his hatred ran, how much danger she and Tom were in.

'I'm sorry, I'm so, so sorry,' she gabbled. 'I had no idea. I didn't know any of this. He told me something completely different.'

'I believe you. I'm sure he didn't breathe a word of the truth. But look at him.' He pointed at Tom who was writhing in his chair, in obvious pain, his feet already showing signs of bruising. 'He knows my version is what really happened.' He sighed, swinging his gaze back to her. 'It's regretful, because I like you, Maddie, but unfortunately you are going to be collateral damage.'

His words turned her blood to ice, her thoughts frozen on those two words. *Collateral damage.*

He looked into the box sitting on the stool and pulled out a hammer. 'Tom is going to watch you die. Not an easy death, I'll be upfront about that, because my father's demise was painfully slow. I'm working on the "eye for an eye, tooth for a tooth" philosophy of justice.' He swung the hammer in his hand, letting it pendulum by the side of his leg, before he suddenly raised his arm and aimed for Maddie's head. She screamed, ducking down, waiting for the blow to land. The whistle of wind ruffled her hair as the hammer flew past the top of her head. Followed by Ed's laugh.

'Oh, quick reactions, Maddie, I'll give you that.' He laughed again. 'This is going to give me so much satisfaction, Tom. You're going to watch. Because you need to know what it's like watching someone you love die, when you are helpless, and you know there's nothing you can do about it. And it's even more painful when they are dying for something that was never their fault.'

He sniffed, his voice all matter-of-fact now. 'Dad took an overdose, and I found him. But it was paracetamol he'd taken, and his liver was damaged beyond repair. It took him another week to die.' The hammer swung in a lazy arc by his side. 'Once poor Maddie here has breathed her last breath, then it'll be your turn, Tom.' He glanced from Tom to Maddie, the smile still playing on his lips. 'The good news is I'm not going to drag this out for a week. No, this has to be done by morning.' He swung the hammer up and slapped it into his hand. 'I think it's time we got properly started, don't you?'

45

Maddie could hardly breathe now that Ed had confirmed her fate. She was going to be killed because of something Tom had done. And what Tom had done had been unforgiveable if Ed was telling the truth. But he had no reason to lie, did he? You wouldn't plan to kidnap and kill random people without a very strong motivation. No, his story rang true. She could hear the anguish in his voice and could imagine how traumatic it must have been witnessing his father's death.

Now she had another lie to add to Tom's list and if the others had been bad, then this one was a total deal-breaker. How could he have done something so callous and cruel for money? But then... how would he know the implications? There it was, that little voice again, giving her the other side of the story. Nobody could have known that his actions would have led Ed's father to take his own life. But he would have known that his actions would have destroyed a man's career and that was bad enough, wasn't it?

It was clear there was a side to Tom that he'd kept hidden, a coldness inside. You'd have to be lacking in empathy to be involved with a stunt like that because it would be clear there would be life-changing consequences. Even if you couldn't foresee exactly how terrible those consequences might be.

Her jaw tightened, her teeth grinding together as she understood how completely she'd been taken in by her partner. All well and good that she now knew Tom's real nature. But that wasn't going to matter if she was dead.

Dead.

Ed's going to kill me.

Just saying it in her head sounded surreal, like it couldn't be happening. But it was. Ed was staring at her, slapping the hammer against his hand, looking as if he was trying to decide where to hit her.

I don't want to die, I don't want to die, I don't want to die.

The words grew louder and louder in her mind, her heart racing so fast she was breathless. *Think, think, think.* Her mind tried to flip her situation on its head, searching for a solution she might not have considered. Ed took a step closer, the hammer swinging in a larger arc as if he was winding himself up to strike.

She used the only weapon she had left. Her voice.

A bloodcurdling scream. As loud and as long as she could manage, putting the full force of her body behind the sound. Hoping that somebody might be walking outside and hear her. Hoping that Alex would find the sound unbearable and come down to help. Hoping for something, anything to happen to make this horror story stop. Because she couldn't just sit there and do nothing. She had to at least try to save her own life.

Ed looked startled, his hand stopping in mid-air. Tom started shouting. 'Let her go! For God's sake, let her go. Please, I'm begging you.'

Maddie carried on screaming, the force of it hurting her throat, making her lungs burn, but this was life or death, and she couldn't let a bit of discomfort stop her. The sound bounced off the low ceiling, filling the room, filling her ears, almost unbearable.

Footsteps hurried down the stairs and Alex appeared. A deep frown creased her forehead, and she looked angry, like she meant business. She came to a halt in front of Ed, hands on hips, putting herself between him and Maddie.

'That's enough, just stop it. That racket's going to bring the police here if you're not careful.' Her chest was heaving and she grabbed for the hammer, catching Ed unawares. But he was taller than she was and after a bit of a tussle, he held it above his head out of her reach.

Her intervention was music to Maddie's ears because she hadn't been sure how well the sound would travel upstairs. She took a deep breath and carried on screaming. Tom seemed to pick up on the plan and started yelling for help too.

Ed seemed oblivious to the noise, his eyes fixed on Alex. He was laughing as if they were playing a game, her intervention appearing to excite him rather than annoy. 'Come to join in, have you?' He pointed to the box. 'Pick your weapon. We've got screwdrivers, wire cutters, lump hammers. And saws. Whatever you fancy.'

'No, I said stop it,' Alex snapped, trying to snatch the hammer out of his hand again, but he danced away and swung it out of her reach, almost over-balancing when it hit the ceiling. He staggered away from her, the laughter gone, replaced by a chilling hardness in his gaze.

Maddie had to stop screaming for a moment to catch her breath and she wanted to hear what Alex and Ed were saying. She had to hope that the noise she and Tom had been making had alerted someone outside to their distress because Ed's next move must surely be to gag the pair of them. Unless he did genuinely believe that nobody outside could hear, however loud they shouted. The thought smothered the hope that her voice was a weapon, something she could use to escape. For the time being, she decided to stay quiet, rest her vocal cords and listen.

'Look, if you don't want to join in, that's fine, but don't get in the way,' Ed snapped. 'We haven't got time for this nonsense. And I'm not stopping. I haven't even got started.'

'This wasn't the deal,' Alex insisted. 'It's not what I signed up to. When we planned it, you were supposed to scare him. That's all. Teach him a lesson that he wouldn't forget.'

She clawed at Ed's arm, trying to reach the hammer, but he shoved her away with a dismissive grunt and she almost ended in Maddie's lap. Maddie put a foot up, keeping Alex in balance, giving her bum a little push to help her stay upright. It appeared that Alex had no taste for violence, which was a very good thing. At least she was in Tom and Maddie's corner now, but Ed didn't want to listen and he was bigger than her. He was in control.

Maddie admired Alex's bravery, because she wasn't sure if she herself would be wrestling with a guy holding a claw hammer. She watched, heart in her mouth, willing Alex on but nervous about the outcome. If Alex got hurt in some way, then Ed might be fired up even more and Maddie and Tom would feel the brunt of his anger. It was like watching a horror movie, not wanting to see what was happening but unable to look away.

Alex squared up to Ed in the middle of the room, where they slowly circled round each other. 'You weren't supposed to really hurt them. Just rough him up a bit. That's all I agreed to, and you know it. I told you Maddie was off limits. I said you could threaten to hurt her but we agreed, Ed. We agreed you wouldn't actually touch her. She was there to taunt him, nothing else. And I trusted you to keep your word.'

Ed laughed. He actually laughed, a sound so out of place it

was jarring. Maddie could hardly breathe, let alone scream, completely hypnotised by the drama playing out in front of her. A drama that could dictate if she lived or died.

'Fun fact, Alex. You're not the boss of me. What you don't understand is I've been working on this for years. Literally years.' They were standing, staring at each other, Ed still with the hammer in his hand. But now he'd lowered it, keeping it behind his back, out of reach. 'It wasn't just a spur of the moment thing when we saw Tom and Maddie on holiday. I organised for us to be there at the same time as them, once I knew that's where they were going. I thought I could make something happen while we were abroad. A tragic drowning at sea, maybe. But my plans came to nothing because the logistics were too risky. I had to think again.'

He gave a slow smile, a nod of recognition. 'All credit to you for coming up with the digital nomad storyline and spotting it was a lure we could use to draw them in. But the apartment swap was all me, wasn't it? Organising the house clearance team to empty their apartment, taking their lives apart. Oh, I have enjoyed inflicting the chaos and trauma, I really have. But that was all my idea.' He sneered at her, his face screwed up like he'd smelt something disgusting. 'I recruited you into *my* scheme knowing your association with Tom. For years, I made you a suspect in all the bad things that were happening to him. I messed with his bike brakes, hoping that would be enough to end him, but unfortunately it wasn't. Then I stalked him. Made his life a misery. Of course he blamed you, why wouldn't he?' He laughed. 'In fact, I made sure the finger pointed to you. And that was fun for a while, but it was never enough to compensate for the dad I'd lost. I needed more.'

He stepped away from Alex, and Maddie wondered if he was

feeling some sort of guilt. She studied his face, but his expression was blank as he carried on speaking.

'Unfortunately, Tom had been a busy boy, trying his hardest to get you sectioned, piling on the pressure as much as he could. I watched and listened from the sidelines. Spyware is a wonderful thing, isn't it? And then you cracked and attacked your co-worker and we all know that led to you being locked up in the psychiatric unit. So he got what he wanted, but it didn't really work for me. It just added an unforeseen delay, which was pretty frustrating, because I couldn't risk being directly linked with killing him. It always had to be you taking the blame if things went wrong.'

He moved towards Alex again. An ugly sneer on his face. 'You were never an equal partner. Not ever, even though you maybe thought you were.' He swiped at Alex with the hammer, making her shy away. 'You've been my fall guy, my shield and now you're my accomplice.'

He laughed at her reaction. 'Scared, are we?' He waved the hammer in her face. 'Now piss off if you're not going to join in. I've things to do.'

The chilling truth made Maddie's blood run cold. It had been a trap all along and she'd been caught like a fly in a spider's web. And it sounded like Alex was a victim in all of this too, used in the most terrible way as someone to blame and to draw Tom and Maddie in.

Alex can't help, Maddie realised and started screaming again, as long and loud as she could muster, surprised that Ed hadn't thought to gag her yet.

He hurtled towards her, the hammer raised to strike. The look of evil in his eyes was so shocking that Maddie screamed even harder, terror in her heart as she shrank back in her chair, making herself as small as possible.

Maybe he'll miss again. Wishful thinking but she had to hold on to some hope, had to believe there was a way to cheat death. Adrenaline pumped round her body, her brain picking up all the details, calculating which way to duck to minimise the impact.

But the hammer didn't hit her.

Ed was so focused on Maddie, he wasn't watching Alex and didn't see the leg she stuck out as he came charging forwards. He tripped and went flying, landing heavily on the concrete floor. The hammer fell out of his hand and Alex dashed to pick it up before he could gather his senses. He seemed to be winded and it took a few moments for him to clamber to his feet. He shook his head, clearly a bit dazed. And absolutely furious.

He gave a low growl, his hands curled into fists, Alex in his sights. But she was quick and nimble and darted to the side, her hand flicking out to catch him on the kneecap with the hammer. Maddie flinched. It was a horrible sound, metal on bone and it made him yell, hopping about on one leg as he clutched at his knee.

'What the fuck are you doing?' he shouted. 'We're on the same side here. Stop attacking me.'

'We're not on the same side if you're going to kill them and put the blame on me,' Alex snarled. 'I can't be involved in murder. That was never my plan, and I wouldn't have helped you if I'd thought it was yours.'

Ed hobbled over to the wall, leaning against it while he massaged his knee, his face contorted in pain.

'Look, I told you before, there's no risk of anyone being to blame. I shouldn't have said that just now. You just got me worked up.' He sighed and straightened up. 'Nobody will know. I told you, I've got this all planned out.' Alex was glaring at him, her body tensed to fight. He held up his hands to calm her. 'Come on, stop behaving like a lunatic.'

He gave a harsh laugh, a mean glint in his eye. 'Oh, sorry, my bad. You can't do that can you, because you *are* a bloody lunatic.' He flung his hands in the air, clearly frustrated. 'Go upstairs if you don't like it. Or even better, just bugger off altogether.' He jabbed a finger at her. 'We're done, you and me. It was never real anyway. A means to an end, that's all you ever were.'

He took a step forwards, bending and straightening his bruised knee. 'Of course, none of this would have happened if your dad hadn't asked Tom to do him a favour. So if anyone's to blame, it's him. But once I'd got rid of your dad in that hit and run, I knew it was possible for me to make everyone involved accountable. The next on my list is Tom and I intend to get this finished.' He flicked a dismissive hand at her. 'Now, I've things to do. Get out of my way.'

Maddie tore herself away from the drama, realising, with a jolt, that she'd run out of time. She took a deep breath. If she was going to die then she'd die screaming.

Ed turned towards her, puffing his chest up, his face going red. 'Right, that's it,' he snarled. 'I can't be having you making that noise.' He grabbed something out of the box, the metal catching the light of the bare bulb as he lunged towards her with a screwdriver.

This is it. I'm going to die, Maddie thought, her scream stuck in her throat.

46

Maddie threw her body sideways as Ed dived towards her. Not far enough though. A piercing pain sliced at her waist, then a splatter of something warm and wet on her face. A grunt. Followed by a loud thump as Ed fell to the floor beside her chair. She looked up to see Alex standing over him, wide-eyed, mouth gaping open, blood dripping from the claw end of the hammer in her hand.

Alex was panting hard, her face turning pale as she stared at Ed's twitching body. He was lying face down on the floor and Maddie could see he was badly injured. The hair at the back of his head was matted with blood, a stream of it oozing down the side of his neck and onto the floor.

'I just wanted to stop him. That's all. I wanted to make him stop.'

Alex burst into tears, the hammer falling from her hand as she crouched on the floor next to him. She put her ear next to his mouth, then felt for a pulse, her movements increasingly frantic. 'Oh no. No, no, no. What have I done?' She was sitting on her heels, rocking backwards and forwards, her hands covering her face. 'But you heard him. He killed my dad. It wasn't an accident, it was him.'

Maddie sat in stunned silence, the events of the last couple of minutes too shocking to accept. She glanced down at Ed, and looked away just as quickly once she'd seen the amount of blood pooling on the floor.

Is he dead? He looked dead. There was now an unnatural stillness about his body. No movement of breathing. But she wasn't an expert and there might still be a chance he could be alive.

At the very least, he was out of action, which meant she and Tom were safe for now, didn't it? She took a few deep breaths, a sharp pain jabbing at her side every time she moved, but she didn't think the screwdriver had done too much damage. Ed had clearly intended to stab her, but Alex had knocked him off balance, making him miss his target. There was blood on her top, slowly seeping through the material, but her hands were still tied so she couldn't investigate. It wasn't loads of blood, she told herself. Probably just a scrape. She could see the screwdriver on the floor, next to Ed's outstretched hand, streaks of blood on the metal.

'You need to call an ambulance,' she said to Alex, who was still rocking, lost in her own world of misery. 'Quickly. It's his only hope.' Personally, she believed Ed was beyond hope, but Tom wasn't and despite everything she now knew about him, she didn't want another person to die.

Alex gazed up at her, fat tears rolling down her face. 'It's too late. I think... I think he's gone.' Her face crumpled. 'I've killed him,' she sobbed. 'Oh God. I've killed him.'

Maddie looked across at Tom, who'd fallen silent while all the drama was playing out. She hadn't been taking much notice of him, her focus on Ed and Alex. But now she could see he was slumped in his chair again, chin on his chest. 'Alex, please. We need an ambulance. I think Tom's hypothermic, or in shock or something. He needs help.'

Alex didn't answer for a few minutes, then she stopped rocking, wiping her face with her sleeve, her eyes on Ed's lifeless body. When she finally looked at Maddie there was a stony glint in her eye, her voice cold and hard.

'Do you honestly think I care what happens to Tom?' she snarled. 'It was you I was worried about. You're innocent in all this, but Tom? You heard what Ed said. You now know what a lying, evil person your partner is. I knew you didn't know the whole truth about him, because he'd never admit to everything he's done.' She looked over at Tom before catching Maddie's eye again. 'He's too much of a coward for that. He can stay and rot in the cellar for all I care.' She spat the words out, hatred seeping through every sound. She gave a sharp nod as she clambered to her feet. 'At least you know now. You're better off without him.'

She marched over to Tom. 'This is your fault.' Her finger jabbed at him as she spoke, poking him in the chest. 'It's your fault Ed's dead. It's your fault my life is ruined.' She carried on poking him, then she started slapping him when he didn't respond, Maddie flinching at every blow. Alex was winding herself up into an hysterical frenzy, the blows coming thick and fast and Tom was helpless to defend himself.

It was unbearable. Tears streamed down Maddie's face, as she witnessed the brutal beating. However angry she was at Tom for his lies, she would never have wished this on him. 'Alex, that's enough,' she shouted. 'You've made your point. Stop it. Please. Just stop.'

But Alex didn't seem to hear her. 'Your fault. It's your fault,' she repeated over and over with every blow. Her slaps became more frenzied, turning into punches and when her hands could apparently take no more, she resorted to kicking.

Maddie started screaming again, as loud as she possibly could, hoping beyond hope that someone walking past might hear and be worried enough to call the police. A roundhouse kick sent Tom's head cracking against the wall with a sickening crunch. It was clear he was unconscious now, his head leaning to the side against the wall, and at that point, it seemed Alex decided enough was enough.

She leant over, hands on her knees, puffing hard as she tried to catch her breath. Maddie carried on screaming, her heart breaking at the state of Tom, his body limp. His eyes were swollen and puffy, his lip was split and blood spatter decorated the walls. His torso was a patchwork of red weals and bruises where he'd been hit.

He didn't look good, not good at all.

Has she killed him too?

Alex shook out her hands, her knuckles red and swollen. She straightened up, her chest still heaving from exertion, a pensive look on her face. 'That sort of feels a bit better. But I'll never forgive him. Never.'

She stared at Maddie and walked towards her.

Maddie's heart stuttered in her chest. She swallowed. *Oh God, is it my turn now?*

47

Alex's T-shirt was flecked with blood, a mean look in her eye. Maddie started to shake, pressing herself as far back in her chair as she could go. Having witnessed Alex's attack on Tom, she felt sick to her stomach, unable to imagine what was in store for her. She flexed her feet, ready to use them to kick out in any way possible as they were her only weapon.

Alex stood in front of her, hands on her hips. 'Tom had that coming.' She glanced down at Ed and nudged him with her foot. 'And so did he, the two-faced bastard. You heard what he said. He played me, pretending we had a relationship when he was just using me to get to Tom and then make me the fall guy. I can't believe it was him who set me up, got me in trouble so many times with the police for stalking, and nobody listened. I told them it wasn't me. Told them 'til I was blue in the face. Even my parents didn't believe me.' Alex huffed. 'I was convinced it was Tom doing it. That's what I told everyone, but then he had alibis.' She shook her head. 'I just couldn't work it out. At least now I know. Not that it makes things any better. It was still Tom who made people think I was a psycho. He tried to get me sectioned for ages. It was the stress that he put me under with his constant barrage of accusations that made me have a breakdown. That was all Tom's doing.'

She looked up and caught Maddie's eye. 'Have you any idea what it's like to be in a secure psychiatric unit, eh? Drugged up to make you compliant, losing years of your life.'

Maddie shook her head. 'It was a terrible thing these two men put you through. Terrible. But I had nothing to do with it. Nothing.'

'I know and that's the sad part. None of this is your fault, but now you're the only witness.'

Maddie gulped, terrified. 'I'll help you if you just let me go,' she pleaded. 'I'll corroborate your story, whatever you want. Just tell me what to say.'

'Let you go?' Alex frowned, her mouth twisting from side to side. She slowly shook her head, the corners of her mouth turned down. 'No, I can't do that. I'm sorry, but I've got to look after myself now. I'm done with depending on other people. I can't trust anyone, because everyone in my life has lied to me. Everyone.'

'I haven't. Everything I ever told you was true.' Maddie could feel her opportunity for freedom slipping from her grasp. 'Please, Alex, you know it's not fair to leave me down here. Just untie me, then you can go, do whatever you need to do.'

Alex stared at her for a long moment, her hands dropping from her hips. Her lips pressed into a thin line, and she shook her head again before turning on her heel and plodding upstairs without another word. Maddie could hear her moving about in the kitchen, the tap running, the sound of footsteps walking to another part of the house.

What's she doing? Is she just going to leave?

Thinking back over the conversation, it sounded like Alex

was going to take off to protect herself. Maddie supposed that was a logical thing to do because it was very clear who was responsible for the death of Ed and the brutal beating of Tom. But if she left the house, she could have two more deaths on her hands. What if nobody had heard Maddie screaming? What if nobody found them for weeks? Tom needed medical help now. And she didn't want to die a slow, horrible death from dehydration.

Maddie started yelling again, the only thing she could do, but her throat was raw, and every sound caused pain. She pulled at her chains, rocked her chair, hoping to loosen the fixings, but they held firm. It was hopeless, and finally, exhausted by her efforts, she fell silent, forced to rest her voice before she could think about trying again.

A few minutes later, footsteps came running down the stairs into the cellar and Alex reappeared, her face blotchy, eyes red-rimmed with crying. She wrapped her hands round each other, like she was giving them a wash and it was clear from her body language that she was conflicted.

'I can't ring for an ambulance.' She glanced across the room to where Tom was slumped in his chair. He hadn't moved at all, and Maddie was seriously concerned it might be too late. He looked very pale, unnaturally so. 'I know Tom needs help, but I can't do it. I've thought about it, honestly I have, and although my conscience is telling me it's what I should do, my gut is saying no.' Her chin puckered, her voice thickening. 'Because I can't go back to the psych ward. I just can't and that's where they'd send me.'

Maddie was so relieved she'd come back, but terrified she might go again and leave her to die as well. 'Let me go.' Her voice was raspy and hoarse after all the screaming. 'Please, Alex.'

'I have nothing against you, Maddie, and I'm sorry we got

you involved in this whole thing, but as Ed said, you were unfortunately collateral damage.' She blinked, quiet for a moment. 'In another time, another place, we could have been proper friends.' She sighed and flicked a glance at the stairs. 'I've got to go now.'

It was clear then, that Alex was not going to call for help. Her intention was to let them die.

48

'Don't leave me.' Maddie's desperation seeped through every word. 'Let me go and I'll say I killed Ed. I'd rather go to prison than die down here.'

'Nope. That's not going to work, is it? Sorry. I've thought about it and there's only one thing I can do.'

Maddie whimpered, fear slicing through her body.

A loud banging on the door upstairs made them both look up. Then a shout. 'Police! Open up or we're coming in.'

Alex looked suddenly frantic, like a cartoon character, turning on the spot like she had no idea which way to run. Maddie felt a surge of hope, warm and energising. She hardly dared believe it was really happening. That she might get out of this alive.

'Help!' Maddie yelled as loud as she possibly could. 'In the cellar.' She started screaming again, as it seemed more effective than shouting, so there could be no mistaking where she was.

There was a loud bang. Hopefully the door being forced open upstairs. Alex ran to the door in the corner of the room. The one that led outside. She yanked on the handle, but it wouldn't turn. Rattled the door in the frame, but it was locked and wouldn't open. In desperation, she turned to run up the stairs, only to meet the figure of a police officer on their way down.

Maddie held her breath, thinking this must be it, the moment Alex was caught, but she slammed her body into the figure on the stairs, knocking them over, and running up into the kitchen. The figure scrambled to their feet and ran after her. There must have been more officers up there though, because Maddie could hear a kerfuffle going on above her head. Shouts and banging and screaming. It sounded like Alex was putting up quite a fight, but eventually it went quiet. Then the clump of footsteps coming down the stairs again and a police officer reappeared. A middle-aged man with a weathered face. He peered around the room, assessing the gory scene, one hand clasped to his radio.

His eyes settled on Maddie. 'Are you okay, love?' he asked as he walked towards her. 'Don't worry, we'll soon have you out of here.' He started speaking into the radio, calling for an ambulance, another officer appearing on the stairs.

Maddie burst into tears.

49

It didn't take long for Maddie to be freed from her chains and handcuffs.

'Are you okay to sit here for a moment while back-up arrives?' the officer said, gently. 'I've called for an ambulance.' He put a reassuring hand on her shoulder. 'It shouldn't be too long. We'll get you to hospital to get checked over.'

Maddie nodded, too numb to speak. Tears rolled down her cheeks, dripping off her chin while she sat motionless, watching the officers at work.

I'm safe. I'm going to be okay. But will Tom?

'Christ, he's cold,' the officer said as he put his fingers to Tom's neck. 'But there's a pulse.' He looked at his colleague, a young man, probably in his early twenties. 'Can you have a scout round upstairs, see if there's anything we can use to keep him warm while we're waiting.'

A few moments later, the officer scurried back down with a duvet, by which time, Tom had been released from his bindings and laid on the floor in the recovery position. They wrapped the duvet round him, making him as comfortable as possible.

It wasn't long before reinforcements and the ambulance arrived. At that point it got overwhelmingly busy in the confined space of the cellar, voices and radios and shouted commands bouncing off the walls and filling Maddie's head with too much noise. She couldn't bear it and clamped her hands over her ears, squeezing her eyes closed until a hand on her arm shook her back into the room.

It was a female paramedic. 'Can you walk, do you think? Shall we get you upstairs where it's quieter and I can check you over?'

Maddie swallowed, her throat so inflamed after the screaming, her voice was a barely audible whisper. 'I'm not— I don't—' She swallowed and tried again, but words wouldn't come as she blinked back tears.

She stumbled as she was gently led up the stairs, her mind replaying the events of the last few hours, her head full of terrible images, things she didn't want to see. It was difficult to hear what people were saying, her thinking woolly and unfocused, her brain not working as it should. She yearned for stillness and quiet. Wanted to go and hide someplace where she didn't have to think or speak or try and make sense of what had happened and what might yet happen to Tom.

As she emerged into the kitchen, she saw there were police officers all over the place, the house a hive of activity, the sound of boots clumping around. But it was as though she was listening through a filter, everything muffled and far away. Confusing. It didn't feel like she was living in a world she knew, everything around her unfamiliar. Her body was shaking, her legs weak and she felt dizzy now she was moving. She clung to the paramedic as she was led out to a waiting ambulance, fearing if she let go, she'd fall.

'Your blood pressure is very low, your pulse is through the

roof and you're all clammy. I think you're in shock,' the paramedic told her after an initial assessment. 'I'm going to give you some fluids and we'll take you to hospital for a proper check, okay?' Maddie nodded, still unable to speak, past caring where she was taken, her mind still in the cellar with Tom.

When she'd been helped up the stairs, another ambulance crew were working on him and from what they were saying, he was hypothermic. It was a relief he was getting medical help because he'd looked like he might be dead. And she couldn't work out how she'd feel about that. Given the ordeal she'd been through, all because of him, and the lies he'd told and the things he'd kept from her, did she still love him? Or was her concern the type of empathy she'd have for any fellow human being in trouble?

Love him? Love him? her brain screeched, appalled that she could even think such a thing. Their relationship was over. Done. Finished. That was the one thing she could be sure about.

The paramedic settled her on the trolley and quickly inserted a cannula in her hand to attach a drip. Maddie had disappeared inside herself, no feelings of pain from the needle, but glad of the blanket that had been draped over her. A hand squeezed her shoulder, and she realised the paramedic was speaking to her, but she couldn't seem to grasp her words and turn them into anything that made sense. She gazed at her, mute. Unable to tell her if she was okay. Unable even to confirm her name. There were no words in her mind, just pictures. Horrible, terrifying pictures.

A police officer walked up to the ambulance and had a conversation with the paramedic, before holding up a bag. 'Is this yours, love?' She nodded and the officer rummaged inside, finding her purse and inside that, her driving licence. He scanned the details. 'Madeleine, is that right?'

Maddie nodded, then indicated that she wanted her bag. She found her phone and her mum's name on her contact list. 'Mum,' she mouthed at the officer, handing him the phone. Thankfully, he understood what Maddie meant.

'You want me to give her a call? I'll let her know which hospital you're going to, shall I?' Maddie nodded again, then sank back on the trolley, closing her eyes, completely spent.

The paramedic checked the wound on her side, where Ed had come at her with the screwdriver, and cleaned it up, telling her she might need a stitch or two, but it wasn't too bad. She'd guessed that already. It wasn't the physical harm that was the problem. It was what had happened to her mind. That's where the real damage had been done. That's where the healing would be needed.

It wasn't going to be easy when everyone around her had been lying. She didn't trust her own instincts any more, given how wrong she'd been about people she'd chosen to trust. But there was still one person she trusted to always be honest with her and that was her mum.

Having an outside view of things would help her to see through the smokescreen and work out how to move on from this. At the moment, she had an empty apartment, her possessions taken to God knows where and only the clothes she'd brought back from holiday to her name. There was going to be a lot to sort out, including talking to the police, and it would take energy she didn't currently have. She was going to need an advocate and the best person for that role was always going to be her mother.

The officer moved away to call Maddie's mum and relay to her what had happened. It was not a quick conversation, which meant her mum had probably been firing questions at the officer, keen to get all the facts. That's what her mum was like.

Always questions. So many questions it often drove Maddie and her dad to distraction, but in situations like this, having her mum by her side was going to be a blessing. Especially while Maddie couldn't speak.

The officer ended the call and put Maddie's phone back in her bag, which the paramedic tucked next to the trolley. 'She's on her way,' the officer said with a quick smile, 'and will meet you at the hospital. We'll be over there to talk to you and take a statement once we've sorted things out here. Probably be a while yet, though.'

That was good, Maddie thought, glad she was going to have a bit of time to sift through her jumbled thoughts before she had to talk to the police. Her evidence was going to be pivotal in terms of how much she incriminated Alex and Tom. Where she laid the blame.

50

Hours later, when her mum's face appeared round the edge of the cubicle curtain, Maddie burst into tears. It was such a relief to have someone she trusted by her side, she clung to her, sobbing into her neck.

Her mum stroked her hair, much like she had when Maddie was a child. 'Hey, love, it's okay.' She kissed the top of her head. 'I saw the doctor on my way in and, my God, am I relieved it's just your voice that's damaged. I wish I'd followed my instincts, then they might have got to you sooner.'

Maddie pulled away. 'What do you mean?' Her voice was no more than a hoarse whisper and even that was an effort. The doctor said she'd damaged her vocal cords with all the screaming and had to drink lots of water and try not to speak. Which was easier said than done when there was so much she wanted to share with her mum.

'I knew there was something wrong when I spoke to you at the Tube station,' her mum said, concern in her eyes as she tucked Maddie's hair behind her ears, studying her face. 'I knew it. The whole set up sounded off to me. And I was going to ignore it, then I was all restless and blurted it out to your dad. I wasn't going to tell him because I didn't want him worrying but...' She shrugged. 'He's always been my rock and old habits die hard. Anyway, I told him, and he said I'd never been wrong. Every time I felt bad about something, it *was* bad.'

'I felt it, too, Mum. That's why I told you what was happening. I thought you might be able to track my phone if I didn't ring when I said I would in the morning.' By the end of the sentence, Maddie's voice was so quiet it was hardly audible. Her throat was throbbing after the effort of speaking and trying to talk, when your voice wouldn't work and every word had to be forced out, was surprisingly tiring. She rubbed at her throat and reached for the plastic cup of water on the cabinet beside her bed, taking a few tentative sips. Even swallowing hurt.

Her mum frowned and tutted, pulling her bag onto her lap to retrieve her iPad, something she never travelled without.

'Oh, sweetheart, your poor voice. Let's use the iPad then you can type instead of speaking. The nurse told me you're not supposed to talk but I instantly forgot.' She rolled her eyes. 'I'm sorry, love. Force of habit.'

She dropped her bag back on the floor before turning on the iPad and opening the Notes app. She passed it to Maddie, who gave her a grateful smile. At least they'd be able to communicate now, and she was desperate to know what had happened to Tom. And Alex. She was hoping her mum might be able to find out.

Her mum took her hand and gave it a squeeze. 'Weirdly, I was just looking at the find my phone app when the police rang to say you were being taken to hospital. It was so strange because I was about to look up the number for the local police station to report my concerns about you because you weren't answering your phone. I mean, you always answer, don't you? In case I'm ringing about Dad.' Her grip tightened. 'That was the only thing I could think of to do. But I'm not sure it would have been enough. Apparently, it was a jogger who heard your screaming and they were so concerned they reported it straight away.'

Silent tears rolled down Maddie's cheeks. The thought of everything she'd endured forced a surge of emotion through her body. Her mum held her tight, while she sobbed her heart out, until she'd finally purged herself. She was sure there were many more tears to come, but for now, she was ready to take the tissue her mum offered her, wipe her face and tell her mum what had happened.

It was hard to explain, even to herself, how she felt. Exhausted above everything else, but anxious and jittery still, even though she knew she was safe. She supposed it would take a while to come down from all that adrenaline pumping round her body, but she didn't feel like she could rest just yet. There were things she needed to know. And things she wanted to share with her mum.

Maddie started to type.

Her mum probed and questioned until a nurse came to sew up the wound in Maddie's side. It just needed a couple of stitches the doctor had said, when he'd checked under the dressing. By this time, there'd been a change of shifts, new staff had appeared and Maddie realised it must be morning. Once her wound had been stitched up, she'd been told she would be discharged, but she was still waiting for news of Tom. Apparently, he was in surgery to address a bleed on the brain. The police wanted to talk to her, too, but nobody had appeared yet, so she had to stay around until they turned up.

'Look, I'm going to leave you to it.' Her mum stood up and stretched as the nurse got everything ready to put the stitches in

Maddie's wound. 'You know how squeamish I am. I'm going to go and get a coffee, have a think and do a bit of research. There seem to be so many inconsistencies in what you've told me. I'll see if I can get some facts.' She gave a determined smile. 'You know I love a project. It's what I've missed about giving up work to look after your dad. Anyway, I'll be back in a little while.'

Maddie gave her a feeble smile, the effort of it feeling too much, her energy levels dwindling by the second. In a way, she would be glad to be alone to sit with her thoughts. Having laid it all out for her mum, she'd realised that she still hadn't managed to sift through all the lies. Alex and Tom's accounts of what had happened in the past didn't match up. Alex's version was probably blurred to make her seem more of a victim and garner sympathy. Tom's version had gaping holes of omission. At least Ed had clarified a few things before he'd died. It appeared he'd been the one trying to make Tom's life difficult, not Alex. But then it sounded like Tom had blamed it all on Alex and that had led to her having a breakdown and being arrested.

There was no doubt in her mind that Ed had been the master manipulator, using Alex as a shield to deflect blame, while hiding in the shadows. She knew what it was like being blamed for things you didn't do and people not believing you. She'd had that for years from the bullies at school and been disciplined multiple times for things she didn't do. It hadn't mattered how hard she'd protested, her voice was never heard. She had a feeling Alex had experienced something similar but in a much more devastating way.

Tom had said Alex had a personality disorder of some sort and if that was true, she supposed it would make her more vulnerable than a person with no mental health issues. He'd also said she'd attacked a co-worker, the police officers arresting her and members of staff in the secure unit, and Maddie could well believe that was true, having seen how she'd attacked Ed and how completely she'd lost control when she'd started giving Tom a beating. She was a seriously dangerous person beneath that charming exterior, a killer now, and it was a good thing she was in custody.

In terms of Tom's misdemeanours, his lies of omission were not telling her he'd been married, or been to prison. But probably the most important one, was that he'd done something illegal for money. And that had destroyed a man's life and resulted in his death. Unforgiveable. Any one of those things would be bad, but taken all together, she knew there was no future for their relationship. That didn't mean she wasn't worried about him though.

She was dozing when the police officer turned up, but when she tried to speak, nothing would come out, so she had to scribble a note, asking them to ring her mum to come back from the hospital café with the iPad. While they were waiting, the nurse came with her discharge papers and asked if they'd mind moving so they could use the bed. There was an empty meeting room they could use for a private conversation. At that point, Maddie just needed to lie down and go to sleep, but she knew it was better to get this interview over with, then she'd done her bit to ensure justice was done.

Her mum arrived, looking a lot fresher than Maddie felt and went into full-on protective mother mode, taking the lead.

'Maddie told me everything earlier and because she can't speak, she wrote everything in Notes on my iPad. Can I just email that to you instead of doing the interview? I mean, look at the poor girl, she's in no state to think clearly. And you know she's been told to rest her voice.'

The officer nodded. 'Fair enough. How about we use that as

a starting point, I can have a read and then see if I've any further questions?'

'Perfect,' her mum said, pulling her iPad out of her bag and typing in the email address on the card passed to her by the officer. She looked up and smiled, all efficient like she was Maddie's PA. 'There, all done.'

'Can I ask what your plans are now?' the officer said. 'I could do with you staying in the hospital until I've had a chance to read through the notes, confer with my colleagues and see if there's anything else we might need to ask.'

'Maddie wants to wait to find out how Tom is after surgery, so we'll probably go and sit in the café for a bit. The nurse thought it would be another hour before there'll be any news. Then I'm taking my daughter back to our home in Sevenoaks.'

'Okay, well if you stay in the café, I'll come and find you in a bit.'

Going back home. Her mum looking after her for a bit. Spending time with her dad. Maddie couldn't think of any place she'd rather be right now. Being so close to death had shifted her priorities and spending time with the people she loved most in the world was all she wanted. Work would have to wait and she was sure Nadia would understand.

She wanted to ask about her apartment and the missing furniture and how on earth that would all be sorted out, but she guessed that was the bottom of the list of priorities for the police. In reality, everything paled into insignificance compared to the question that kept flying back into her mind like a boomerang: will Tom survive?

51

Maddie's mum bought her a hot chocolate, in lieu of comfort food, because the doctor had suggested she stick to liquids for now to take it easy on her throat. They sat at a table by the window, in companiable silence for a little while, watching people scurrying to and fro. It was a pleasant distraction and Maddie was happy to just people watch and close her mind to everything that had happened.

Her mum finished her coffee and popped the last piece of her bacon bap in her mouth, studying Maddie's face as she chewed. 'Look, I've got to say this. I've always liked Tom. Right from the start, I just felt he was a good match for you. I've been thinking about everything you told me, and I can honestly forgive him for not telling you he'd been married. I can understand it's a shock, but the relationship was over, there was no love lingering for his ex – quite the opposite, in fact, and I can see why he wouldn't tell you about Alex.'

Maddie frowned. That was fine her mum forgiving him, but she wasn't anywhere near that point herself. If nothing else, it was dishonest, and she'd come to realise over the last couple of weeks that honesty was important to her. His past with Alex was a part of Tom and look where it had led. No, forgiving wasn't happening any time soon, she was sure of that.

'I'm finding it hard to believe he would do anything malicious,' her mum continued. 'That seems out of character, doesn't it?'

Maddie considered that, then nodded. Her mum was right and she realised now that was one of the things that had jarred with her. She slid her mum's iPad in front of her and tapped out the questions she still wanted answering, then slid it back towards her mum.

'Hmm, yes.' Her mum scanned down the list. 'I think you're right. Let's see what we can find out.' She got busy Googling to see what evidence there might be of Tom and Alex's past on the internet and Maddie left her to it, knowing what her mum was like once she got stuck into a bit of research. Similar to a terrier with a stick, not wanting to let go until she had the answer.

A little while later, when she was gazing out of the window, her mind in free fall, her mum gave her a nudge.

'Look what I found... I know you searched Alex under her married name, but I searched under her full maiden name. Tom told you who her father was, didn't he? So, I followed that trail, starting with the report of Tom's conviction and I've found a couple of things. Firstly, Tom was telling the truth about Alex being arrested for attacking someone and being committed to a secure mental hospital. She was released six months ago.

'And I can confirm that her father was indeed Tom's employer. And Tom was convicted of insider trading. He pleaded guilty so it never went to court and that reduced the time he served. Knowing everything else you know now, do you think he might have been set up by her dad? The timing seems awfully convenient, roughly about the time he and Alex split up.

I've done a timeline and not long after he came out of prison, he must have then got involved in changing the video. I found a news report about it. Big scandal at the time. It seems like Alex's dad was a nasty piece of work and maybe he's behind the wrongs that Tom is accused of doing.'

Maddie grabbed the iPad and typed:

He's dead. Alex's dad. Ed killed him.

And now it seemed like rough justice.

Of course, it had been wrong of Tom to agree to change the video and implicate someone else of a crime, but was he coerced into doing it? He was probably scared of Alex and scared of her father. Stuck between a rock and a hard place. It still didn't absolve him of blame though. He'd had a choice. He could have said no. Then Ed's father would still be alive, and Alex's dad, too, and she wouldn't have been through such a horrifying ordeal. Three people died because of that decision. Actions have consequences, but she could imagine Tom not thinking it through, just desperate to get Alex and her father off his back. *How could he have imagined what the terrible consequences would be?*

At that point, the two officers appeared in the café and her mum waved them over to the table. Their faces were grim.

'We'd like to give you an update. Something... unfortunate has happened.'

52

Maddie's world grew still. *Unfortunate? What was that code for?* Whatever it was, the expression on their faces suggested she wasn't going to think it was good news. Her mum grabbed hold of her arm and they both gazed at the officers, waiting.

'I'm afraid to tell you there's been a fatality.'

'A fatality,' her mum repeated, her voice wavering. 'Not Tom. They said he was stable.' Those were Maddie's sentiments exactly and she held her breath, waiting for the bad news to hit her.

'No. It was Alexandra Hargreaves. I'm afraid she briefly managed to escape from custody. She headbutted the officer who was getting her out of the vehicle at the station, and ran off. We're not entirely sure what was in her mind, but a witness said she ran straight out into the road and then a van hit her. The witness thought... well their view is... it was deliberate. The van had no chance of stopping, probably didn't even see her. We think it might have been suicide.'

Maddie's mum released her grip on Maddie's arm. 'Oh,

that's… sad,' she said. Maddie nodded her agreement. It *was* sad. But it fitted with what Alex had said about not being able to face being in a secure psychiatric unit again. With Ed dead as well, it seemed this chapter was closing.

Nobody would be brought to justice. It was over. Apart from tidying up the loose ends, like where her possessions might be, she now needed to try and come to terms with what had happened.

Later that day, once it was confirmed that Tom was out of surgery and comfortable, Maddie went back to Sevenoaks with her mum. She slept on and off for most of the next three days, by which time, her voice had slowly started to recover. The police had managed to track down the majority of their possessions to a house clearance company, who had nothing to do with Ed. His story that the apartment had been cleared out in error was a complete fabrication.

Unfortunately, a lot of personal items had been thrown away, but at least she was able to retrieve most of the furniture and soft furnishings. A few days later, when Maddie had started to recover some of her energy, her possessions were returned and her mum helped to put everything back in its rightful place. But the apartment didn't feel like home any more and she went back to stay with her parents for a while.

It was what she needed at that point in her life, while she was processing her trauma, and although she knew it wasn't a long-term solution, living in London had suddenly lost its appeal. Thankfully, Nadia was happy for her to work from home and only come in if she was needed at a client meeting, but most of her work could be done over Zoom.

It was six weeks before Tom was allowed out of hospital and Maddie suggested he live in the apartment for the time being. It felt mean to kick him out when he was down, and he needed a bit of support. Her conscience wouldn't let her desert him completely, even though her love for him had died amidst the revelations in that cellar.

EPILOGUE
A YEAR LATER

Maddie sat on the promenade gazing out to sea, studying the necklace of islands on the horizon. She'd been to most of them now and smiled as she remembered each trip. She was back in Split, Croatia, and it was a year to the day since she'd first arrived here on that fateful getaway with Tom. It seemed a fitting anniversary to celebrate because not only had she survived a terrifying ordeal, but she'd reinvented herself. Now she was chasing her own dreams and living a life she'd never dared to believe she could have.

Six months ago, she'd finally sold her apartment, once Tom had finished his rehab and had moved out to take a job in Newcastle. But instead of investing that money in another property, she'd bought herself a campervan, determined to fulfil her promise to herself. Today she was a fully-fledged digital nomad, having travelled across Europe to get here and gathering a whole bunch of new friends with a similar outlook on life. Finally, she'd found her tribe. She was still working for the agency but had the flexibility to set her own hours and she'd blossomed

The Getaway

with that freedom, her design ideas getting stronger with all the new influences in her life.

She enjoyed being on her own and not having to compromise. And if she wanted company, all she had to do was visit one of the nomad hubs to hook up with fellow travellers. There were plenty of social media groups to join that kept her connected and gave the low down on the best places to visit. She'd met so many interesting people, with fascinating stories to tell, but she'd told nobody the whole truth about her past and her reason for being on the road. That was her story, to keep to herself and she had no desire to relive the ordeal in the telling. Anyway, she'd moved on and could honestly say she was happy, fulfilled and pretty content with the way things were going.

On the positive side, the kidnapping and imprisonment had shown her that she was resilient and resourceful. She had courage and resolve. All the things she needed to live this nomad lifestyle.

She knew she wouldn't be living like this forever, because her family were such an important part of her life, but her parents were doing great now and didn't need her for the time being. Her dad had recovered from his heart attack, so she didn't have to worry about him so much. And her mum had gone back to work. She had a busy brain, just like Maddie and always needed a project to be getting on with.

Living back at home for a while had been exactly what Maddie had needed at the time, and she'd been able to help with her dad's rehab and take the pressure off her mum. But once the apartment was sold, they'd encouraged her to go and live her life just the way she wanted.

Tomorrow she was moving on. Catching the ferry over to Italy to meet up with a friend for a little while. Then she was travelling up to the Dolomites to get some mountain air. And after that? She'd no real plans and would go where the fancy took her.

Life was better than she could have imagined a year ago. Different, yes, but better in a lot of ways. A year ago, she'd been here on a getaway with Tom, trying to escape from disappointments and worries. Today she was on an adventure, here to experience the best that life had to offer. A completely different mindset. Not running away. Not escaping but embracing the possibilities and thriving in the process. One couldn't have happened without the other though, and that, she'd discovered was the irony of life. The bad was the springboard to dive into the good. And to her, at this moment in time, life was pretty much perfect. No need to get away from anything.

Her phone beeped with a message and she smiled as she read the text. It was from her new friend, Debbie. A middle-aged lady she'd bumped into on her travels. They'd hit it off immediately and had spent a few days getting to know each other while Maddie had been in Italy and Debbie's boat had been in the docks getting some repairs. She was a fun companion, old enough to be Maddie's mother but with an adventurous spirit and a cheeky sense of humour. She reminded her of someone but she couldn't quite work out who it was.

They'd arranged to catch up with each other in Split this evening. Debbie was sailing into port and had invited her to dinner on the boat, which felt like an exciting treat. Lobster. That's what she'd promised her. And champagne. They'd sail out into the bay and enjoy the sunset while they ate, how exciting was that? It was certainly an offer she couldn't refuse.

Apparently, Debbie's husband had tragically died just two years previously and she always did something special on the anniversary of his death to honour her love for him and the life they'd had together. She'd invited Maddie to join her and her daughter, Philippa, who was flying over from the UK for a few days. Their plan was to sail to Sicily and then Corsica, Debbie had said, then on to Naples where her daughter would fly home. It sounded like a fabulous adventure and Maddie quite envied her the freedom of the seas.

It felt like a fitting end to her Croatia trip, reacquainting herself with the places she'd enjoyed the last time she was here, when Alex had been her new friend. It was good to come back and lay the start of that whole episode to rest. She'd forgiven herself now for not recognising the sort of people Alex and Ed really were. How could she have known? They were master manipulators and she, for her sins, was someone who always saw the good in others, not the potential bad. She'd stopped beating herself up about it because what was the point? Accept and move on, that was her mantra when her thoughts got bogged down in those terrible events.

Thinking about Alex now, picturing her face in her mind, brought a sudden thunderbolt of clarity to Maddie's thoughts. A connection was made and her heart did a weird flip, making her catch her breath. Now she knew exactly who Debbie reminded her of. And it wasn't just her looks, but her mannerisms too. That couldn't be coincidence, could it?

She went onto Google and started searching and it didn't take long to confirm her suspicions. Debbie was Alex's mum. Her sister – Philippa, was the Pippa that Tom had spoken about. Now why would the two of them be so keen for Maddie to go on the boat for dinner, hmm? And could she really believe that they'd met by coincidence? That they didn't know who she was?

She stared into space for quite a while, trying to work out how Debbie had tracked her down. But then Maddie had made no secret of her whereabouts on her social media, posting regular updates of her travels. In any case, what did any of that matter? Her gut was telling her to get back in her van, right this minute and skedaddle. Cancel the ferry crossing she'd booked and get a refund. Re-organise things with her friend.

She was a free agent, she could go anywhere.

Her heart was racing, her mind replaying flashbacks of her incarceration in the cellar with Alex. How she'd watched her kill Ed and almost kill Tom. Had that been genetics at play? Were her mum and sister cast from the same mould? The idea made her shudder.

She'd been caught out by Alex's charm and that was bad enough, but to be caught out by her mother and sister too, well that would be careless. She had to have learnt something from the past, and she didn't need to understand what Debbie's plans might really be. Her senses told her that boat would be a death trap and she was going to trust her gut. Enticing her with lobster and champagne. Ha! How stupid did they think she was?

* * *

Debbie

Debbie checked her watch again, looking down the pontoon towards the entrance to the marina. Maddie should be here by now. In fact, she should have been here half an hour ago and that girl was never late. Not even a minute. She was either slightly early or bang on time.

'Mum, shall I put the lobster on yet?' Pippa popped her head out from the galley where she'd taken charge of preparing the food. They'd been so excited, the two of them, to finally have this chance to put everything right. Oh, the hours they'd spent daydreaming of ways to end the one threat that existed in their lives. So many wild schemes they'd come up with until the perfect opportunity had arisen and they'd grabbed it with both hands.

'I don't think she's coming,' Debbie said, her eyes still on the marina entrance.

'What do you mean?' There was no mistaking the panic in Pippa's voice. If anything, she was more worried than Debbie about the threat Maddie posed to their lifestyles. There had been no newspaper reports after Alex and Ed's deaths, no publicity at all. Nobody knew what had happened except those involved and the family wanted to keep it that way. Unfortunately, they knew Maddie could go to the press with her story any time she wanted. A sensational, mind-blowing story, and then the whole world would know about Alex and what she'd done. How could that not damage both Debbie and Pippa, given the circles they moved in? Reputation was everything and any hint of tarnish would see you ghosted and dropped like a stone. It was a terrible thing to have hanging over you, waking up every day and wondering if this was the day your life would crumble to dust.

It had been bad enough when Debbie's husband, Peter, had been killed. But every cloud has a silver lining and he was very well insured, leaving her able to live the privileged life she'd been accustomed to. In many ways, she was actually happier without him. He could be a bit of a bully, involved in shady deals that she turned a blind eye to. Better not to know, just in case it blew up in his face. That had been her strategy.

She didn't know the half of what he got up to but now the police had told her the full story, she knew it was his actions that had ultimately led to Alex's death. It was a story in which Maddie had played a leading role and she must surely be thinking of monetising her experience. Everybody would do that, wouldn't they? It was just a matter of time, but Debbie and

Pippa were determined to act before that happened. Snuff that story out so nobody would ever know.

'Why don't you ring her?' Pippa said, breaking into Debbie's thoughts. 'Then we'll know if she's been held up for some reason.'

Debbie nodded, but when the call went to voicemail, her suspicions were confirmed. She shook her head when Pippa gave her a quizzical look. 'No answer.'

Pippa slammed her hand against the door frame, her face contorted in a ferocious snarl. She was so like her sister, Debbie thought, knowing she'd have to tread carefully until her daughter had calmed down. 'Look, don't worry about it, sweetheart. We missed our chance this time, but we can try again. Obviously, we'll have to take a different approach because something must have spooked her.' She smiled and pulled her daughter into a hug, smoothing her hair as she kissed her forehead. 'We can do this. I've got a tracker on her phone.' She laughed. 'We're not going to let her get away, are we?'

* * *

Maddie

Much later, Maddie sat on a bench overlooking the bay. It had been an eventful evening and she was too wired to go to bed just yet. Police sirens sounded in the distance and she watched the flashing lights get closer before pulling up outside the marina. Two officers walked down the pontoon, stopping beside Debbie's boat. She smiled to herself, glad the police had been true to their word.

When she'd decided that instead of running away, she needed to confront the issue, talking to the police had seemed like her best option. It hadn't taken them long to find the tracker app on her phone and it appeared Debbie and Pippa would be spending the rest of the night at the police station. Once they understood they'd been outplayed, Maddie hoped, that would be an end to it. But she was going to be a bit more careful about publicising her movements from now on.

She stood up, turned and walked away. It was time to move on.

* * *

MORE FROM RONA HALSALL

Another book from Rona Halsall, *The Soulmate*, is available to order now here:

https://mybook.to/SoulmateBackAd

ACKNOWLEDGEMENTS

I feel so lucky that I get to write books for a living and want firstly to thank all my readers for buying, sharing and shouting about my books. I write them for you and I love to hear your feedback, so an even bigger thank you to everyone who leaves reviews on Amazon, Goodreads and Instagram and those of you who post on Facebook reading groups. You are the best and that is why this book is dedicated to all you lovely people!

A book is a team effort and I'd like to thank everyone at my publisher, Boldwood, who has had an input to this project. Firstly my wonderful editor, Isobel Akenhead, who had to work doubly hard with this one, untangling all the lies and making sure it all made sense. A massive thanks for the fabulous cover. Got to be my favourite so far. I do love hot-pink!!!

Thanks also to the rest of the team at Boldwood including Jenna Houston for marketing support, Wendy Neale on sales and all of the production team and backroom staff for everything they do. Also thanks to the copyeditor and proofreader for their attention to detail – not my strong point!

A big thank you to Mark Fearn and Sandra Henderson for your feedback on an early draft, which helped to shape the finished book.

Finally thanks to my children, John, Amy and Oscar, who are always there for moral support and don't mind when I have to cancel get-togethers because I have a deadline to meet.

As always, thanks to my dogs, Maid, Evie and new recruit, Sandy, who are my writing support team. They are in charge of my mental health and make sure I get outside several times a day, get plenty of exercise and enjoy the wonderful place where I live.

ABOUT THE AUTHOR

Rona Halsall is a #1 bestselling author of psychological thrillers including, most recently, *The Bigamist* and *Bride & Groom*. She lives in Wales with her mad little Border Collie, Maid and Romanian rescue dog, Evie.

Sign up to Rona Halsall's mailing list for news, competitions and updates on future books.

Visit Rona Halsall's website: www.ronahalsall.com

Follow Rona on social media here:

- facebook.com/RonaHalsallAuthor
- x.com/RonaHalsallAuth
- instagram.com/ronahalsall
- bookbub.com/authors/ronahalsall

ALSO BY RONA HALSALL

Keep You Safe

Love You Gone

The Honeymoon

Her Mother's Lies

One Mistake

The Ex Boyfriend

The Liar's Daughter

The Guest Room

The Wife Next Door

The Bigamist

Bride and Groom

The Fiancé

The Soulmate

The Getaway

THE *Murder* LIST

THE MURDER LIST IS A NEWSLETTER DEDICATED TO SPINE-CHILLING FICTION AND GRIPPING PAGE-TURNERS!

SIGN UP TO MAKE SURE YOU'RE ON OUR HIT LIST FOR EXCLUSIVE DEALS, AUTHOR CONTENT, AND COMPETITIONS.

SIGN UP TO OUR NEWSLETTER

BIT.LY/THEMURDERLISTNEWS

Boldwood

Boldwood Books is an award-winning fiction publishing company seeking out the best stories from around the world.

Find out more at www.boldwoodbooks.com

Join our reader community for brilliant books, competitions and offers!

Follow us
@BoldwoodBooks
@TheBoldBookClub

Sign up to our weekly deals newsletter

https://bit.ly/BoldwoodBNewsletter

Printed in Dunstable, United Kingdom